Leaving the Comfort Zone

Ian Kennedy Williams is the author of three previous collections of stories and three novels. He has also written for the stage and worked on film and TV initiatives for Screen Australia and Screen Queensland. His work has garnered numerous awards and he is a recipient of an Australian Film Institute nomination for screenwriting. He lives in Launceston, Tasmania, with his wife Liz and two cats.

I0742668

Also by Ian Kennedy Williams and published by Ginninderra Press
Fugitive Places

Ian Kennedy Williams

Leaving the
Comfort Zone

Acknowledgements

Stories in this collection were originally published in *Meanjin* ('The Methuselah Gardens'), *Outrider* ('When You Have To Go There'), *Antipodes*, USA ('Traces', 'Nin's Father'), *Narrator International* ('Hares', 'Garrison Town', 'A Firestarter Speaks of His Love').

A reading of 'Nin's Father' was broadcast on *Writers' Radio*, Radio 5UV Adelaide.

Leaving the Comfort Zone
ISBN 978 1 76041 362 0
Copyright © Ian Kennedy Williams 2017
Cover photo: Danger No Swimming Sign © photogoodwin

First published 2017 by
GINNINDERRA PRESS
PO Box 3461 Port Adelaide 5015
www.ginninderrapress.com.au

Contents

For Bev and Rick, Paul and Pauline, old friends

And for Kelly Davis, who got me started

Eidolon

A Ghost Story

Eidolon: 1. an unsubstantial image;
Apparition; phantom.
2. an ideal or idealised figure.

'Unprepossessing,' Donny says. 'Is that a word? Not much to look at, you know. Smart but introverted. Cruise and Dustin Hoffman in that *Rain Man* flick. That's me and Carl.'

He lies naked on the bed, dragging on a smoke. His devouring gaze is on Beth, sitting in her underwear, putting on a face. He's just a little crazy about her. Twenty-five, with the kind of cold porcelain beauty you see on fashion models.

She gives him a sharp look. 'Just remember why we're going.'

'How'd he do it?' Donny says. 'All these years a pathetic little loser, and then he hits the jackpot. Last time I saw him he was rooming in some fleapit in the valley.'

'You'd better get dressed,' Beth says. She's finished her make-up. 'We'll miss the flight.' She pulls a couple of dresses from the wardrobe, holds them out for Donny to see. 'It'll be hot, won't it?'

Donny's still venting about his brother. 'Tarts and potheads hanging around the stairs,' he says. 'Place reeked of dope and spermy French letters. He belongs here, that's what I thought. This shit hole. He's in his natural element.'

Beth drops the dresses over a chair. 'Donny…you're going to talk me out of this.' She stares at her anxious reflection in the mirror.

Donny stubs his smoke and slides off the bed. He comes up behind her, slips his arm around her waist. 'He's expecting you, babe. I promised… He wants to meet you. We need to do this together.'

Beth breathes deeply. 'Just a day, you reckon…'

'Tops,' Donny says. 'You'll charm him.' He kisses her neck. 'Maybe he'll charm you…' He slips his hand down her pants.

Beth resists. 'We don't have time.'

Donny doesn't want to hear. He edges her back onto the bed, drags her pants down. 'Thirty-eight,' he murmurs.

'What?'

'Weather on the Gold Coast…'

'That's hot…' Beth sighs.

'Yeah,' Donny says. 'So dress cool…'

The plane touches down late afternoon. The sky is a deep, clear blue, the road shimmering in the heat.

Carl's place is a ten-minute taxi ride from the airport, a bleached white sprawling walled mansion, guarded by two-metre iron gates. Donny barks into the intercom and a gate slides back. A small, pale long-faced man opens the front door. Carl. The moment is strange, almost surreal. Donny wants to laugh at the absurdity of it. He introduces Beth to his baby brother. Carl's gaze is tentative, almost reluctant.

Inside, the house is refreshingly cool.

Carl ushers them into a vast, open-planned living space. 'It came furnished,' he says.

Spare, minimalist, Donny notes. A large sofa dominates the room, facing a huge plasma TV. There are no drapes at the window. An expensive exercise bike stands in the corner.

Donny's eye is caught by a sequence of prints on the wall. 'Jesus,' he says. 'Is this stuff legal?'

'Japanese erotica,' Carl says. 'Copies. Originals would cost a mint.' He glances at Beth, who is standing at the window, taking in the Gold Coast vista.

'Porn with a fancy price tag,' Donny says.

'Pornography debases women,' Carl says softly. 'Erotica…celebrates the art of love…'

Donny smirks. He sees Beth pull her jacket round her shoulders. She's shivering.

'You cold, babe?'

Beth comes into the room. She avoids looking at Carl.

'I need to use the bathroom.'

'It's at the top of the stairs,' Carl says. He stares after her as she climbs the broad stairway, out of sight. 'She's nice.'

'Yeah,' Donny says. He rubs his arms. 'It's forty degrees on the street,' he says. 'It's like a morgue in here.'

'It's the air con,' Carl says. 'It's a bit temperamental. I need to get a technician to check it out.' He glances up the stairs to see if Beth is returning. 'I don't think Beth likes me.'

Donny is checking out the prints on the wall again. He rubs his crotch, absently. 'Sure she does. It's just the situation, you know.'

Carl nods. He doesn't ask. 'You want a drink?'

'Scotch.'

'I don't keep spirits,' Carl says. 'I got some red wine in the cellar.'

Donny looks at him. He doesn't know whether to laugh or give him a hard smack. A fucking wine cellar. The kid's living the dream.

He follows Carl through the kitchen and down to the cellar. A solitary light illuminates rows of mostly bare racks. There's a table and two chairs and a large free-standing pantry unit which has been pushed up against the back wall. Donny pulls a cleanskin from the rack.

'Jesus, mate. Two dollar chucks.'

'I don't drink so much,' Carl says. 'It inhibits your performance.'

'What performance would that be, Carl?'

Carl smiles thinly. He looks nervous. 'You're not here for my wine.'

'I need a loan,' Donny says.

'I don't have much cash,' Carl says. 'You know what they pay a hospital orderly?'

'You've got this fuckin' great mansion,' Donny says. 'You could raise fifty thou overnight.'

Carl whistles. 'Fifty thousand dollars. I'd need some kind of collateral.'

'Are you kidding me?'

'What if you can't pay it back? I'd have to sell up.'

'It's just bricks and mortar,' Donny says. He's trying to keep his cool. 'What d'you want a place this size for, anyway? When was the last time you chucked a society ball?'

'I can't leave here,' Carl says. 'It's my home.'

'You won it five months ago in a lottery.'

Carl looks a little smug. 'I know. I never even won a raffle before.'

'You could get a string of units for what you'd get for this place,' Donny says. 'Live off the rentals.'

'I like my work,' Carl says. 'You know...?'

Donny doesn't know. He grabs a second bottle of wine from the rack to curb his frustration. There's a hum he hadn't noticed before, a murmur like a fridge kicking in. 'What's that?'

Carl listens for a moment. 'It's the air con.'

'Down here?'

'Ducted,' Carl says. 'It's everywhere.'

Beth flushes the toilet, adjusts her dress. The bathroom, she thinks jealously, would fill half the space of her Sydney unit: double shower, bidet, spa, his and her washbasins. A solitary hand towel hangs over the rail. She washes her hands under the basin tap. Facing the mirror, she sees how pale and sickly she looks. She shivers. It's not just the cold. A day, Donny reckoned; she could handle a day. Taking a lipstick from her bag, she leans forward to touch up her mouth. Her breath frosts the glass.

Leaving the bathroom, she pauses a moment on the wide landing. There are more pictures on the wall, the same weirdo stuff that had caught Donny's eye downstairs. It's too refined to repulse her, but she doesn't like it. She doesn't much like Carl. What normal guy would hang erotica on his living room wall? She can't help it, though; she has to look. An Oriental woman straddles a man. She stares out of the frame, inviting Beth's voyeuristic scrutiny. Just for an instant, it's as if the picture is animated, the man thrusting up into the woman. Beth blinks and looks again. Her pulse has quickened.

She's cute, Carl thinks. His gaze is on Beth, taking a smoke on the patio outside. It's early evening, but dark already.

Donny opens another bottle of wine. He's doing most of the drinking. 'You getting any, Carl?'

Carl drags his gaze away from Beth. 'You mean sex.'

'Yeah, sex. You ever bring girls to this great fancy mansion of yours?'

Carl sighs. 'I don't go in for casual sex.'

'Doesn't have to be casual. A regular girl to share your home comforts. Be quite an attraction, eh? How many bedrooms…?'

'Four,' Carl says carelessly. 'Or five. I forget.'

Donny looks sour. Having his nose rubbed in it.

Carl can't help himself. He sips his wine. 'Still Mr Bigshot Property Speculator…?'

Donny's smile is a little cool. 'Might try my luck here. Get you top dollar for this place.' He swallows a mouthful of wine. 'Sydney went off the boil. Had to bring in a partner to stay afloat. Truth is, I took a few quid out of the business to cover the cards, which I neglected to mention to my partner. She's kinda pissed…'

She… Carl thinks. He keeps his thought to himself.

Beth comes in to show Donny a mosquito bite on her wrist. 'Fat little bloodsucker.'

'It's the canals,' Carl explains. 'And the heat.'

Donny kisses the bite. He draws her close, running his paws over her body. Carl looks away for a second. When he looks back, she's staring at him.

'I'm going to bed,' she says.

'Sure,' Donny says. 'I'll be right up, babe. Warm the sheets.'

Beth draws her jacket around her shoulders. She moves around the table, pausing behind Carl. As she leans over, he smells the cigarette on her breath. She brushes the corner of his mouth with her lips.

Donny stares after her as she walks off. 'How about it?' he says.

Carl takes a moment. 'How about what?'

'The fifty grand.'

Carl's gaze drifts after Beth, but she's gone. 'I'll think about it.'

Beth drops her jacket on the bed. She's got goosebumps from the cold. If it wasn't for the humidity and the mosquitoes, she reckons she would've slept on the patio. The bedroom fittingly is expansive and, apart from the huge TV, sparely furnished. The same soft porn prints on the walls. She doesn't want to look at them again. She'd come up earlier to take a shower and change her clothes. She can hear the shower still dripping. She tightens the tap and returns to the bedroom, observing her reflection on the blank TV screen for a second before pulling back the bed covers. The TV remote is lying on a pillow. The bedding looks new or freshly laundered. It reassures her a little. She's unbuttoning her shirt when Donny comes in.

'Will he lend you the money?'

Donny doesn't say. He's checking out the prints on the walls. 'Only thing he collected when we were kids was beer coasters,' he says.

Beth shivers. 'I am so fucking cold.'

'It's the air con,' Donny says. 'It's fucked. Can't turn it off – we'll roast.'

'What if he won't give you the money?' Beth says. 'I'll freeze to death if I have to stay in this mausoleum more than a day.'

Donny takes a closer look at one of the prints. It's turning him on, she can see.

'He wants something,' he says. 'He wants collateral.'

Beth stares at him. What would Donny have that would back up fifty thousand dollars? She sits on the bed. A sudden groan startles her. The TV has switched itself on. It's a porn movie, a close-up torso shot of a couple having sex. She grabs the remote and hits the close button.

Donny is still mesmerised by the performance on the screen. 'What the fuck was that?' He sits with her, kisses her, starts caressing her. He's really worked up now.

She's too freaked out. 'I need a drink,' she says.

Donny looks pissed, but he keeps his cool. 'Sure, babe, I'll see what I can find.' He pauses at the door. 'We'll be out of here tomorrow. Promise.'

Beth lights a cigarette. There's no ashtray; she goes into the en suite so she can ash into the basin. The shower is still dripping. She tightens the tap again and then jumps with fright. A woman's voice is coming from the bedroom. 'Hello. My name is Noriko.' Beth drops her smoke in the basin. The voice is coming from the TV. 'I am twenty-three years old and I would like to meet an Australian…' A sexy-looking Asian woman is speaking directly to camera. 'I am very artistic and I like to play games…' She smiles, a little too archly.

The house is quiet when Donny goes down. Carl has gone to his room. Without drapes at the window, the place is half lit by the lights of the Gold Coast. He stands a moment, taking in the night view. The empty wine bottles from earlier are still on the kitchen table. It's not as cold here, the air con seemingly working better downstairs. His mobile rings briefly. He checks the display, but it's blank. He puts the phone to his ear: nothing. He checks the display again, but the light has gone. Shoving the phone back in his pocket, he heads for the cellar.

Something about the house is starting to get to him. The air con playing up, the TV turning on of its own accord. Carl didn't have the smarts to play games like that. Screwing with them or not, Donny thinks, as long as he comes up with the money. Grabbing another bottle of wine from the rack, he notices the air con seems louder than earlier. Again his mobile rings. The display lights up: Beth. It's getting to him now.

'Jesus, Beth, get a grip, will you.' He listens to silence. 'Beth…?'

Still nothing. The connection drops out. He takes the stairs two at a time.

Beth is sitting on the end of the bed, flicking through the TV channels with the remote.

'What the fuck are you playing at?'

Beth is fixated on the channel jumping.

Donny grabs the remote and turns the TV off. 'What's the matter with you? Why'd you phone me?'

'I can't find it!' Beth says. She's almost sobbing with frustration. 'It was there, and it's gone!'

'What d'you want to watch that shit for?' Donny says. He laughs. 'Like we need it!'

'She was there,' Beth says. 'I watched her, and then she just…'

Donny sighs. He unscrews the wine cap and fetches two glasses from the en suite. Beth is still staring at the blank TV screen.

'Hey,' he says, a little too sharply.

She takes the glass of wine.

'What was so urgent?'

She stares at him, like he's the one losing it.

'You rang my mobile,' he says.

She shakes her head, slowly. Now she just looks confused. And a little scared. 'Just…don't leave me alone,' she says.

Donny sits on the bed next to her. He kisses her, caresses her breast. She resists at first, then slowly submits.

He eases her back onto the bed, reaches under her skirt. 'Still cold?' he murmurs.

'No,' she says.

He knows from the change in the light in the room that the TV has come on again.

She's gone, when he wakes, though her side of the bed is still warm. He switches on a side light, checks his watch: a little after two. The en suite door is open, but there's no light. He can hear the shower dripping.

Pulling on a shirt and a pair of pants, he goes downstairs. The house is moonlit and bitterly cold. He checks the air con control in the lobby; it's reading eight degrees. He tries to adjust the thermostat, but it won't respond. Heading back towards the kitchen, he sees a figure through the window, moving across the side patio towards the front gate. It's Beth, dressed in the same clothes she arrived in. By the time he gets to her, she's at the gate, gripping the rail and staring across the dimly lit street. She seems oblivious to his approach, barely responding when he calls her name. It's only when he touches her arm that she flinches, as if stung. It hits him, then, what she's doing out of bed. She's sleepwalking.

She's awake once he gets her back inside the house, but a little spaced out. He sits her at the kitchen table and boils water for coffee.

She sleepwalked when she was a small girl, she tells him, until she was twelve when her parents finally split. 'It screwed me up, them fighting all the time. Nightmares... One night I woke up and I was halfway down the street. Like I was running away...' She can't think why she should start again now, except that the stuff with the TV and the air con going crazy had spooked her. She's hot, now, burning up. Donny realises how warm the house is. Million bucks worth of property, he thinks, and his dumb brother gets a jerry-built air con system.

'You know what really spooked me?' Beth says. 'When I woke up by the gate? Seeing that woman over the road. Just standing there... staring at me...'

'Yeah?' Donny lights a couple of cigarettes. Carl didn't like them smoking inside, but what the fuck.

'You didn't see her?'

'Babe, I didn't know what was going on. You walking out there like a zombie.'

'It seemed like she'd just left here,' Beth says. 'And was waiting for me to follow...'

'Left here? You were dreaming.'

Beth presses her palm to her forehead. 'Christ, I've got a head. I need a pill.'

'You want a tab?'

'Just an aspirin...something.' She gives him a desperate look.

Donny checks the kitchen drawers and cupboards. Apart from a few bits of cutlery and crockery, each one is empty.

'She was probably some tart heading home,' he says. 'Would've scared the shit out of her, you appearing like that at the gate.'

'I don't know…' Beth's jittery gaze follows his search of the empty cupboards. 'You sure anyone lives here…?'

'My brother has simple needs,' Donny says dryly.

He checks the pantry, a room off the kitchen as big as a shed. There's nothing much in the way of provisions, just a few tins and packet meals. He drags a box from the back of a low shelf and flips the lid. Inside is a small cache of tablet jars. He brings the box into the kitchen and tips the jars onto the table. The pills are blues, greens and yellows, labels all in some Asian language. Caught between the jars is a bubble strip, half the tablets gone.

'Are these what I think they are?'

'Contraceptives,' Beth says.

She's still asleep when he wakes. It's a little after seven. He leaves her to sleep, takes a shower and goes downstairs. Carl is sitting in shorts and T-shirt, stuffing cornflakes into his mouth. He looks a little bleary-eyed, as if he hasn't slept well.

'Not working today?

'It's my rostered day off.'

Donny helps himself to cereal. The radio's giving the weather report, predicting a sweltering forty degrees. 'You going to call that air con technician?'

'It's working okay, now,' Carl says. He finishes his cereal. 'Beth must have thin blood. To feel the cold so much.'

'Beth's blood is just fine,' Donny says. 'She reckons this place has all the charm of a mausoleum.'

Carl says nothing. He drops his cereal bowl in the sink.

Donny pulls the pill strip from his pocket and drops it on the table. 'Is that why she left?'

Carl looks at the strip. He seems only slightly fazed. Maybe he just doesn't like Donny poking his nose around. 'Noriko's,' he says evenly. 'She posed for me.'

Donny laughs. 'Yeah, right.'

'I'll show you,' Carl says. 'Maybe Beth too…later.'

Donny follows him upstairs, along the hall past the guest bedrooms. A door, more distant than the others, opens onto a long gallery that runs the full back of the house. Apart from a red leather sofa, the room is empty. It's the long wall that catches the eye, white and windowless, hung with dozens of erotic drawings, each one done in the Oriental style of the prints in the rest of the house.

Donny moves from one to another, gazing in sheer wonder. 'You drew all these?'

'Uh-huh.'

He examines one up close. A woman sits on a chair, her lover's head between her thighs. 'That Noriko?'

'Yes.'

'Who's the lucky guy?'

'Me,' Carl says.

Donny looks at Carl. He examines the picture again. Not that he can tell from the back of the guy's head, but no way was that baby brother Carl.

'I set up a video camera and then select a frame to work from,' Carl explains. His delivery is instructive, oddly detached.

Donny moves on, checking out one marvellous drawing after another. He squeezes his balls absently. 'You never drew squat when we were kids,' he says. 'Where'd you learn this?'

'Night classes,' Carl says. It could have been a joke. 'I discovered I had a talent.'

Donny finds another drawing to scrutinise. The male lover is dominant here. While the body could be Carl's, the face is oddly obscured, as if the charcoal had been smudged.

'This you?'

'They're all me,' Carl says. He's getting a little testy. 'I told you.'

'All your own work, eh!' Donny laughs. He stands back, surveys the whole collection. Loser Carl, he can't get his head around it. He views one more picture. His gaze meets the woman's, lost in sexual ecstasy. 'So why'd she leave?'

Waking, it takes Beth a moment to remember where she is. Donny's side of the bed is cold and there is a slight chill to the room. A dream she'd had has left her feeling uneasy, but she can't remember what it was about. The en suite is even chillier; she turns the heat up on the shower as hard as she can bear. For a few seconds after she steps out, she luxuriates in the steamy atmosphere before the bathroom begins to rapidly cool again. By the time she has wrapped herself in a robe, her teeth are chattering and the mirror and metal bathroom fixtures are running with water. Returning to the bedroom, she draws back the drapes. Beyond the glass, the Gold Coast landscape simmers already in the bright hazy sunshine.

She's dressed when Donny comes in. He's got a look on his face, like he's had a win at the tables.

'You got the money?'

Donny shakes his head. 'Those pills,' he says. 'Carl had a Japanese girl here. Picked her up from some Internet dating service. Hot little sweetie!'

'She'd have to be,' Beth says. 'Living in this ice bucket.' She shivers a little, glancing at the blank TV screen. 'What was her name…?'

'Noriko.'

'Artistic…and likes to play games…'

She feels his arm around her, his warm breath in her ear.

'Come and see,' he murmurs.

It disturbs her, what she sees. She doesn't know what to feel. She has no eye for art, no taste for pornography, yet it moves her. It arouses and confuses her. She gazes at the drawings, her mind caught between the artist's seductive talent and his creepy presence. Sitting on the patio later, she watches Donny do laps of the pool. Carl has brought her coffee, juice, toast and marmalade elaborately set on a tray.

'I'm a lousy host,' he confesses. 'I don't get too many visitors…' He hands her the juice. 'Of course, I had Noriko to stay…' He watches Donny for a moment. 'She liked the pool,' he says. 'I don't use it so much, now. She may have left one of her costumes, if you'd like –'

'I can't swim,' Beth says. She looks at the toast. She feels she would choke on it. 'I've seen her,' she says.

Carl says nothing. He slips into the chair next to her.

'The video,' Beth says. She doesn't look at him. 'The TV in the bedroom. It just came on…'

'She left me,' Carl says. 'I paid her flight out from Japan. I gave her all this… Anything she wanted… She said she loved me.'

'The drawings,' Beth says. 'Maybe…'

'She posed willingly,' Carl says. 'Dare I say…enthusiastically. She taught me the art.'

'Drawing.'

'Love,' Carl says. 'Physical love. Pleasure.' He pours coffee.

Beth stares at the dark, swirling surface. 'The drawings,' she says, 'they're…' She's conscious of Carl's steady gaze, his bated breath. 'Very impressive…'

Finishing her coffee, she leans back in her chair and closes her eyes. Carl watches her for a while and then takes the breakfast tray into the kitchen. What she said…about Noriko appearing to her on the TV… Flirting with them, playing games. That was Noriko. But why Beth? What was Beth to Noriko…?

He finishes the toast Beth left and puts the dishes in the sink. He can see Donny is out of the pool and drying himself. He talks with Beth for a few moments, but it doesn't look like she's in a mood for conversation. Carl looks away, not wanting to be caught staring. He checks the thermostat on the air con, which seems to be steady, then returns to the kitchen.

Donny is swigging from the bottle of juice. 'I could sell a few of your porno pics,' he says. 'Guy I know. Nice little intimate gallery up the Cross.'

'They're not for sale,' Carl says. He watches Donny as he wipes his mouth. 'I can't give you the money,' he says. 'I'm sorry.'

Donny sighs. 'Fuck, Carl. We're family. I'd do it for you.'

'You've never done anything for me.'

'I looked out for you when we were kids. Never got picked on, did you? Not when your big brother was around.'

'I remember you being around,' Carl says. 'Even when I didn't want you around.'

'You always wanted me around. It was Donny who got the girls, right?'

'I didn't want your girls,' Carl says. 'I had my own girls. Not as many – or as pretty – as yours. But they were mine…'

Donny looks a little rueful. 'Okay, so I fucked them. I'd have fucked them anyway. What's the big deal?'

'You owe me,' Carl says. He sticks the juice bottle back into the fridge. 'That's the deal.'

It's a hard sell. He can't see her going for it, but it's worth a shot. It's not like she hasn't done it before. She was working the tables, when he met her, dealing cards and moonlighting as an escort to pay for coke. She was off the drugs now and the hooking was behind her. He loves her, she knows it. And she loves him. Which is why he has to ask.

'I can't,' she says. 'He gives me the creeps.'

'Sure,' he says. 'No sweat.' He paces the room, stands at the window. It's like staring across some Moroccan city, baking under a fierce Mediterranean sun.

'Don't make me do it, Donny.'

He can't bear to hear that plea in her voice. He grabs his bag, tosses it on the bed and unzips it.

'What're you doing?

'No point in hanging around, is there.' He flips open the bag, drags out a clean singlet. Half a dozen casino chips spill onto the floor. He stares at them a moment before gathering them up and checking their paltry value. 'Bit short of fifty grand…'

He's sitting on the sofa, when she goes in. He's so still, she thinks he's meditating. Or maybe it's just the drawing in front of him that he's contemplating. She imagines herself someplace she hasn't been in a while, a hotel room with a punter, some lean business guy in a crumpled suit.

Carl rises as she approaches. He looks nervous, like a tongue-tied teenager about to get his first taste of sex. He doesn't look like anyone she's ever fucked for money. Standing close, she sees, she thinks, just the ghost of Donny in his face. She takes a deep breath.

'Are you cold?'

She shakes her head.

'It's always warm in here,' Carl says.

He makes no attempt to kiss her. She averts her gaze. Facing her is the reclining Noriko with her lover's head between her thighs.

'Hello. My name is Noriko…' Donny's pedalling hard, trying to work off his frustration and self-loathing on Carl's exercise bike; the voice barely registers. 'I am twenty-three years old, and I would like to meet an Australian…' His heart's pounding and the tension makes his head spin. The lounge is half-lit, the air humid and uncomfortably warm. 'I am very artistic and I like to play games…' He sees her then, smiling archly at him from the TV. A few seconds ago it had been some nature doco screening, the sound muted. He slides from the bike, moves in for a closer look. Perspiration blurs his vision, but there's no mistaking that come-on look. It holds him for the barest second before the image flickers and disappears, sending him back to the African savannah. He grabs the remote, runs through channel after channel, but she's gone, slipped into the ether, if not back into his twisted imagination. But he knows what he saw and heard. She was there, reaching out to him…

He's calmed a little by the time he returns to the bedroom. It's some glitch on the DVD hard drive, he decides, a fragment of the dating programme Carl was into. Carl… His guilt kicks in again. For a few moments there, it had almost slipped from his mind.

Beth is in the spa. She doesn't look at him.

'I'm sorry, babe…putting you through that.' He begins to strip; he's sweating so bad he needs to shower.

She lifts her head a little. Her teeth are chattering. 'Get me out of here,' she says. 'I'm freezing…'

'You want to go to a motel?'

They're sitting in a quiet corner of a bar about five minutes' walk from the house. Soon as she was out of the spa and wrapped in a towel, Beth said she had to get out. She needed a drink, a shot of hard liquor. She needed to be somewhere normal for a couple of hours.

'Tonight,' Donny says. 'I'm just saying, babe, you don't have to go back. Leave Carl to me. I don't want this to fuck us up.'

'It won't,' Beth says. She sips her Scotch. 'I'm good, now.'

Donny nods. 'It was just sex,' he says. 'A dream. A bad sex dream.'

Beth takes another sip. 'It wasn't so bad.'

What does that mean? Donny's phone rings before he can push it. He checks the display. NORIKO CALLING. He stares, confounded.

'Who is it?' Beth says.

'Louise,' he says. 'I'll call her later.'

'She still wants you,' Beth says. There's an edge to her voice.

'She wants her money. She gets that and we're free. I promise.'

The bar is starting to fill with a late-night crowd. They finish their drinks in silence.

'We should go back,' Beth says.

'You sure?'

'Yes.'

The tree-lined street is deserted, poorly lit. Their footsteps echo eerily through the silence.

Approaching the house, Beth stops suddenly. 'There's something I have to tell you…'

Donny pulls up short. A figure – barely more than a shadow – was slipping through the gate into the house. 'Did you see that?'

'See what?'

He strides across the road, stands at the gate. Moonlight sweeps the front of the house. The grounds are deserted. He was sure…

Beth comes up behind him. 'What is it?'

'Nothing,' he says. He slips the gate latch. 'What did you want to tell me?'

'It doesn't matter,' she says. 'I'll tell you later.'

Inside, the house is dark and silent. The only sound is the low hum of the air con. Beth shivers.

'Go to bed,' Donny says. 'I need another drink.'

He watches until she's up the stairs and then heads for the cellar. The light flickers a couple of times before staying on. There's no sound except the faint humming of the air con. As he grabs a bottle of wine from the rack, he hears something. It's so soft – a whisper – he's not even sure he heard it. It comes again. 'Donny…' Someone is whispering his name. He can feel the hairs at the base of his neck rising. It comes again. 'Donny…' Beth. It has to be Beth. But he watched Beth go up the stairs. He couldn't swear it was Beth's voice, anyway. It's too… ethereal.

He stands for a long moment, waiting for it to come again. There's nothing, just the steady drone of the air con. He starts towards the stairs. Again he hears something – not his whispered name this time, but a tight girlish laugh. He looks around. The cellar is so brightly lit, there are no shadows to hide in. There's only the pantry unit, standing against the far wall. What would Carl want with a pantry unit down here? The erratic hum of the air con sounds almost human. Like someone's heavy breathing. It's all in your head… It's the house, the business with Carl and Beth. It's getting to him. The temperature is dropping; he's not imagining that. He can see his panting breath.

He flips the pantry door open. It's empty, bar two pink suitcases stuffed in the bottom, under the lower shelf. Dragging them out, he's aware that the air con has returned to its regular rhythm. He flicks the catch on the first. Unlocked. Nothing but a jumble of women's clothes and underwear. The second is the same, as well as cosmetics and various pairs of shoes. He pulls out a red knee-high leather boot and tentatively inhales. A stale muskiness… He breathes out, strangely calmed. There's no moisture on his breath. The air is warming.

Pushing the suitcases aside, he takes a closer look at the pantry. He sees then the edge of a door jamb behind it. It's hiding another entrance into the cellar. He drags the unit forward and reaches the handle to the closed door. He's barely put his finger on it when his phone messages him. For a long moment he stands with his hand on the handle. He can't do it. He can't open the door. He hasn't the will to try. Pulling his phone from his pocket, he checks the display. Beth. 'where r u?'

He pushes the pantry back and shuts the door on the suitcases. Upstairs, a bluish light illuminates the lounge as he passes. It's the TV, displaying a blank blue screen. He stares at it for a few precious seconds, willing it to flicker into life. There's nothing, just the mesmerising blue screen.

Beth is sitting on the side of the bed, still dressed. 'What took you so long? Jesus, Donny. You're scaring me.' She can see the unease on his face.

Unease. Fear. He doesn't know what he feels. He puts the wine bottle on the bedside table and fetches glasses from the en suite. He strains for sounds, whispers in his ear. He pours the wine, sits next to Beth. She shudders.

'Are you cold?'

She shakes her head. 'Not now.'

He tells her, 'Tomorrow. First thing. We're out of here.'

'Not without the money,' she says. 'I've earned it.'

'You want to tell me about that stuff in the cupboard downstairs?'

It's before seven. Carl was hoping to be out of the house before Donny came down.

'Later,' he says. 'I have to go to work.'

Donny grips his arm. 'What did you do to her?'

'Nothing. She left.'

'Why'd she leave her gear behind?'

'She didn't want it. It was old. I bought her a heap of new stuff. She took that.'

Donny releases his grip. 'She flipped you.' He grins.

Carl checks his watch. He's rostered for eight. 'How's Beth this morning?'

The grin's gone. Donny looks ready to throw a punch. 'Fifty grand. That was the deal.'

Carl nods. He wants to say that Beth was worth every cent, but he doesn't believe it. And he doesn't want Donny's fist in his face. 'I'll get you a bank cheque,' he says.

Donny calls after him. 'Noriko. You sure she left?'

Carl doesn't answer.

Upstairs, Donny finds Beth standing at the window in her underwear. She's watching Carl drive out the gate. He slips his arm around her and kisses her neck. There's a smell about her, sour, unpleasant.

'You okay, babe? You don't look so good.'

'I'm pregnant.'

It takes a moment to register. 'Since when?'

She pulls away. 'Are you kidding?'

'I mean…how long have you known?'

'A while. It's yours, Donny. I want it. I want us to have it.'

'You should've said.' He's angry. With himself. With her, for what she let him do. 'I'd never…'

'It doesn't matter,' she says. 'It's done. I just want to get out of here.'

He nods. 'He's getting a bank cheque. We'll be out of here tonight.' He tries to hold her again, but she pushes him away.

25

'I need a shower.' She moves towards the en suite. 'Don't leave me,' she pleads. 'Don't leave this room till I'm out.'

She looks so scared, it's freaking him.

'I'll never leave you, Beth,' he says. 'Never.'

She luxuriates a little under the shower. She's told him, he's good with it. They're going to have a kid together. They're going to be like normal people. All the other shit, the drugs, the dodgy business ventures, the sex for money: that's all behind them. Physically, she feels crap, but her head for once is in the right space.

She's aware of a slight chill when she gets out the shower. The air con again, or maybe she just had the water too hot. Donny's watching some reality show on the TV. He's put his jacket on; he's feeling it too.

'Let's go outside,' she says. 'When will Carl have the money?'

'He's working a shift. Four o'clock, maybe.'

They go outside. Beth settles on a lounge in a shaded part of the patio.

Donny brings her juice, coffee, a couple of slices of toast. 'We'll go out someplace for lunch,' he says. 'Bottle of bubbly, eh! We've got something to celebrate.'

'Sure,' she says. She sips the juice. Her lids feel heavy. She slept badly and now she's out of the house, and with Carl gone, she feels more relaxed. 'I'm going to have a nap,' she says. 'You okay?'

'I'll call Louise,' he says. 'Tell her we're good for the money.' He gazes at her. He's still taking it in, she can see. He's going to be a father. 'I love you, babe,' he says.

Louise isn't picking up. He leaves a message, promising he'll have her money in twenty-four hours. He's pissed with Carl, making them wait for the cheque. He takes a shower and dresses in the last of his fresh gear. He'd expected to be gone by now. The bedroom is cold, the air con on the blink again. It's a little warmer in the hall. He should go down, check that Beth's okay. He tries Carl's door. Locked. What dirty secrets you hiding in there, little brother? He moves down the hall to the gallery. He's feeling the heat again, though maybe it's anticipation. There's no denying Carl's talent with a pencil, even if the execution is all in his head. He enters, taking his time to revisit the drawings. Maybe his concentration was misplaced, but it's not until the fourth or fifth drawing that he notices the change. The features are more plainly drawn. The woman is clearly Asian, but her lover… He swears it's him. Just in one or two, his head turned as if inviting the artist's gaze. And then in another, what stops him dead is Noriko, naked but for a pair of knee-high red boots. He can feel his heart beating. The air is so hot and close, he can barely breathe. He loosens his shirt buttons, stumbles towards the door. The thermostat on the wall reads 37, flicking to 38 as he watches.

Those red boots… Out of the gallery, he breathes a little more easily. The air cools rapidly as he descends the stairs. The heightened hum of the air con follows him through the house and down into the cellar. He pulls the suitcases from the cupboard, tips the contents onto the floor. One red boot… It hadn't struck him before. Why would she leave one boot…? He's shaking, the air in the cellar is freezing. It's as if the rise and fall of the air con hum is whispering to him so cold, so cold… Kicking the suitcases aside, he drags the cupboard away from the wall. The door gives at a touch. Pushing it open, he enters pitch darkness and an Arctic chill. A cold room. The cupboard was hiding the door to a cold room… He runs his hand down the jamb for the light switch.

A corpse lies under a sheet on the autopsy table. It disgusted Noriko a little that he worked in the mortuary. You touch dead bodies… Disgusted and excited a little, if she were honest. He was just an orderly, he told her, porter and cleaner. It was no big deal. All the same, Carl's heart always beats a little faster when he's alone with a cadaver. He draws the cover back from the face. A woman well past her prime. The face of a hard grafter, he thinks.

He's about to cover her again when his phone rings. He flips it open, but there's no display. He presses various keys, to no effect. Despite the continuous ringing, the phone appears to be dead. He snaps it shut and opens it again. Still no display, just the constant ringing. He's uneasy, now. Fearful. He's sure it's Noriko, teasing him. Last night was the first in weeks she hadn't come to him. Not even a shiver of her presence. She's jealous, he thinks. Because he had sex with Beth. Was this why she'd appeared to Beth? To warn her off? Scare her away? He takes the phone outside and the ringing stops. He walks to the end of the corridor and flips the top again. There's no display, no life in it. Still uneasy, he slips the phone into his pocket and returns to the autopsy room.

The air seems cooler than a moment ago. Maybe it was because the corridor seemed unnaturally warm. His eye is drawn to the corpse on the autopsy table. He was sure he'd left the face uncovered. There are voices in the corridor, a sudden burst of laughter that quickly drifts away. He stands over the table, his hand on the cover. The cold is making his skin crawl. He draws the cover back.

Beth wakes with a start. Someone was calling her. Donny. Or was she dreaming? She slips off the lounge, sips the dregs of the warm juice. A car burns up the street. Lorikeets are squawking in a flowering bush. A fleeting movement behind an upper floor window. It's nothing, a flash of sunlight on the glass. She hears it then, the slap of water. Donny's in the pool. She crosses the patio and slips through the gate. The glare from the water is almost blinding. She can just make out the swimmer, gliding stiffly under the water. It's not Donny, not in that lipstick pink costume. A neighbour's kid, maybe, small and shapeless. She glides to the end of the pool. As she nudges the edge, she rises to the surface, face down, as if drowned. She floats there, the hot sun glistening on her bare back. Beth can't stop herself, she kneels, reaches out. The body turns suddenly. A hand shoots out, grasping Beth's, hauling her from her knees into the pool.

Noriko. Pale face, pale, pale lips. Eyes closed, as if resting in repose, waiting for the coffin lid to shut her in everlasting darkness. He knows it's not her lying on the table. She's in his head, playing with his perception. He closes his eyes and opens them again. He swears there's a touch of colour come to her lips. She's in his head, still, whispering to him, kiss me… At night, when she comes to him, her lips are deathly cold. He leans over her. It's like kissing ice. It burns.

Maybe it's the baby… She's not conscious of anything, except that she's drowning. Being drowned. Dragged down and held under in a grip so tight she feels her chest being crushed. Maybe it is the baby… Some instinct deeper than naked fear that makes her fight so hard to free herself. And yet the more she struggles, the tighter the grip seems, her last choking breath surely almost upon her. And then suddenly it's gone. Whatever monstrous being is holding her under vanishes in a freezing eddy of water and she's gasping for air, her hand grasping for the pool rail, her head barely above the swirling surface. It's then she thinks, my baby… And then again, arms around her, crushing the breath from her, and a voice hoarse in her ear, 'I've got you, babe, I've got you… Quit struggling…'

'I've called a cab,' Donny says. 'Take you to a motel, couple of blocks away. Riviera. I'll get there as soon as I can.'

She won't go inside the house. Even after he's stripped and rubbed her down, she's still shaking, jabbering like a lunatic. He finally gets her to settle on the patio lounge while he goes back inside to change back into old clothes and make the phone calls. The house is so cold, his wet shirt and pants stick to him like ice.

By the time she's dressed, the cab's at the gate.

'I'll need your phone,' he says. 'Mine's fucked. Stay in your room. Call me when you get there.'

'It was her,' she says. 'Noriko.' She's staring at the pool, its cool, glass-like surface.

29

'Noriko's dead,' he says.

The cabbie's getting impatient, banging on his horn.

'I'm not going without you,' she says. 'This place… It's evil. It's trying to kill us.'

'Soon as I get that cheque,' he says. 'We've got him, babe. We've got a hold over him he'll never wriggle out of.' And then he tells her what he found in the cold room.

It's late afternoon when Carl returns. He looks strung out, like he's had a bad day. Donny's not looking to make it better.

'You want to tell me what a dead girl's doing under your house?'

It's a question Carl seemed to be expecting. He takes a moment to get his answer straight. 'I brought her here,' he says. He seems resigned, almost anxious to confess. 'I paid her airfare. I bought her clothes. I got her whatever she wanted… All I wanted in return was a little loving…'

'You wanted sex,' Donny says. 'That's what you paid for. Then she flipped you.'

Carl smiles, ruefully. 'She said I was a poor lover. Timid. Dull. Unadventurous. She wanted other men. Lots of other men… At first she just stayed out all night. Then she started bringing them home.'

'So you killed her.'

'Sometimes she'd still let me make love to her. But I couldn't perform…unless she was passive. I had to make her passive…'

'You throttled her.'

'She liked it, at first. And then…the last time…she kind of panicked… So I just kept pressing my fingers to her throat till she passed out.'

Donny feels sick. He's been drinking Carl's wine since he put Beth in the taxi. It was all he could do to re-enter the cellar. Nothing would have taken him back into the cold room. Nothing would get that vision of her out of his head: dead, frozen, naked but for that one red boot.

'I knew she'd never stay after that,' Carl says. 'I thought she might go to the police. So I took her downstairs. Carried her. She was as light as a feather. I tried to put her boots on, because she really liked those boots. But she started to come round, so I just…shut the door and left her there. I didn't even look in for about a week. I thought…what's the point…? It's over…' He runs his fingers tenderly across his lips, disfigured by a string of tiny sores. 'Except, that's the thing, it's not… over…'

Donny knows. 'She's still here,' he says tightly. 'Some…thing… that was her… She tried to drown Beth in the pool.'

The sores on Carl's lips have begun to bleed. 'Is she okay?'

'She's gone to a motel. Where that crazy spook can't reach her.'

The air con has started to crank up. The house is rapidly cooling. Carl opens the door to the patio. 'She comes to me,' he says. 'At night… It's like it was in the beginning, when she was instructing me in the art of lovemaking…'

Donny snorts. 'That's all in your head, Carl. You're dreaming. She's messing with your head.'

'No.' He's blunt. Insistent. 'She's there. It's…terrifying…and exhilarating…'

A cold draught is licking at the back of Donny's neck. What Beth told him – that some phantom dragged her into the pool… He hesitated to believe it. It was her eyes that convinced him. The lingering fear. The terror. There's something of that terror in Carl's eyes. And something else…almost playful…

'You always took my girls, Donny,' he says. 'You afraid to take Noriko…?'

He goes outside to phone Beth. She's anxious.

'When are you coming? Did you get the money?'

'Tomorrow. He said the bank needs a day. It's bullshit, but it doesn't matter. I'm pushing him for eighty. He can get it. He's got a dead body in his cellar.'

He can hear Beth's fear in her breathing.

'Don't leave me here alone.'

'I'm stuck here, babe,' he says. 'I'm stuck with Carl. I don't trust him.'

'Please,' she says. 'Donny. I'm scared.'

'You're safe there,' he says. 'Take a pill, get a takeaway delivered. Just chill out, okay? This time tomorrow we'll be flying back to Sydney. And we'll be eighty grand sweeter.'

Carl turns the bed covers down. His bedroom, like the rest of the house, is sparely furnished, dusted and spotlessly clean. Before Noriko came, he paid a Filipina woman to clean and launder, but she pried and stole cutlery, so he let her go. Noriko was scrupulous about housekeeping, though she herself never cleaned; it wasn't what she was there for. Sometimes, in the early hours after she's left and his blood is pumping and the room is still icy from her presence, he hears, he thinks, a teasing reminder to change the sheets. Pausing now before the closet mirror, he inspects his blistered lips, dabbed with antiseptic cream. She's never come to him outside the house before, never come to him in any form other than his spectral lover in the darkest hours. It's Donny's intrusion that has caused the disturbance, piqued her curiosity and playfulness. Already the room temperature is falling, surely in anticipation of his playboy brother's sexual prowess. It's what the apparition on the autopsy table signalled that concerns him. That his crime had been discovered? Or that, as in life, in that ethereal space she now occupies, she has finally tired of him? He should never have allowed Donny into the cellar. The consequence of that he can, at least – belatedly – deal with.

Beth orders takeaway and crawls under the bedsheets to watch TV. She's on the third floor, a three-star motel with tea-making facilities, a mini bar in the fridge and a picture of Uluru on the wall. A bedside clock ticks over the minutes. Her watch still runs, but water has got under the face, misting the glass. She drinks her way through the mini bar and falls asleep with the TV droning in her ear. When the phone rings, she wakes with a start, the room in darkness. She listens to static for a few seconds and hangs up. The clock reads 11.32. She mutes the TV and punches her mobile number into the phone. The clock ticks over to 11.34. How come she missed a minute?

'Hey, babe. You okay?'

'Did you just ring me?'

'Not since an hour ago.'

She feels her breath tighten. 'What time is it?'

'Bit past eleven-thirty.'

'What are you doing?'

'About to jump into bed, babe. Wishing you were here.'

11.36.

'I'm cold,' she says.

'Turn the air con down.'

She watches the ceiling fan working its way through the frigid air. 'There isn't one.'

Donny hangs up. He gets it, she's still spooked. There's nothing he can do except try and soothe her fears. Maybe Carl's right; she's thin-blooded. This other thing with Carl he's not so sure of.

Stripped off, he's alert to every sound and movement, but there's nothing to arouse his senses. He grabs the bed covers, throwing them back to reveal a plain, ice-blue sheet. Satin he was hoping for, nothing as utilitarian as cotton. It strikes him then that the walls are bare, none of the fancy erotica that decorates the other walls. Not even a couple of examples of his own juicy handiwork. He rifles through bedside cabinet drawers, expecting some porn and a cache of little coloured pills that would explain his brother's nightly visitations. Socks, jocks and singlets. In the bottom drawer he roots out a brown envelope hiding a Japanese passport. He flips it open. Noriko's plain, childlike face draws his gaze. A pang of disappointment. She's nothing like the idealised figure of Carl's carefully executed drawings. Even more remote is the frozen naked corpse in the cold room, sporting its one red boot. This nightly visitant…some figment, conjured from Carl's fevered bad conscience. He drops the passport back into the drawer. It comes, then, a long drawn-out sigh whispering in his ear. 'Donny…' The hairs at the nape of his neck rise. He looks around. He's alone, there's no other presence in the room other than his reflected image in the closet mirror. There's nothing to see, but he can feel it, a touch, light as a fingernail tickling his groin. Almost against his will, he's hardening. The light flickers and dies. The sudden deep chill takes his breath. 'Donny…' She's here.

05.03. The phone is ringing. Donny.

'Where are you? The cab's waiting.'

She struggles to wake. 'It's the middle of the night.'

Donny laughs. 'Babe, it's a bright sunny day.'

She peers at the clock. 08.03. She throws back the covers, opens the blind. It's dark outside.

The phone rings.

'Where are you? The cab's waiting.'

'I'm dreaming. Wake me up.'

Donny laughs. 'You know what to do, babe.'

She goes outside, stands at the rail. The motel sign blinks in the dark. Down below the cab is waiting. A hand reaches from the passenger window, beckoning. Beth hooks her leg over the rail. She's dreaming. She knows what to do.

Donny phones Louise; she'll get her money, soon as he sells Beth's unit. Two days back and Sydney's as hot as the Gold Coast. It's like she's reaching out to him, making him sweat for her. Noriko. He can't stop thinking about her. Her. It. Whatever it was came to him in Carl's room. Nothing human. But alive, burning with such fiery passion.

Isn't she something…? Carl's sly gaze in the morning. He's been out already, moving Noriko's body. No body, no leverage. No cheque. Donny wants to punch his face to pulp. He phones the motel.

The receptionist takes the call. 'The police are here,' she says. 'They want to talk to you.'

When he hangs up, there's a message from a missed call. 'I love you…' It's not Beth.

Carl's almost gleeful. 'She won't let you go,' he says. 'Not once she's had you. She's got both of us now.'

'She's here,' Beth says. 'I've seen her. In the street, just staring up at the apartment. She's coming after me.'

'It's your nerves,' Donny says. 'You're still freaked from the motel.'

'It's her,' she says. 'It was her at the motel. She wanted me to jump.'

'You were sleepwalking, babe.'

A pharmaceuticals rep leaving for an early morning flight saw her climbing the rail. He caught her just as she was about to jump. She woke with such a start, she lost it, lashed out, screamed like a banshee. The rep reckoned she was on ice, told the receptionist to call the cops.

'I phoned Louise,' Donny says. 'She'll wait till the unit's sold.'

She's noted the change in him since their return to Sydney. He's pissed about Carl doing the dirty on them, but it's not that. It's not because she slept with Carl; she never wanted that in the first place. He's wary of her. He's almost afraid to touch her.

'I don't care about the unit,' she says. 'I just want you. Us. The baby.'

He nods. 'Let's go out,' he says. 'Get drunk.'

She waits until she hears the shower run and then goes to the window. He believed her when he pulled her half drowned from pool. Now, after the motel, he's conflicted. He thinks being pregnant has turned her a little crazy. She knows what's come between them. It's not the baby.

Cars are jammed back from the busy corner, the sidewalk dense with late afternoon shoppers sweating in the unnatural heat. She's there, exotic and waiflike, standing in the shade of the deli awning, so still she might have been superimposed on the street scene. Watching.

Carl wraps the mortician's saw and cleaver in cloth and places them in his backpack. He needs to return them before they're missed. The pieces of Noriko's roughly dissected body lie in the chest freezer in the outhouse, waiting to be discreetly burnt in the mortuary furnace. He should have done it weeks ago, before Donny came snooping around. Now she's gone. Two nights now she hasn't come to him. Donny's taken her, as he always took his girls.

He finishes his wine and drops the glass in the sink. The house is quiet, just the regular hum of the air con. He checks the time display on the stove: 11.36. He kills the downstairs lights and prepares for bed. If she comes, it'll be just after midnight. With the drapes drawn back, moonlight illuminates the room. A slight chill piques his expectation. Just once more... He slides naked between the sheets. The moon slips behind clouds, plunging the room in sudden darkness. His heart begins to race, anticipating her feathery touch. He's begun to sweat. It shouldn't be like this. Her breath comes like a blast of hot air. Her fingers scratch and burn. It's as if his skin is on fire. He's never felt such scorching pain. Such terror. He's burning alive.

It's the TV that wakes him. He slips from the bed, barely aware of Beth under the covers. He's groggy from too much booze, his joints stiff from vigorous lovemaking. It's what he needed, what they both needed, to reconnect in sex. He shuffles into the lounge, mutes the TV. Some breakfast news programme. He swigs some juice from the fridge, takes a glass for Beth. The fierce morning sun almost bursts through the blinds; the bedroom is as steamy as a hothouse. The TV nags at him. Who turned it on? He draws the bed covers back, runs a finger over Beth's shoulder. She's cold.

He grips her shoulder, pushing her onto her back. 'Babe...?'

She stares up at him, her wide open eyes glassy, opaque. Like orbs of ice. A sob stops his breath. The TV...

A siren voice calls to him. 'Hello... My name is Noriko...'

A Fire Starter Speaks of His Love

It's her hair makes you want to laugh, the reddest hair you ever saw, except maybe for the picture on the box of matches which Pop says looks like some pasty-faced tart peering through lipstick-red curtains, hanging out for some guy to come and pay for a poke. You can't wait to tell Pop about the red-haired lady. Like she had flames shooting out of the top of her head, you'll say, you could almost hear them crackle and hiss, the same as that scabby brown dog you found dead in the yard crackled and hissed when you poured diesel over it and set it alight. That was something to watch, but nothing like watching the red-haired lady crying and punching Sergeant O'Rourke, begging him to let her through. You can see the smoke billowing across the bottom of the street where her house is, and then, just as the wind whips up and dies again, you get a glimpse of the Juna fire tender and two Yellowskins rolling the hose across the kerb.

Jeez, you wish you were down there with them. The red-haired lady is giving O'Rourke such a hard time you could almost slip through without him seeing.

'Hey, hey, hey,' O'Rourke keeps saying to her, soothing like, trying to hold onto her.

She's as slippery as an eel, wriggling and crying, and O'Rourke's hey hey heying getting him nowhere until he grabs hold of her wrists, real tight, like he wants to play some dumb kids' game. She goes kinda limp, then, time enough for O'Rourke to push her up against the side of the squad car and hold her there.

'Please,' she says, 'please...' but O'Rourke still has hold of her.

'You can't go down there,' he tells her, shouting it now, like she's deaf or stupid.

He has his face right up close to hers, but she isn't looking at him. She's looking down the street to where her house is, and the fire burning all around it, the flames jumping and crackling and hissing. Laughing.

That's my girl for you, laughing at you, laughing and licking her fiery lips, just burning (ha ha) to eat you up. You think you can stop me? she says. No one can stop me. The Yellowskins can't stop me. I laugh at them. I laugh at them rolling out their hoses. They turn their tanks of water on me and it's no more than a squirt of piss on a blazing log. Stone walls can't stop me. I can jump roads and rivers. I'm on my own in gullies, racing across the tops of trees. I can move through an open paddock quicker than a mad snake. Fences and chook pens and lean-to sheds are just a taste. Lady, you've got no hope. I'm on the roof of your place now, licking out your gutters. I'm tasting the walls, running my fingers under the eaves, along the windowsills. I'm so hungry I could eat the bricks from your chimney. Hear me. Hear me burn your house down. I'm burning your pretty curtains, the rugs on your floor. I'm burning your books and your bed and the long dresses hanging in your wardrobe. I've boiled your goldfish. I know everything about you. I know the pattern on your plates and saucers. I know the movies you keep, the CDs you bought. I know what pictures you like, the photos you took of your Mum and Dad. I've seen the notes you write yourself, the bills you haven't paid, the dirty washing piling up in the laundry basket. If you've got letters from some smooth-talking guy who's been into your pants, I've burnt them. I've burnt the termites under the floorboards, I've barbecued the lamb chops in the fridge, melted the honey mango ice cream. I've cleaned out the pantry...

Red Hair knows it. O'Rourke's still got hold of her, but sort of loosely, like they're positioning themselves for a country music dance. He's talking at her, jaw jaw jaw, the old business...fire...heat... smoke...suffocation...death... It's like he's telling her a bad news story, getting his side in before she hears it on the Six o'clock Report. Red Hair shakes her head. No, she says, this isn't happening to me...

Down at the creek where it started there'd be just ash now. Ash and baked earth and smouldering splinters of fence posts hanging from blackened wire. And silence. Except for the crows, maybe, always the first to return to pick the steaming flesh from a possum or lizard or a brush turkey, fat as Nan's Sunday joint. Poor little creatures, Nan always says, watching TV with Pop sitting in his old chair, crunching on peanuts. 'Poor little creatures,' Nan says, waiting for the news guy to say, '…caught in the conflagration…'

Conflagration…deflagration…phlegethon… You know these words from Pop's thesaurus. So many words, you never knew half of them existed. When no one's around, you sing some of them out loud, like it's a poem you're reading.

Fiery…flagrant…ignescent…piceous…

Emblaze…incinerate…cremate…

Some don't sound like fire words at all, but you sing them all the same.

Calcinate…cauterise…self-immolate…

How would it be, you keep thinking, to burn to death? Pop says no one ever died from burning because the smoke or the heat gets to you first. Best thing, if you know it's coming, is for your heart to give out. Just the fear of it. Pop says he's seen more burnt bodies than charred steaks on the barbecue, but you'd be dumb to believe that. Pop always takes charge of the barbecue, and how Pop likes his steaks is with the moo cooked right out of them. Pop can't take the taste of blood in his mouth. But give Pop a beer and get him talking, and Nan'll be saying, 'You watching them steaks, Pop?' And you'd smell them. You'd smell the fat crisping to a cinder. You'd think Pop would notice, but he always says human flesh burning has a smell of its own. Those times you've lit a match under your calloused fingertips, you know what he means.

If you'd been Red Hair, you'd never have left the house. You know the drill, see, you know what to do to survive. It's the same as that list of words for fire which you can recite like a poem. You know it by heart –

Protect yourself from radiant heat –

Keep away from windows –

Fill big containers with water –

Watch for embers –

Control mini fires –

Don't hide –

Don't run –

Stay near an outside door for when the fire front has passed –

Maybe (Pop's advice) say a little prayer –

A Yellowskin comes running up the street, waving his arms and hollering at O'Rourke. 'Move back! Move back! Move back!'

You can feel it, like someone blowing on the back of your neck, making your skin prickle. The wind's on the change.

It's just a big game, sporting with nature, Pop says. After October till the autumn rains come, it's the only game to play.

When You Have To Go There

You do not know me. I hope it does not disturb you, my writing like this. I am not a crank. The thing is, you are living in the house I was born in. That was a long time ago now, almost fifty years. Then my parents fell on hard times (as they say) and we moved away. I was only five years old so my memories are a little uncertain. I wonder, has the house changed much? I do apologise for the intrusion, and for addressing you so formally (sir/madam, indeed!). I should not have written but lately I have been feeling sentimental about my childhood. It is the curse of my age group, I suspect. If it is not too much trouble, would you care to write a few words by return and make a sentimental middle-aged fool happy? I would dearly love to see the old place but it really is too far to travel.

With kind regards.

PS. I selected this card especially. My father had a keen interest in the natural world. Our Botanical gardens are rather fine, don't you think? Perhaps you have visited them…

You can't imagine what a pleasure it was to receive your kind letter. The moment I popped my card into the box I thought, Baruch my son, you will regret this. Either there will be no reply or the reply will fill you with such maudlin nostalgia (for a place, let it be said, you hardly remember) you will wish you had never written. See how the Devil sports with me? My dear Miss Linacre, you have restored my faith in – well, myself really. And you have done it with such grace and understanding. And such words! I wept when I read your description of my old home. Such beautiful prose, surely this is no mere talent. You are a journalist, perhaps, a writer. A poet certainly. You write so little of yourself and yet so feelingly of your home. I can see how much you love it. It is just as I remember it (though you are right, the conservatory is new – does it get so cold in that part of the world? I don't recall). My deepest apologies for the brevity of this note. I have business to attend to and I know you will be anxiously awaiting my response. And yes please, a photograph would be much appreciated.

With kind regards.

Do you know, it is not as I remember it at all. When you described the porch and the three steps into the garden, and the brick path that angled around the outhouse, I could see myself there as a toddler making those first tentative steps into the outside world. And yet this photograph you have sent, I look at it and I think, did Baruch live there? It strikes no chord, plucks no string of emotion. It is just a common little suburban house, your neighbour's perhaps, similar in design, but – ah, here we have it! You think Baruch is not who he says he is! We will give him a little test, you say! Well, you are sprung, Miss Linacre, admit it! Shall we try again?

I did enjoy your most interesting letter. How coincidental that we are of a similar age. I too live alone, though I have my diversions…

Cheers.

It was not my intention to question your integrity. Forgive me. I am so ashamed of my boorishness I can barely write. This poor card must suffice. Do you like it? How magnificent the plane trees look in bloom! The town is rather proud of them. The partly obscured building behind is the municipal library. You would find me there – if you cared to look! – every Saturday morning. Do you like to read, Miss Linacre? (Of course you do!) I imagine the rooms of your house filled with books. In Baruch's time, alas, there were but a few: Frost's *Poems* – a favourite of my father's (I still have it!), a children's encyclopedia, an Oxford dictionary, some romantic novels much loved by my mother, and three or four largely unread nineteenth-century volumes on self-improvement. The books of childhood, indeed, stay with you forever! My father, I blush to confess, was a free-thinker, so there were no works of a theological nature – not even a Bible!

Kindest regards.

Though you have not replied to my card, I feel composed enough to write a little further. I have re-examined your photograph and all my original doubts have returned (not about your photograph – what a fool I was!). It was short-sighted of me to expect the house you have so lovingly maintained (or is it restored?) to be the same house I remember from more than forty years ago. Each year, as it fades a little more in my memory, so it grows in my imagination. In truth, bearing in mind my parents' impoverished circumstances when we left, it would have been an ugly little place, in need of a coat of paint, windows stuck fast from the damp (your note about cyclical weather patterns was most revealing).

I will tell you something I have told no one before. My father had a small butchers business which got into difficulties. In the end the house and nearly everything in it had to be sold to pay off his debts. I still have the auctioneer's notice which lists the household effects. It is a curious and painful document to read, even after all these years. It has occurred to me I could write it out for you (I have this childish weakness for lists!) though I doubt that you would find it of more than academic interest. I have only the haziest recollections of those dark days, though I do remember one afternoon a fellow from the estate agent called, a flash sort with silver caps on his teeth and wearing a wide-brimmed hat (the small things that stay in your memory!). My mother was so distressed she shut herself in the pantry. My poor father went to the pub… Do you have much use for the old pantry these days, Miss Linacre? I can see where it is on your photograph, the smaller of the two windows on the (east?) side, above the rhododendrons…

With kind regards.

Certainly I do not tell lies. Nor do I invent stories to impress you. My memory, I am sure, is no better or worse than the next man's. I thought we had been through all that. Of course I cannot remember the books I mentioned from such an early age (the emphasis was particularly noted), but certainly from my later childhood, by which time, I can assure you, Miss Linacre, they would have been in the family a great number of years, at least since the time we occupied the house you now own. The one exception (for which I regret having misled you) being the children's encyclopedia. That was given me on my seventh birthday. I remember it distinctly: each volume had a clean bookplate pasted over the name of the previous owner.

My apologies for the card. It is the only one I have at hand. The building in the picture, however, is of historical interest. I believe the last person hanged there was a brute convicted of sodomising and mutilating a schoolteacher's wife in 1944.

Yours regretfully.

Teasing – I should have realised… You did not strike me as that sort of person, but I am getting to know you better…

As we are friends again, I thought it would be interesting to test my memory a little further. I knew I was right about the pantry window! My earliest memory, you know, is of that enormous pantry (well, it seemed enormous to me). In fact, of all the rooms in the house it is the only place I remember with any certainty. I can see it now as if I were standing again on the bare boards: sacks of potatoes, sugar bags, strings of onions (I told you I had a weakness for lists!), on the shelves jars and containers of all shapes and sizes, biscuit tins (one of which my mother kept for toffees – oh, how I remember those toffees!). And the smells! Is it likely, do you think, that I should still smell that pantry after so long? If the truth were known, it was probably the damp I could smell, a mustiness made all the more pungent by the odour of rotting vegetables.

My mother, I have to say, was not a good housekeeper. She was very beautiful but frivolous and untidy. After my father died, she squandered what little money he left her on expensive clothes and holidays at the coast with Uncle Pete and Uncle Jack and Uncle Arnie.

You know what I'm saying, Miss Linacre. My mother was a tart. When I was twelve, she sent me to live with some dreadful aunt of hers while she went west with a traveller in imported ladies' underwear. Fancy knickers and stuff, just the sort of business a tart like her would be interested in. She said to me, 'I'll send for you, sweetie, when I'm settled.' She was sitting on her bed in her fancy knickers and stockings, with her blouse undone. That fly boy was packing her bags. She wrote once or twice, and then nothing. I didn't care. My mother the tart, why should I care? I like to think she was found dead in a seedy hotel room some place, a long silk stocking knotted tightly around her neck…

Excuse the crease. My landlady was here a moment ago, pressing me for the rent (it isn't due until Friday). She has noticed that I have begun writing to someone and is consumed by curiosity, but hasn't the courage to speak. We were good friends once, and then last Christmas she came drunk to my room and kissed and fondled me and spoke of the great emptiness in her soul that only poetry could fill. She had seen my father's copy of Robert Frost on the shelf beside the bed and thought I was a poet (ha!). We have not spoken much since. I have lived most of my life in hotel rooms, Miss Linacre, since I was fifteen in fact, when I gave my mother's aunt the slip. There is usually a sad individual like my landlady in one of them. It's a cock up the cunt they're after, that's their kind of poetry, not my father's beloved Robert Frost. Did I say how pleased I was to learn that you have read him? I was sure you would have. Do you recall that poem about the hired man who returns sick to the farm he's been absent from for some years? 'He has come home to die,' the wife says. 'Home,' the farmer muses (he mocks gently). 'Home is the place where, when you have to go there, they have to take you in.' And his wife says, 'I should have called it something you somehow haven't to deserve…' Do you know where I think of when I read and reread those lines, Miss Linacre…?

With fondest regards.

You have not answered my letter. Are you unwell? I can't bear to think of you lying in pain or discomfort and no one to care for you. You live like a recluse, you told me so yourself, and it is not good for you. Think of your heart! (How is that little murmur?) Should I come to you? Perhaps it's not so far to travel after all (though a little something towards the fare would be welcome). I suggest you give me your answer by return or else I'll pack my bags regardless, simply to come and satisfy myself you are in no danger. You can depend on Baruch, Miss L: he is a meticulous man, clean in his habits, and has a fondness for Dvorak's *New World Symphony*, which he likes to play on a portable record player bought for twenty dollars at Mr Singh's (licensed dealer in second-hand goods and books).

Did that make you smile? You must keep a sense of humour at all costs. Remember your little tease…?

I trust this card will cheer you. The illustration is interesting, don't you think, though Oriental erotica is not entirely to my taste…

Yours.

You disappoint me. If you wished to end our correspondence, you simply had to say. A letter from your solicitor was not warranted. An unnecessarily threatening letter, I might add. It was the card I sent, wasn't it? I knew it was a bad choice. Mr Singh let me have it. He keeps a selection of such items under the counter for his 'scholarly' customers. Mr Singh numbers me among his 'scholarly' customers, though I fear he deludes himself. I prefer an action novel, myself, or a nice fat popular biography of a military figure, such as Alexander the Great.

I was at Mr Singh's yesterday when he drew me aside. 'This will interest you, Mr Baruch,' he said. 'It is about a fellow accused of murdering a young lady and then disposing of her body. The fellow claims it is all an unfortunate mistake. Death occurred during sexual congress, he says. It transpires the young lady was performing a certain act and tragically choked on his semen. A terrible miscarriage of justice averted,' Mr Singh said. 'The poor fellow might have hanged for his dubious pleasures.'

It is goodbye then, Miss Linacre. Your solicitor employs some fine language, though I think it is largely bluff. In parting, I include the list I promised you earlier (I trust you'll find it a little more than of academic interest…)

Beds (1 double, 1 single), wardrobes (1 large, 1 small), chests of drawers (2), tall boy, side lamps, rugs, roller blinds,

enamel piss pot,

horsehair sofa, easy chairs (2), sideboard, glass cabinet (cracked), lamp standard, ass. bric-a-brac, net curtains,

laminated table, ladder-backed chairs (4), cabinet (painted, no glass), bench, butcher's knives,

hat stand (incl. gentleman's wide-brimmed hat),

tea chests (4), sacks, ass. storage jars, biscuit tins, rug, skirt, knickers, gentleman's single-breasted jacket, trousers (including braces), white underpants, toffee paper.

(toffee paper?)

prophylactic wrapper.

With compliments.

Traces

She would be fifty-five, he thought, maybe sixty. A shapeless rag of a woman, all skin and bones. She was watching him warily from behind the screen door, her free hand playing nervously with the latch. He could understand her nervousness. Standing under the veranda with the sun behind him, his face would be in shadow. She would be one of those women who could read a bloke's character in the shape of his face – the position of his eyes, the angle of his jaw. He had her at a disadvantage, all right. She had snibbed the lock on the screen door, hoping he hadn't noticed. Out here with only the cane fields around them, and even the flies resting from the heat, it was like a rifle shot in the dark. She knew he'd heard.

She withdrew a little, stepping back into the gloom of the house, taking something of his advantage. He wasn't concerned. He was used to peering into dark corners. His eyes were still as keen as a young cat's. She lifted her good arm and rested it across her chest. Defensive. He knew all about body language, he'd read books on it. He saw the way her long bony fingers picked absently at a scab on her neck. Bad habits. He was interested in people's bad habits. He'd spent almost ten years studying people's bad habits. He let his eyes rest for a moment on a small angular tear in the screen door. What really interested him right now, what excited his curiosity, was why this scrawny woman's left arm was strapped in a sling.

'Work,' she said. 'What sort of work?'

'Fencing, painting. Anything mechanical. I'm a good all-rounder.'

She approached the screen door again, gaining confidence. He was careful not to look away because people who avoided your eye were not to be trusted. That's what she'd think. She scrutinised his face – or as much of it as she could make out. He was wearing a wide-brimmed straw hat that he'd picked up at a market for two dollars. It gave his advantage that slight edge, but he thought he could do without it now. She was wavering. She was interested. She was… He moved back towards the veranda step, into the sun. The hat he lifted with a little flourish that she might have thought just a touch old-fashioned. He shouldn't overdo it. He didn't want her thinking she was being manipulated. He couldn't afford it. He needed the work. Badly.

'What's your name?' she said.

'McNeil.'

'I got a few jobs need doing, but I got no money to pay you.'

He shrugged. 'A bite to eat, somewhere to kip for a few days. I'm easy.'

She unlatched the screen door and stepped out onto the veranda. She was wearing weathered denims and a loose sleeveless top. Her skin had a flaky, mottled look which made him think of an old tree stump shedding its bark. She stood for a moment without saying anything, without even looking at him, directly, though he was sure she would be aware of the most subtle movement, the tiniest facial tic.

He flopped the hat onto his head again and backed against the veranda post. 'Bit of a handicap you've got there.'

She smiled uncertainly. For just a second it was as if she hadn't a clue what he was referring to. Then she said, 'You'd be surprised the mischief I can get up to with one hand tied.'

He didn't know whether he was supposed to laugh, so he just nodded. She was telling him to keep his distance, he could understand that. A part of him wanted to reassure her, tell her that at his age sex was something he used to have with street girls when he still had the money and the need. But then there was that other part, the part that said to keep his mouth shut; the part that wanted to keep her guessing.

'You'd better come through,' she said. 'That all you've got?'

He reached for the bag that he'd dumped on the bottom step earlier. 'Everything I need.'

There was that flicker of nervousness again as if inside the bag, beneath the change of clothes, the underwear, the shaving kit, there might be magazines that she wouldn't like the look of, hoods and straps, knives honed to a razor's edge. Tools of his trade. He threw the bag lightly over his shoulder and followed her into the house. The screen banging behind them might have been a cell door closing.

It was a small property, a squat, ugly little house, not unlike ones he'd lived in as a boy, some crumbling outhouses, and two large paddocks of long dry grass. There was another house about a kilometre away, owned by a one-armed man, she told him, who kept exotic birds. He was interested in the exotic birds, but she couldn't tell him anything about them. She'd fallen out with her neighbour over the grass in her paddocks which he wanted burnt off before the heat of summer made it too risky. She was more interested in the loss of her neighbour's arm than concerned about the fire hazard. People's disabilities held a peculiar fascination for her. She noticed at once that he had two fingers missing. A sister of hers (now dead) had been born with a club foot, and a cousin had been blinded at school trying to make a bomb. She told him all this while she was brewing tea in the large untidy kitchen. Her own handicap she dismissed as 'a bit of a nuisance'. She'd slipped on the back step coming up in the dark and had sprained her wrist trying to break her fall. He guessed that she'd been drunk. There was a near empty bottle of Scotch on the sink and he'd noticed two full bottles in the cupboard when she'd been taking down the tea. It was more than ten years since he'd last had a drink, though he wasn't going to tell her that. He didn't want her thinking he was some kind of puritan.

She showed him the jobs that needed doing – some roofing iron had come loose, the septic was backing up into the house (he'd noticed the smell), and there was an old Valiant in the garage that she wanted stripping for its parts. He reckoned there was a week's work in it at least. She was interested to know what he thought the parts from the

Valiant would fetch – men knew about these things, didn't they? He gave her some figures off the top of his head and she seemed satisfied. He was a bit out of touch with the cost and value of things. There wasn't much buying and selling where he'd been recently. Not buying and selling as she would understand it.

Next to the garage there was a caravan with dented aluminium panels and a shrivelled grapevine clinging to the roof. She gave him a broom and sheets and a musty smelling pillow. Except for his meals, she didn't want him inside the house. She made that quite clear. He could wash and use the toilet in the laundry. He told her that was fine by him, he knew his place. She wasn't too sure what to make of that.

There was one thing he liked about her – she didn't seem too nosy. He couldn't stand those inquisitive types, the ones who wanted to know every small detail of your life. There was a couple he'd done some odd jobs for, an elderly couple, more generous than he would've expected. He could have worked for them permanently, mowed their lawns, cut logs, painted, cleaned the gutters. He had it in his hand. The old man had a heart complaint, and she was crippled with arthritis. They needed someone like him, not so young, not too old. Experienced. They shared their meals with him and let him sleep in a quiet enclosed part of the veranda which had once been their daughter's bedroom. They'd had two sons but they'd both died, one in a car crash, the other of some rare disease. They told him everything about it. They included him as if he were one of the family too. He was flattered by this, but he didn't like it. It was nothing to do with him. He only listened because they were kind and generous and didn't mean him any harm. But he hardly knew them. They told him all these things – these private things – as if he were a priest or something. As if it was something they had to get off their chest. He couldn't bear it. And then, when they'd told him all these things, they began to ask him questions about himself. He wasn't a young man, and he didn't appear to have anywhere permanent to live. That interested them. That excited their curiosity. Not in the way the woman's arm in a sling had excited his curiosity earlier. That was different. That was business, knowing the score. This old couple were taking a personal interest in his life. His whole life, every changing year of it. And he wasn't having that. No, sir. He wasn't having that at all.

It was late September. He hadn't expected this sort of heat. He'd come north for the winter, thinking of his age, his health. The terrain constantly surprised him. He'd never seen fields of cane before, hills webbed with banana plants. He was a foreigner in his own country.

'How'd you lose them fingers?'

It was the second day; he was eating breakfast. She cooked porridge for breakfast, winter and summer; he'd have to put up with it.

He wiped the bowl clean with a slice of limp bread. 'Rip saw. I got careless.'

'Wouldn't have took you for the careless sort.'

He'd cleared the septic and begun to strip the Valiant. It was stifling in the garage, but at least it was out of the sun. She told him the roof could wait. She was thinking in terms of the likelihood of rain, but he was counting the days. He'd have to stretch the work out a bit if he wanted to stay. And he did want to stay. He could see how he could make himself useful around the place. He wasn't taken in by her talk of having no money. She'd see how useful he was and make him stay. She'd need him because she was in a bad way. Sprained wrist one day, fractured skull the next. He'd heard her rolling around in there after dark, singing to herself. Singing and talking to herself. Two nights he'd heard her. The first night he'd thought she was calling out to him and nearly went in. He'd stopped at the kitchen door. Her voice became strangely subdued. She sang off-key, but he'd had to listen to worse. She sang, 'Hold me tight as the nights grow colder.'

The nights were growing warmer.

He didn't think about sex, not much. She wasn't so old, but she hadn't taken care of herself. It wasn't just the drinking. It was the way she lived, as if she'd given up. He guessed something in her life had turned sour. He knew he was going to hear about it when she brought him a mug of coffee as he worked on the car. She stuck around. He didn't like it, but what could he do? She had him captive, so to speak.

'You ever been married, McNeil?'

'Not me.'

'I been married,' she said. 'That's his vehicle you're taking apart.'

He gathered from the way she said it that he was long gone. Dead or run off, she wasn't telling. He'd noted the registration label on the windscreen – 1999. The year he went away. It was something they shared, then, the same wasted years. At least he'd kept himself fit, read books, learnt things.

She watched him closely as he drank his coffee. 'You know what this place used to be?' she said. 'Church property. And up the street there were houses and shops and a coupla pubs.'

It was her use of the word street that interested him. They were still there, those houses and shops and pubs, still a living part of her memories. Or nightmares. Even in the poor light of the garage he could see the strain on her face.

'Nothing left now,' she said after a moment. 'Not a trace.' She seemed almost cheerful about it.

He went back to his work.

She emptied the dregs of his coffee into the dirt. 'I don't need no one to look after me,' she said, knowing what he was thinking. 'I can look after meself.'

'Cept when you fall on your arse,' he said.

Her laugh was like the squawk of a duck with the dogs on its tail.

The following day he drove her into town. She had a ute with a blowing muffler. He'd tell her about it later, he thought. Something to keep in reserve. The motor didn't sound too hot either. He could see the work piling up. Another week, at least.

She bought a few provisions at the supermarket – milk, potatoes, bread, sausages. More porridge. She didn't ask him what he liked. She walked past the bottle shop. Later she directed him into a side street. He saw a brass plaque on a brick wall.

'I gotta see the quack,' she said. 'About me arm.'

He understood why she'd put on a smart dress that morning, done something with her hair. It wasn't for the benefit of the check-out girls in the supermarket. He looked at the name on the brass plaque. Dr A.J.C. Symons. He'd read about a doctor who'd checked some woman's pulse by squeezing her nipples. You'd think any woman would be so dumb?

After about forty minutes he saw her come out. Her arm was still in the sling. He saw that the bandage had been changed and secured with a shiny safety pin that matched the buttons on her dress.

'Monday,' she said.

He turned the ignition. Four days. He could work something by then. She'd wonder how she'd ever managed without him.

'Stop at the servo on the way home,' she said. 'I forgot to buy smokes.'

The heat was oppressive now. He fiddled with the vent on the dash and got a blast of hot air, as foul as dog's breath. She was sitting next to him with her legs apart, the hem of her smart dress pulled up past her knees. Like a fifteen-year-old tart, he thought. Inviting. He shifted gear to take a bend. This was where he'd hitched a ride three days ago. A back road going nowhere, cane fields, a small mill gone to the wall. He should've stuck to the coast. That's what he was thinking. He'd watched a milk truck turn out of sight. Further up the road he'd seen the house with the fading pink weatherboards, the gate hanging off its hinges.

He shifted gear again. There was a line of perspiration along her top lip. Her forehead shone. She hadn't spoken since she'd left the servo. She hadn't even offered him a smoke. Bad habits again. He didn't think so badly of her bad habits now. He liked her better. It must have been the smart dress and the trouble she'd taken with her hair. He even liked the way she smoked, the shape of her mouth, the look of deep satisfaction on her face as she blew a shot of smoke across the windscreen. She looked at him hardly at all. He was aware of how far up she'd drawn the hem of her dress. He could touch her now and he'd be there before she even knew what he was about.

'You ever handled a firearm, McNeil?'

He concentrated his thoughts on the road.

'I reckon I must've shot more snakes and foxes than you've had hot dinners,' she said.

He didn't dispute it. He imagined her drunk, or half drunk, shooting at shadows in the corners.

She laughed, misunderstanding his silence, and boasted, 'One-handed, too.'

They came to the street where the houses had been, the shops and pubs.

'Bastard!'

There was smoke rising from behind the house. A thick, black choking cloud had turned the bright day into dusk. He'd never seen a fire like that, never seen grass burn with such fierce intensity. It was like a field full of cane burning, it was as if the land itself had sprung alight. They pulled up at the house. The air was filled with ash, some of it still glowing, little satellites of flame spiralling to the ground. There was a sound like a great rush of wind as the fire swept through the long parched grass.

'That bastard!' she screamed. 'That cripple bastard has set my paddocks on fire!'

Martians, he thought, strange figures in yellow came looming out of the smoke. He heard the sound of a truck. A water tender was moving slowly along the fence, soaking the ground behind it.

'It's all right!' he shouted at her. 'They've got it under control.'

She wasn't listening to him. She ran towards the smoke and for a moment was lost from sight. He wasn't fool enough to go after her. It's just a grass fire, he thought. It's nothing to get excited about. This is the way things are done. He was the one who should have been affected about it, exhilarated, a little fearful. He was the outsider.

All at once, the fire seemed to burn itself out. The air was heavy with smoke; it was difficult to breathe. He could see her standing beside the water tender. She was gesturing wildly and shouting. There was no sign of the one-armed neighbour. The water tender turned and drove back across the smouldering paddock.

In the evening, she got drunk. There was no hiding it this time. She sat on the back step with the bottle and called out to him. 'McNeil! Come and keep a lady company.'

She was wearing the same dress, the smart dress. It didn't look so smart now. She'd slipped her arm free of the sling. He guessed she'd drunk so much she could no longer feel the pain.

He lay on his bunk in the caravan and listened to her. She finished the bottle and threw it across the yard.

'McNeil!' she called out. 'Come and fetch a lady a drink.' She was growing maudlin. 'I got songs in my head and misery in my heart,' she moaned.

When she began to weep, he turned his face to the wall.

He woke early. He was aware of a strange light and the lingering smell of burnt grass. He pulled on a pair of strides and a sweater, and stepped out into the yard. The blackened paddocks were like a waste land, a moonscape. The air was still thick with smoke, or it might have been mist rising from the dew wet earth.

He'd half expected to see her slumped over the back step, dead to the world. The back door was shut. He walked to the fence. Some of the posts had been singed, but it was a marvel how the fire had been contained. He imagined looking down on the scene from a great height and seeing two overlapping black patches, like postage stamps. He ducked under the fence and picked his way across the scorched earth. In places, thick clumps of grass continued to smoulder.

He walked to the centre of the paddock and stopped. He was standing on a rectangular slab of stone. There were others within spitting distance, some broken, some half buried, all weathered and blackened by the fire. Gravestones. He was struck by the absurdity of it, as if he'd stumbled onto the film set of some horror movie. But it wasn't horror he felt. Not even unease. It was a sort of numbness, an emptiness. He couldn't really describe it. He looked down at the stone. He wondered if her name were inscribed on it, the name of her father, a grandfather. He had no way of telling. The names had long worn away, and anyway, he knew her only by the name of the absent Valiant owner. Looking back at the house, he saw that a light had come on in the kitchen. And he saw himself as she might see him, if she were inclined to the supernatural. A spectre rising from its tomb.

It was then that he became afraid.

Real Estate

1

'Hello', she says. 'Have you come about the room?'

'Well, I haven't come to read the meter,' I say, and we both laugh.

That's a good start. Break the ice before it has a chance to set. Not that she strikes me as the frosty sort. Lovely smile. A little condescending, perhaps, so I keep my guard up, just in case. I needn't have worried. As soon as she tells me she teaches the tots at Riverdale Primary, I relax. Can't be grim with the kiddies. I do like her face. Very pretty (and doesn't she know it), but in a girlish rather than a handsome sort of way. Wedding band. Insignificant little engagement ring. She plays with it absently while I look over the room. A monk's cell, warmed by a little morning sunlight coming through the blinds. The faintest whiff of some cleansing agent.

'Laundry's included with the rent. Did I say?'

I take it.

They're an odd pair, Jodi and Trent. Trent and Jodi. I never know who to say first. In any marriage, one partner usually dominates. Isn't that true? These two are more like brother and sister. The way they tease each other, crack jokes, make puns. The banter. It's almost childlike. Never sexual. Good clean fun. I've never heard a murmur come from their bedroom at night. Not that I make a point of listening. And the house: 1960s red-brick shoebox, nondescript but solid.

I eat with them most evenings. This wasn't part of the arrangement, but we all get on so well, being much the same age (twenty-somethings) and liking the same TV programmes, it just kind of happened. Right from that first night when they insisted I share dinner with them. Just to help me settle in, feel at home. Of course I pay a little extra.

Sometimes, if they're both working late (Trent sells computers), or have some private business to attend to, I knock up a quick stir-fry when they come in. Fresh vegies, leftover chicken, noodles. They appreciate it. That I muck in. The situation – it's more like a share house, really. I don't feel like their lodger. Sometimes I bring home doughnuts for supper, or rent a video (romantic comedy for Jodi, something a little arty for Trent). We sit in the TV room, drinking beer, Trent and Jodi on the sofa, holding hands, me in the painted wicker chair.

We watch the credits roll.

'Top show, Franz,' Trent says (invariably).

He calls me Franz. They both do. That's cool. I kind of like it.

Most mornings, Jodi leaves for work before Trent. Trent is not really a morning person. He's not a breakfast person, either. A glass of juice and two cups of black coffee. That's Trent's breakfast. And neither is he much of a conversationalist at that hour. He does like a smoke, though. It's funny, that. Two cigarettes each morning, one before breakfast (juice and coffee) and one afterwards. Not inside the house. In the garden. Under the clothes hoist, usually, where there's a little early morning winter sun. I watch him from the kitchen window, standing under the clothes hoist, smoking his cigarette and looking reflective. Thinking. Thinking about computers, I imagine, though he's not what you might call a computer bore. You know the type: hard drive, software, gigabytes, soundcard, ram, jabber jabber jabber. A foreign language to most of us. A second language to the computer geek. But that's not Trent. His job's his job. He loves it, but it's rarely a dinner table topic. Probably because Jodi doesn't know one end of a computer from the other. Like me, I say. Which is not altogether true; they're an essential tool of my trade, after all. But that's work. It's Trent's work too, of course, but that's different. It's his livelihood.

The one time I see Trent and Jodi unhappy with each other is when he rather stupidly brings the subject of computers up over dinner. He couldn't help himself. A new model, all the bells and whistles. No sooner had he started (hadn't got past gigabyte) than Jodi slaps her hands to her ears and shrieks, 'Nerd attack! Nerd attack! Nerd attack!'

Did I laugh, or what?

Trent didn't. He looked quite put out. Po-faced, I guess you'd say. Hurt.

Jodi was just a touch regretful. But she couldn't resist a giggle. 'Franz thought it was funny, didn't you, Franz.'

Franz grins, but thinks it best to say nothing.

It seems for a moment that Trent will leave the table, go to their bedroom and sulk. But he settles for a little snort of indignation, and then smiles. Not altogether warmly, but still. A young lovers' tiff averted.

Usually I'm the last one home from work, but some days, if business is quiet, I'll finish early. I let myself in through the back door, and if I hear the radio playing, I know Jodi's home. She's slicing onions or scrubbing potatoes, putting together something delicious for dinner.

'Hello, Franz,' she says, always pleased to see me. 'How's your day been?'

I tell her about my day. This is one of the strange things about Trent and Jodi. They're day-to-day people. I don't know anything about their past, their background: where they met, whether they have brothers or sisters, what their fathers do or did, whether they grew up in Riverdale or hereabouts. As a couple they're oddly self-contained. I never ask. I don't like to seem to be prying. Neither do they talk much about their hopes or plans for the future, though Jodi did let slip that, if she were to fall pregnant, I would have to move into the 'junk room', as they'd always intended my room to be the nursery. The oddest part of this was hearing her say 'fall pregnant', which made me think of them having sex, when nothing in their day-to-day behaviour – apart from the hand holding on the sofa while watching TV – suggested the remotest sexual interest in each other. The other thing that struck me was the understanding that, once they had a baby, there was no suggestion that I should leave. Of course, they would need the extra money then. I knew they were finding it a bit of a struggle already to keep up with the mortgage payments on the house.

This particular day that I tell her about has not much going on in it, so I feel I'm boring her. She looks kind of down. I wash and prepare a lettuce for a salad while she trims the lamb cutlets she's bought for dinner.

She opens a bottle of cheap red wine. 'Let's have a drink, Franz. Do you feel like one?'

I don't really, but I say yes.

'I'm not very happy today, Franz. I'm sure you realise.'

We're sitting across the table from each other. I reach for her hand and give it a gentle squeeze. I can feel a slight resistance, and I think she's going to pull away, but she doesn't. After a moment, I withdraw my hand.

She wipes her nose with a tissue. 'I saw a little dog run over this morning,' she says. 'It was horrible.'

Riverdale Primary is two blocks from Jodi and Trent's house. Jodi always walks to work, even if it's raining. She strides off down the street, the rain splashing off her huge bright red umbrella.

'It ran out from a garden. A terrier of some sort. A little girl was calling after it. It just went shooting across the road and a car ran right over it. Poor thing. Poor little thing. Thankfully it didn't suffer. The girl was absolutely distraught. I should've stopped, but I couldn't bear it. And there were people there, neighbours and the girl's mother. I just kept going. But all day, I haven't been able to get it out of my mind. I wanted to cry. All day I've just wanted to cry. Mrs Parsons, the principal, said I should come home. I was upsetting the children.' She begins to cry. Little sobs of grief for a little dead dog.

I get up and walk round the table to her, put my hand on her shoulder. She reaches for my free hand and holds onto it, a bit tight.

I think of something to say. 'It was just the little girl's dog,' I tell her. 'It could have been the little girl.'

It's difficult to tell at first what effect this has had on her. Her sobs have eased to a kind of flu-like snuffle. I squeeze her shoulder. She squeezes my hand. She doesn't seem to want to let go.

'Yes,' she says. 'I'm being silly. A little dog. It's sad, but I'm being much too emotional about it. I should be thinking of that little girl. She's the one who'll be heartbroken.' She releases her grip on my hand.

I tactfully withdraw, resume my seat. We drink our wine in silence for a few moments. She looks quite sad still, but at least she's over the sobbing. She wipes her eyes and blows her nose into a fresh tissue.

I refill the glasses. The bottle is almost empty. I look up to catch her staring at me.

'Don't tell Trent, please.'

'Tell Trent what?'

'Anything. About the poor little dog. And…that I was upset.'

Of course I won't tell Trent, if that's what she wants. Lips sealed. Not a whisper.

She seems uneasy. Unconvinced. My acquiescence was maybe a bit too…unquestioning.

'Trent hates it when I cry. If I get weepy over something, a bit teary…he gets really angry. He can't cope. It was his mother… She was a bit of a drama queen, apparently. Highly strung. She took tablets in the end… You know…'

'Killed herself.'

'Yes.'

It's the first piece of personal history I've heard from either of them. What a shocker.

'My mother could be a bit of a drama queen too,' I confess. 'But she didn't kill herself. Alas.'

It's as if I swore at her. Insulted her. Gave her a sharp slap across the cheeks. That one tiny word. Teasing appendage.

She's horrified. 'What a horrible thing to say!'

I laugh lightly. Ha ha. She's not mollified. It's not something to joke about. Not with these two, at any rate.

We hear Trent's car in the drive. Jodi gives me an anxious look.

I shan't tell. I shan't.

Trent has been to the bottle shop. Another bottle of wine. Jodi has already dropped the empty bottle in the recycle bin. The glasses have been rinsed, wiped and put away.

'Hello, Franz,' Trent says cheerfully. 'How's your day been?'

Jodi moves round the table, takes the wine from him.

He looks at her. 'You okay, Sweets? You look kinda fraught.'

She sighs. 'Those kids. Little devils, sometimes.'

It's not the same, though, after this. Nothing has changed, not on the surface of things, but it's like we're different people. Different not in ourselves, but as we are to each other. Jodi and Trent have become more self-contained. More than they were, though I wouldn't have thought it possible. I've become the lodger, the guy who's renting the spare room. Like I say, it's not as if we're doing things differently. I still pick up the odd movie, surprise them with an innovative stir-fry. But there's a distance between us. Between me and Jodi, really, but then it's not as if she can be separated from Trent. I thought at first it was my stupid remark about my mother. That dumb joke. Like Jodi knows it wasn't a joke, and I honestly don't give a shit about the stupid woman. But I don't think it's that at all. I think she's pissed off with herself for letting slip that little gem of info about Trent's loony mother. Exposed his wound, so to speak. Made him bleed. Because what makes Trent bleed makes both of them bleed. Weakens them.

Trent doesn't know any of this. Leastways, that is what I assume, as we still kind of muck around together as if nothing's changed. Until…

'You'll have to leave, Franz,' he says, waking me early, and standing stiffly at the end of my bed. 'Jodi doesn't want you here any more. She feels uncomfortable being close to you. I've sensed it myself, for a while now. This feeling you have for her. She's my wife, fuck you, and if you ever make a move on her I'll smash your face to pulp.'

I don't argue. I just leave. I don't even get a chance to say goodbye to Jodi. Trent makes sure of that. I give it a couple of days. And then, as luck will have it, an opportunity presents itself.

'Hi, Jodi. How are you?'

'Oh, Franz, you shouldn't phone. What if Trent had answered?'

63

'He isn't there, Jodi. I just saw him driving up City Road.'

'He's gone to get a movie. How are you, Franz? I feel so awful about what happened.'

'It wasn't your fault.'

'I know. I don't know what got into Trent. I can't understand why he'd even think such a thing. Me and you, Franz. How ridiculous. Trent's not normally a jealous guy, you know. He's never accused me of anything like this before. There was this one guy, John, single dad. I met him at a P&C. We kind of clicked. I mean – I didn't feel anything for him, not sexually, but he was a lovely guy. I really liked his company. I know he fancied me. I told Trent because…well, you know, I didn't want any misunderstanding. And Trent was okay about it. I think he rather liked it, actually, that there was this guy sweet on me. And having a little boy… I don't know. But it happens sometimes with young fathers and their children's teachers… But Trent trusts me, Franz. He always has. He knows I'd never, never be unfaithful to him. Which is why I find his attitude to you so extraordinary…'

'He said I made you feel uncomfortable. He said you didn't like me being close to you. Like I repulsed you. Do I repulse you, Jodi?'

'No, Franz, of course you don't! It's nothing you did. Or I did. It's just Trent. He got it into his head you wanted to sleep with me. He can be very pigheaded when he gets a notion about something. Doesn't matter how unreasonable or irrational it is.'

'As long as I don't repulse you, Jodi.'

'You're quite a gorgeous-looking boy, Franz, you know you are. If you were attracted to me, well… I guess I'd be kind of flattered. If you said you loved me, and I wasn't with Trent, and… Oh, a hundred other things… I suppose… I mean… I reckon, you know…'

I'm not attracted to her. Not particularly. But that's not the point, is it?

We agree to meet. That is, she agrees. She's not altogether keen. She doesn't like going behind Trent's back, deceiving him. It's not deceit, I tell her. She's not being unfaithful. We're just friends. We like each other's company. If she can be friends with her single dad from school, she can be friends with me. If Trent doesn't see it that way, then it's best he doesn't know. And it's for Jodi, really. It's not as if she needs my friendship, but she just can't bear to leave things the way they are. All that bad feeling. Suspicion. Misunderstanding. Jealousy. Friendship is important to her, she says. She values it above all else except love. She's a little pissed off with Trent for being such a prick. For thinking what he thinks. She feels compromised having to balance her love for Trent with her wish to choose her own friends. And because it's made her do something she's never done before: keep something secret from him.

And this is the thing, isn't it? The irony (or is it a paradox?) – that to maintain our friendship, we have to behave like illicit lovers.

I wait for her across the road from the school entrance. She waves when she sees me, then stops a moment to talk to some tot's mother. The boy whines and tugs at the woman's arm. I can see her face. She'd love to smack the little brat's ear.

'Where shall we go?'

'Let's go to the park,' Jodi says.

As we walk, she tells me about the boy. It's as I thought: he's disruptive in class. The mother's recently separated from her husband. She works at the chicken processing plant.

'How depressing,' I say. I'm careful not to say the wrong thing again.

Jodi nods. She's feeling a bit down. Sometimes she wonders if she really wants children. I think of Trent making love to her, getting her pregnant. She says they've been trying for a while, but nothing's happened.

We walk down to the park lake where Jodi feeds the ducks with pieces of a bread roll she's saved from lunch. I sit on a bench and watch her. It's quite cool; the sun is going down. When she's finished scattering the bread, she comes and sits next to me. I wonder if she's warm enough; she's only wearing a shirt and a skirt. I tell her she can have my jacket, if she's cold.

'I'm okay, Franz. But thank you.'

She calls me 'Franz' now and there's none of that self-consciousness I used to hear from them before. Particularly Trent. She's got so used to it I can imagine she's forgotten what my name really is. It's not a dumb joke any more. I've become Franz. As if Franz is different from me.

'Where are you staying?' she asks.

'I have a room at the Riverdale Hotel,' I tell her. 'But it's not permanent. I've been looking at the accommodation ads in the paper. I've marked four or five "looking to share" notices. Two are across the river in Tramontane Park.'

'Why don't you get your own place?' she suggests. 'Your job's secure, isn't it? You're doing all right.'

'I am doing all right. I'm doing good, actually. My best month so far for commission. But the idea of a place of my own is kind of scary. Papers to sign, bond money and advance rent to find. Furniture to hire. I don't feel settled enough to make that kind of commitment.' I let this float between us for a few seconds, and then I make a confession. 'I grew up in Tramontane Park, but I've been away for some time. I'm not entirely sure how I feel about coming back.'

Jodi gives me a strange look. 'You make it sound quite dire! Do you have a dark secret, Franz? How intriguing!'

I keep her guessing for a moment longer, and then I say, almost offhand, 'I was raped. An older guy I thought was my friend.'

Jodi hardly knows what to say. Here's something to rival Trent's suicidal mother.

'Oh, Franz, how awful! Did he go to jail?'

I shake my head. 'I didn't tell anyone,' I explain. 'Not for months. I was too ashamed. My mother knew something was wrong. My schoolwork went to pot. I was so screwed up inside. When I did tell her, she said it was my own fault. For being so naïve. He was a real friendly guy.'

Jodi is momentarily stuck for words. 'The beast…' she hisses finally. 'And your mother…'

'Ah, my mother. Couldn't face the scandal, could she? Said he'd deny it anyway. It had been months… My father would've killed the guy, so we never told him. He thought I'd been brooding over some girl.'

It's almost dark.

Jodi stands, brushes out her skirt. 'I have to go, Franz. Trent will be home shortly.'

We walk slowly back up the path to the park gates.

She slips her arm through mine and rests her head against my shoulder. 'Is he still here?' she asks when we're almost at the top of the path. 'In Tramontane Park?'

'I don't know. Ever since I got here I've been thinking about finding out. Something's stopping me. I haven't even looked him up in the phone book. I know it's best to leave well alone, but I keep asking myself…if that's the case, what am I doing here? Why have I returned?'

At the bottom of Riverdale Park Road, we go our separate ways.

Jodi holds my hand for a moment. 'I always felt there was some sadness deep inside you, Franz. Some great emptiness. An abyss that can only be filled with love. I hope you haven't come back for the wrong reasons. Maybe you feel you need to confront this guy, I don't know. To do him some harm. To punish him for the harm he did you. You can still go to the police, you know. Whatever your stupid mother might have said, it's never too late. Or if you have faith, you can trust in God to exact the penalty this beastly man must pay. I'm touched… I'm deeply touched that you've confided in me, Franz. It's a true sign of trust and friendship. I'm here for you, I want you to know that. If you want to talk some more…you know…'

I nod soberly. I can't look her in the eye.

She squeezes my hand and – after a split second hesitation – kisses my cheek. 'I'll call you, Franz. The Riverdale. And I have your mobile number.'

I sleep well that night. I'm feeling uncommonly content. I feel as if I'm progressing. Tomorrow I'll check out those share house ads. I have phone calls to make.

2

Jodi has seen where I used to live. She phoned this afternoon, wanting to know if I was still at the Riverdale. I was with a client, so I was a bit short with her. I said I'd meet her outside the school. I was late getting there (another client), but she didn't complain. She understands: my clients come first. It was too late to go to the park, and it's not so warm today, so we go for a drive. She likes my little Hyundai Getz. Trent drives an old Renault, which Jodi hates, because whenever it breaks down (every few weeks, it seems), he has trouble getting it fixed. Trent's fairly handy himself, but he can't always get the right parts.

'Why doesn't he just get rid of it?' I say. 'Buy something more reliable.'

Jodi laughs as if I've just said the dumbest thing. Guys and their cars, don't you know? Trent and his Renault. He's had it since he learned to drive. In the early days, when they first started going out together, he had their names TRENT and JODI across the top of the windscreen. When they got engaged, Jodi made him take them off. She thought it was too juvenile. The disappointment was, he didn't get rid of the Renault too. He's told her if they have a baby he'll get something more suitable for a young family.

We drive over to Tramontane Park. That is, I drive while Jodi tells me about her day. Which is not very interesting – not to me, at any rate – so I take advantage of a sigh dropping on the heels of a whinge about obnoxious parents, to say, 'I want to show you something. A house.'

'A house!' she says, sounding quite ridiculously excited. 'Is this where you're going to live? Have you found somewhere nice, Franz? Oh, I do hope so.'

'It's not where I'm going to live,' I tell her. 'It's where I used to live.'

She doesn't know this part of Tramontane Park. You can live all the years of your life in a suburb and there will always be streets you never drive down, districts you never have any reason to visit. Since my return, I've probably seen more of Tramontane Park in a few months than I saw in my whole childhood growing up here. All the same, this is one street that has yet to come up on my professional radar. Until today, it's never occurred to me to just drive through and take a look. I'm not sentimental about houses. Homes. I've had a few since we moved away.

The street's much as I remember it, but it still seems oddly unfamiliar. Not quite real, as if I've only seen it in pictures. Of course there are superficial differences: landscaped gardens, new and fancy gates. The trees lining the street are so much bigger. Jodi tells me they're jacarandas. She's surprised I didn't know. They're bare now, but come the end of October the street will be ablaze with purple blossom. I remember. Slimy rotting flowers covering the footpath. An old lady – Mrs Morecombe – across the street slipped and broke her ankle. My mother said she should sue the council.

'There,' I say, pulling up behind a blue Audi. 'That's the one. Number 18.'

Jodi stares at our old house. It's been painted yellow and green. Federation colours. A wisp of smoke comes from the kitchen flue.

'Weren't too many Audis in the street when we lived here,' I report.

'Do you have good memories of living here?' Jodi says.

I don't say anything.

Jodi looks at me. Mortified. 'I mean – apart from – Oh, shit. I'm so thoughtless.'

'It's okay,' I say lightly. 'Yes. I do. Generally, you know.'

'It wasn't there where it happened, then… In your house.'

'No.'

'I thought he might've been a friend of the family. You hear about it so much, don't you. Family trust…betrayed.'

'My parents didn't know him,' I say. 'He was just someone I met.'

I start up the motor. The street lights have just gone on.

'I don't know why I brought you here,' I say. 'I'm stupid.'

She rests her hand on my knee. 'You're very fragile, Franz. Emotionally. And psychologically. If it had been reported…properly dealt with… You know.'

We sit for a moment, the motor idling.

Jodi removes her hand from my knee. She's a little anxious, fumbling absently with her engagement ring again. 'You're still at the Riverdale, then,' she says, just to change the subject, I think.

I nod. None of the places I looked at appealed much. The rooms were okay, nicely furnished. Colourful (posters and stuff). It was the company I didn't take to, the guys (mostly) I'd have to share with. I just couldn't see myself living amongst them, eating with them, sharing a few beers over a rental movie. Listening to their inane chatter about their tedious jobs, their sex lives. Their miserable life stories. I'd been spoilt. Spoilt for Jodi and Trent. The perfect share house.

Jodi is silent. I shift the little Getz into gear. Neither of us looks at my old (heritage green and yellow) house as we drive off.

Back in Riverdale, I drop Jodi at the top of City Road.

'I can walk from here, Franz, thank you.'

I wait for her to kiss me on the cheek again. She seems to be in two minds. I tell her I wish it could be the way it used to be. Jodi, Trent and Franz. The three of us together. Like the three equal sides of a triangle, I say. Making a whole.

'It can't ever be like that again,' she says with a little regretful sigh. 'You know it can't.'

'Because of Trent.'

'Yes. Because of Trent. And because…'

I wait to hear the detail of that tantalising 'because', but it doesn't come. Her mind is elsewhere. Some old guy sitting on a street bench has caught her attention. He's wearing trousers and a pullover over a short sleeve shirt. He might've been waiting for a bus, except that the stop was a block down the street.

'He looks lost,' Jodi says, as if it were a dog she'd found wandering aimlessly. 'I think I should see if he's all right.'

I sit in the car and observe their rather comical intercourse. Jodi does all the talking. The old guy listens and shakes his head. Jodi glances over at me and then helps the old duffer to his feet. She holds his arm and they shuffle slowly over to the car.

'His name's Fred. He's awfully cold and a little disoriented, I think. He says he lives up Ridge Road in Tramontane Park. Will you take him home, Franz?'

As if I'd say no. I want her to come with me, but she says Trent will be missing her. She hates lying to him. It's better that she doesn't give him reasons to ask awkward questions.

'Franz is going to take you home,' she tells Fred. 'Isn't he a Samaritan?' She secures his seatbelt. 'I'll phone you tomorrow, Franz. Okay?'

She thumps the door shut. No kiss tonight.

Fred says not a word while we drive back across the river to Tramontane Park. This little sad-eyed man with tufts of silvery white hair and snot dribbling from his nose. He's breathing heavily, and his hands are shaking, so I turn up the heating. Don't want to be taking piss-stained seat covers to the dry cleaners in the morning, do we, Fred.

Fred's silence makes me edgy. Uncomfortable. It makes me want to jab my fingers in his ribs, and shout, Hey Fred! Look at me, Fred! I'm here. I'm your Samaritan, remember? I'm taking you home where (let me guess) some fretting unlovely and unloved daughter is waiting to give you an earful of grief for going out without your coat. An egg and buttered bread for tea, a cup of Milo, a quick sprinkle under the shower, and then safely tucked up in bed.

He hears me. Didn't he hear Jodi well enough? Shaking his head to her gentle, Jodi-like interrogation (as if she were cajoling one of her sulky primary tots). Giving up his name.

Luckily I know Ridge Road. 'Some very desirable properties along Ridge Road,' I tell Fred. 'I have memories of coming up here as a small boy, bouncing up the road in my father's utility, winding our way to the lookout with its panoramic views of the valley. A picture postcard scene,' I tell Fred in my picture postcard prose. I have, I think, Fred's attention.

'There was one Sunday – I was five or six – we were the only people there. It was a sunny winter afternoon, but cold. A bitter south westerly blowing right across The Heights. My parents sat in the ute, Dad listening to the footy, my mother reading the Sunday paper. Stay close, my mother warns me, don't wander off. She hid herself behind her newspaper. As if she knew. Secretly hoped… Hearing that, what's the little guy going to do? I wandered over the top of The Heights, out of the wind. The scrub had been thinned out, but there was still plenty of shelter. I followed a dog track for a couple of minutes, and then I got scared. It crossed my five- or six-year-old mind that Mum and Dad might just take advantage of my absence and drive home without me. I never did feel particularly loved, you have to understand. So I started running back, but I took a wrong turn, and there, right in front of me was this young guy and his girl fucking. She had her legs wrapped around his arse, and he was humping away, and grunting, and she was singing in his ear, oh sweetie, oh sweetie, oh sweetie… Five or six I was, I remember it like it was yesterday. He still had his pants on, but her knickers were spread out next to them, lovely white knickers spread out on the ground, like they'd got wet and were drying in the sun. I just stood there and gawked. As a five-year-old would. Or maybe I was seven or eight. She sees me then, looking over his shoulder. She never said a word. No more oh sweeties, just that look-at-me stare, like it was giving her pleasure that little bit of extra juice…'

Fred is getting agitated. Fidgeting in his seat like an antsy brat. He jabs a finger at the windscreen. 'Here! Stop! Stop!'

I pull the Getz to the side of the road, under a dull street lamp.

'Here, Fred? Out you get, then.' I unfasten his seatbelt.

Fred sits. Does he expect me to walk him to his front door? Wherever that is. There's a gate, and beyond it there is only the night. No lighted windows, no lit porch. Not the most welcoming of homecomings, is it, Fred.

Fred continues to sit. A little gasp of air slips from his throat, like a kind of death rattle. A touch of reflux.

'I'll walk you in, Fred.' A Samaritan would.

I unfasten my seatbelt.

Fred grips my hand. His face is so close to mine our noses almost touch. His breath is strangely odourless. 'Filthy… Filthy-mouthed… Dirt… Dirty, dirty-minded…' He gives another little gasp, withdraws his face from mine.

'That's not nice, Fred,' I say. 'That's not nice at all. No way to talk to a Samaritan.'

Fred isn't listening. He twists round, scratches at the door for the handle. He scrambles out, snapping his seatbelt strap back in his haste to get out of the car. I watch him stumble across the grass verge and through the narrow gate. Gone.

Demented old prick. I'll tell Jodi I delivered him home safely.

The door has not latched properly, the interior light is still on. A little plastic gizmo on the floor catches my eye. It's one of those puffer devices asthmatics use. I peer into the direction Fred disappeared, but there is nothing to see. It's as if he never existed. I drop the puffer gizmo into the gutter.

Securing the door, I spin the wheel (the Hyundai Getz, you know, turns on the proverbial sixpence) and speed off down the street.

3

I've been thinking about Trent's mother. Killing herself. Jodi didn't say, but I got the impression it was while Trent was still at school. Last years of high school, I'd guess. Those years of your life, they're kind of hypersensitive times. Having something like that happen in your family would really screw a young guy up.

We meet by chance in the Plaza. I'm checking the real estate windows when Trent walks past. Riverdale Technics, the computer store where Trent works, is shop 12.

'Hey, Trent, how're you doing?'

Trent has his head down, hoping not to catch my eye. It's awkward for him, I can understand that. I guess he wouldn't expect me to want to acknowledge him either. He nods, slows briefly, before walking on. I catch up with him. We walk side by side.

'Can we talk, Trent? Just for a moment?'

Trent presses on.

'I don't think so,' he says. 'What would be the point?'

'I don't want to talk about Jodi,' I tell him. 'I know there's nothing I can say to make things right there. I want to talk to you. About your mum.'

He stops abruptly. I almost walk on.

'What's Jodi said to you about my mother?'

Trent is a little heavier than me. A touch taller. He might be handy with his fists, I don't know, but he did threaten to bash my face to pulp. So when he confronts me with his fists clenched, I back off a bit.

'Cool it,' I say. 'She didn't mean to be indiscreet. She was just kind of empathising, you know. My mother...'

'What about her?'

He's unclenched his fists, but he still looks like he's ready to deck me. I shrug.

'Look, mate, I'm sorry, I shouldn't have said anything. It's none of my business, I just thought...despite, you know... Well, it's not something you can talk to just anyone about...'

He stares at me a moment. There's a cop, just come out of a takeaway, watching us as he walks across the Plaza to his squad car.

'Your mum killed herself...?'

'No. Least ways, not so far.'

He lets me take him for a beer. The Freemasons is just across the road from the Plaza. It's noisy in the bar so we take our beers into the garden. It's mild enough. There's an earthy dampness about the evening air.

Trent lights up a smoke. He's wary still. He doesn't really want to get to like me again. If he feels something for me, kind of engages with me, he'll start thinking he's got me wrong. Or he'll feel he'll have to make allowances. It'll be less about Jodi and more about me.

'Jodi never said,' he says after he's lit up. 'About you telling her about your mum. She tells you about mine, but what you tell her she keeps to herself. You can see how I might be a bit pissed off about that.'

'She was a bit strung out that day,' I explain. 'She wasn't in control of her emotions.'

I tell him about the little dog she saw killed in the road. It was just a dog, but it's still upsetting. For someone as sensitive as Jodi. You have to talk these things through. There'd be a lot of out of work counsellors if people didn't need to talk the traumatic moments of their lives through.

It's not my place to say it, I say (but I'm going to say it anyway): Trent let his wife down that day. He wasn't there for her when she needed him. Franz made a poor substitute.

Trent has almost finished his beer, which surprises me because he's not really much of a beer drinker. Not unless he's at home, watching a video.

'I don't get it,' he says. 'She saw some dumb dog get killed. Gets run over by a car, right? I can see it would upset her a bit. That maybe she'd want to talk about it. Okay, talk to me. And she gets you. So how come you get from there to talking about my mum? Or yours?'

I'm surprised at how insensitive he is. And how stupid.

I tell a small lie. 'My mother ran over someone. A friend of hers. Killed her. It wasn't Mum's fault, but she's never got over it. She's been on medication ever since.'

'Jesus,' Trent says. 'What a bummer.'

Not the sort of response I would have got from Jodi. But Trent's Trent. He stares gloomily into his glass of beer. He doesn't really want to ask. But he's hooked.

'How'd it happen?'

'Pure fluke,' I say. 'But kind of tragic, you know. They were real close, best mates. They worked together. In the same building, at any rate. Different departments. The thing is, all the years they'd known each other, all the good times, going out, having a laugh together and stuff… And then they have this big falling out. Big blue over this guy she was seeing. Mum's mate. She wasn't married, but she fucked around a bit. Certain types of guys she liked… Anyway, they fell out.

Weren't talking. And then, this night, Mum's driving home from work. It's dark, she's running late. Turns into our drive, maybe a bit too fast, and whack! Didn't even see her. Must've been walking back down the drive after calling at the house. She wasn't on duty that day, so she wouldn't have known Mum was working late. That was what made it so hard. Why would she have come to the house unless she wanted to make her peace with Mum? Try, anyway. Stupid row, all over this guy she was fucking... Mum should never have found out.'

'What did it matter to your mum who her mate was screwing with?' Trent asks. 'Wasn't your dad, was it?'

'God no!' I laugh. He should hope.

Trent narrows his eyes. Thinking. 'It was you, you horny little bastard. It was you, wasn't it? You and your mum's mate...'

'I was eighteen. Old enough to do as I pleased. And she didn't seem so much older to me... It was Mum who had the problem with it. Still has. Because of what happened.'

Trent gets a second round of beer in. I pinch one of his ciggies while he's up at the bar. I like the occasional smoke.

'What's your story?' I ask Trent when he returns. 'Why'd your mum do it?'

For a moment I think he's going to pike out. He takes his time dragging a cigarette out of his pack and lighting up.

He takes a deep breath. 'My mother was a real performance artist. The smallest difference of opinion became a big drama moment. My father just couldn't hack it any more. He met this woman...and told Mum he was moving out. Mum said if he left her, she'd kill herself. Dad went anyway. I don't know if he thought she'd do it or not. She did it. Sleeping tablets. No mess.'

I like this story. I like it for its brevity and simplicity. I like the way he called her bluff...and probably got just what he wanted.

'How old were you?' I ask.

'Fourteen. I haven't seen my dad since the funeral. I lived with an aunt until I left school and started work. Then I met Jodi.'

'Your rock,' I say.

He looks at me strangely for a second, and then nods. 'Yeah. Jodi's my rock. Without Jodi…'

A couple with a small boy on a harness walk through the garden, making their way to the dining room. Trent follows their slow progress with the same gloomy expression he'd engaged earlier, contemplating his beer.

'A rock in a stormy sea,' I say, running with my metaphor. I'm kind of pleased with it.

'Stormy sea…' Trent drags his attention away from the couple and their small boy.

'Stormy sea of emotion… Family turmoil. Losing your mum… Your dad going off like that. You'd be pretty vulnerable. You wouldn't want a relationship with someone who wasn't pretty solid. Jodi…she's really got it together, hasn't she?' I say. 'You've made a good choice there. She'll be good with the kids. When they come.'

Trent has finished his second beer. Not good. He's starting to slur his speech. 'Jodi told you…'

'She told me you'd been trying,' I reveal. 'But so far, nothing doing.'

He stares at me through his glassy eyes. His expression hardens. 'She shouldn't have told you. It's private. Fuckin' bitch…'

It surprises me to hear him say this. Shocks me. His rock. I shake my head.

He grips my arm. 'I know what you're doing. Bastard. She won't have you. She won't. She'd die before she'd let you put a finger on her.'

I extract my arm. His grip is painfully tight.

'I'm not doing anything,' I tell him. 'I think you're a little paranoid.'

He says nothing to this. He stands unsteadily, and looks around as if getting his bearings. As if he's forgotten which pub it is he's in. He lurches off.

I phone Jodi. It's hard to say whether she's pleased to hear my voice or not. Naturally she's waiting for Trent to come home. I tell her we've had a couple of beers at the Freemasons.

'We were getting on real fine,' I explain. 'I think he was starting to see he'd got it wrong about us. Him thinking I wanted to sleep with you. Then I said something really dumb. I'm real sorry, Jodi. I let it slip out that you'd told me you and Trent wanted a baby, and, you know, nothing was happening…'

She's uncommonly quiet for a long few seconds. Then she says, 'It's okay, Franz. It doesn't matter.'

'I hope I haven't made trouble for you,' I say. 'The last thing I'd want in the world is to come between you and Trent. It's a real shame Trent's the way he is. We could be such friends, the three of us, couldn't we?'

'I don't quite know what you mean,' Jodi says, sounding uncomfortable. 'The way Trent is… What way d'you mean?'

'Well,' I say, 'he's carrying a lot of emotional baggage, isn't he? What his mum did…and being estranged from his dad. He's bottled it up. He's not working it through, getting some kind of, you know… closure on it. The way he behaves with you…kind of over-protective. It's because he's insecure. He's a little paranoid, don't you think? A little crazy…'

'He's not paranoid,' Jodi says, getting angry. 'And he's not the least bit crazy. He loves me. And maybe that makes him seem possessive. Over-protective, like you say. What his parents did was unforgivable. Selfish. It nearly destroyed him. If it wasn't for his aunt who looked after him –'

'And you,' I cut in. 'If he's got someone in his life to hold onto, it's you, Jodi. You're his rock. He told me that.'

'You're dead right, Franz,' Jodi says. 'I am his rock. You don't know him, not as deeply as I do. I know he's got…stuff in his head he has to manage. And he might be kind of insecure. He was betrayed. The people closest to him, the ones he loved the most let him down. He was only fourteen. That's a terrible thing to happen to anyone at fourteen. But he's not crazy. He's not paranoid. That's a stupid conclusion to make, if you don't mind me saying. I thought you were smarter than that.'

'Consider me chastised,' I say evenly. 'You're right. What do I know about the two of you? I can't see inside your heads. Or your hearts. I love the both of you, you know that. But if I can't have you as my close friends, then so be it. I guess the best thing would be for me to just leave you alone. Accept the situation. I'm just complicating your relationship, I know that. I just wish it could be different.'

'Franz,' she says, 'I don't know what to say. You're right, you are complicating our relationship, but... I have to think about it.'

'I'll leave the both of you alone, Jodi,' I say firmly. 'I really think I should, don't you? It's best we don't call each other again.'

'I have to go, Franz,' she says with sudden determination. 'Trent's just driven up.'

I buy myself another beer, which I drink in the dining room with a bowl of spaghetti carbonara. The couple with the little boy are sitting at the next table. I was thinking of having apple and custard for dessert, but watching the kid stuffing chocolate ice cream into his mouth put me off.

Walking back to the Riverdale, a light drizzle sets in.

4

'Oh, Franz! Can we meet? I know I shouldn't, but I have to talk to you. It's been horrible. Please, Franz!'

We meet in the park a little after nine a.m. Nine-o-seven, to be precise. I check my watch as I saunter down the path. I can see Jodi sitting alone on the bench, the same bench by the lake we sat on the other day. The ducks are gone this morning. Across the lake a couple of young guys are kicking a ball around. The grass is still damp from the shower of rain overnight, but the sky is a seamless sheet of uninterrupted blue.

I'm in an exceptionally good mood. Jodi needs me.

'Hello, Jodi,' I say as I approach the bench.

She turns to me as I sit next to her. Her lip is swollen and she has a deep bruise on her cheek. Her eyes are wet, though she's holding back. She looks quite ugly.

'Trent,' I murmur. 'The bastard.'

Jodi nods. 'He was so worked up when he got home last night. He's never hit me before.'

'If he's hit you once, he'll hit you again,' I tell her. 'It's in his nature. He's just kept it in check up until now.'

'I don't believe that, Franz. I don't want to believe it.' Her eyes well with tears. She brushes them away. 'I was so frightened. It was like a horrible dream. I couldn't believe it was happening.'

I take her hand and hold it between mine. Give it a little consoling squeeze.

Jodi stares a moment across the lake. The boys chasing the ball are yelling obscenities at each other.

'It's my fault,' I say. 'I shouldn't have taken Trent to the pub. He only drank two beers. He did kind of gulp them down, though.'

'He brought a six-pack home with him,' Jodi says quietly. 'He'd already had one in the car. I knew there was going to be a scene. We've never fought like that before.'

'I can't picture you and Trent ever fighting,' I say, mindful of how shocked I was to hear Trent call Jodi a 'fucking bitch'. 'I always thought of the two of you as the perfect couple.'

Jodi manages a light giggle. Like a hiccup. 'I shouldn't imagine there's any such creature,' she says. 'The Perfect Couple...'

'It's still all my doing,' I contend. 'Trent hates me. Taking him for a beer was a dumb move. Everything I said just made things worse.'

'You tried,' Jodi says generously. 'Your intentions were good, Franz, but I think you're right. What you said last night. Trent is a little... unbalanced.'

'Families...' I sigh. 'Sometimes they really fuck you up.'

Jodi is silent. I keep expecting her to withdraw her hand, but she doesn't.

'It's not what you think,' she says presently. 'The row we had – it wasn't anything to do with his frightful parents. It was because I told you we were trying to have a baby.'

'That was lousy of me,' I confess. 'I didn't think. I didn't realise he was so touchy about it. Have you had, you know, tests and stuff…?'

'We've barely talked about it,' Jodi says. 'Like we never really talk about anything that's important. We stopped using contraception about this time last year. It wasn't that we were ready particularly to start a family. It was just…we felt…if a baby comes now, it'll be nice. We just felt good about it, you know? I'd get maternity leave. We'd manage. And you know, it was kind of a sexy idea…having a baby. We were making love every night. And every month… I'd wait for my period to stop.'

She wriggles her hand free. Without realising it, I'd drawn it into my lap, close enough to my genitals to give them a fondle, if she'd been so inclined. I cast my eyes across the lake. The boys with their ball and obscene banter have gone.

'I guess…' I begin uncertainly… 'I mean…not knowing…which of you…'

'It's not me,' she says, quite sharp. 'I've had a baby already. When I was thirteen. Trent never knew. I never told him. Last night…well, that's what we had the fight about.'

I allow myself a moment to take this in. I'm not quite sure how I feel about it. 'Thirteen…' I say. 'I suppose you were too young to keep it.'

'Of course.'

I gaze at her. She has a small nose, turned up slightly at the tip, which is only really apparent when you see her in profile.

'Well, at least you know,' I say. 'I mean – which one of you has the problem.'

She looks at me, a little askance. 'It's not really the issue, is it, Franz? You have to have openness and trust in a marriage, don't you think? How can I devote my life to Trent and keep something as important as this from him? That's the issue. I never told him because I'm a coward. Because I thought it would disgust him, what I'd done. And he wouldn't want me. I chose to live a lie. I'm despicable. I'm not worthy of him.'

I want to comfort her, hold her hand again, but I feel it would be a bad move. Of course she's got it quite wrong. The issue for Trent is his watery sperm. That she's already had another guy's baby is simply one more squeeze of his neutered balls.

'You've told him now,' I say. 'That's good, isn't it?'

'Yes, it's good,' she agrees. 'It's much, much too late, but it's good. I've done the right thing. I'm happy about that. I don't know if it'll save our marriage... Maybe...if we give it time. A few days...he'll have had time to absorb it. We can talk, then. I think we love each other enough to get over this, Franz. I really do. I'm an optimist, you see. I believe in goodness and kindness and forgiveness, all those wonderful human things... I couldn't live if I didn't. I couldn't face the world each day.'

She looks at her watch. 'I should be getting home.'

'Aren't you at school?' I ask.

'I rang in sick. I wouldn't be any use to anyone today. Trent's at work. He's plenty to do. That'll be good for him. First time this morning he went out without kissing me. Without saying he loved me. That was harder for me, Franz, harder to bear than the smack he gave me last night. In a way I welcomed that. It was like someone shaking me out of a long sleep, and shouting, Wake up! Wake up! It's time...' She sighs deeply.

I can see she's calmer now. She's talked it through a bit with good ol' Franz, and she feels better for it. I should be happy about this, but for some reason I am not. Not at all, really.

'Do you want me to take you home?' I ask with a little sigh of my own.

She touches my arm. 'You sound sad, Franz. I'm sorry. I shouldn't have burdened you with this.'

'Of course you should,' I say, quite fervently. 'I'll always be here for you Jodi, you know that. Whatever happens between you and Trent.'

It's unclear whether this is the appropriate thing to say. But I think – just for the moment – it's what she wants to hear.

'Do you have to go straight home?' I ask tentatively.

'I guess not. What did you have in mind? Don't you have to be back at work?'

'A coffee,' I suggest,' and a slice of chocolate gateau. Work can wait.'

She laughs. 'Oh, I don't think so. I only have to look at cake…' She tugs at my sleeve. 'Take me for a drive. You can show me where that funny little man lives. Fred. Did you get him home all right?'

We walk slowly back up the path to the gate. Jodi slips her arm through mine. She's almost happy. Her world is not collapsing after all. She's sure of that. She's equally sure it's how Trent will feel, once he's calmed down. She's already forgiven him the punch he threw at her. What concerns her is whether he can ever forgive himself.

We'll drive up to The Heights, I decide. 'I used to picnic up there when I was a kid,' I tell her. 'There was nothing there, then. No houses, no development. Just a cairn of stones marking the highest point.'

When we're in the car, Jodi asks suddenly, 'What did you think? Tell me the truth, Franz. What did you think when I told you I'd had a baby at thirteen? I wasn't much over thirteen. I was only twelve when I conceived.'

'I don't know the circumstances,' I say tactfully. 'And it's not for me to make moral judgements, anyway.'

'No, it's not,' she agrees. 'But you must've thought something. You must've felt something. About me. I think you have a sort of idealised picture of me, Franz. Somebody nice. Sexually pure, only giving myself to my husband. You must've felt a little disappointed, at least. Let down.'

I let the question hang there a moment. We turn off City Road and onto Bridge Road.

'I don't know what I felt,' I say. 'It came so out of the blue. And you seemed…despite everything else, kind of matter-of-fact about it.'

'I know. I know. I shouldn't, but… I guess I've lived my life again since then. It's all kind of distant…and unreal… But still painful, you know? My little baby boy. I didn't even get to see him. Not after the birth. I could've, but my parents thought it better to just let him go…'

'The guy,' I say, 'the father. I guess he was just a kid too.'

'Not really,' she says. She doesn't elaborate.

We drive over the river. It's muddy looking, the roots of the mangroves exposed along the banks.

'It might have been less painful if you'd had an abortion,' I say. It hadn't occurred to me that Jodi's family maybe were Catholics. Neither Trent nor Jodi had struck me as being the least bit religious.

'Yes,' Jodi says, 'it might have been...in the long term. But I'm glad I didn't. Didn't have to, that is. I was quite plump, you know, when I was in my puberty. Not fat, but decidedly chubby. I was in hell when I realised I was pregnant, but I never told anyone. By the time the baby was starting to show, it was too late. There was no question of me keeping it, so my parents arranged for me to sign the adoption papers. It was all very...mundane... Like selling a car.'

We cruise into Tramontane Park. I try to imagine Jodi at thirteen, plump and pregnant, braces on her teeth, inky fingers pushing a pen across adoption papers. She's right, it's not my idealised picture of her at all. It's hard enough imagining Trent fucking her. This other image, this unholy vision of pubescent outrage, fills me with a kind of fury. I can't speak for her making me think of her like that.

We're halfway up Ridge Road before I realise how far we've gone. I pull the car to the side of the road.

Jodi winds down the window. 'Is this the place? Is this where you brought Fred?'

Fred's place, I think, is further back. This property has a long drive. There's a commercial vehicle parked at the side of a shabby-looking timber and iron cottage. Not exactly des-res, I think, noting the name painted on the back of the van. Announcing itself. Shouting itself down the drive at me. Down the years, down old memory lane.

I grab Jodi's hand and squeeze it tight. 'Do you know who that guy is?' I say. 'Vincent Cornish? He's the guy who raped me.'

'Cats,' Jodi says, pointing an accusing finger down Vincent Cornish's long drive. 'Next to the van. Three – no four of them. D'you think they're all his? I detest cats. I really do. They're such cruel, self-centred creatures. I've never understood why some people have such a thing about cats.'

I don't comment. I don't have an opinion on cats. Jodi naturally thinks it's the painful memories that keep me from speaking. The hurt and humiliation.

'Poor Franz,' she murmurs. 'Has it brought it all back?'

'It's never gone away,' I say, a slight quiver to my voice. 'I just live with it.'

Jodi observes the cats for a moment or two. 'Why did you stop the car here?' she asks. 'Is it because…?'

'No,' I say. 'I've never been in his house, thank God. I knew he lived along here somewhere, but I wasn't sure of the number…'

We sit a moment longer. The cats have drifted off.

'I'll show you where it happened,' I say impulsively. 'It's not far from here.'

We drive back down Ridge Road, and then onto the service road, heading north. Jodi sits in silence, her hands clasped tightly in her lap. She's not sure about this. Her own sad situation is enough for her. Some new horror I might conjure up could be more than she can bear.

I brake suddenly, again almost driving past my intended destination. The tyres burn as I swing the little Getz sharply onto the forecourt of the Francis Tramontane Memorial Hall. As it is properly known.

'The scene of my ruin,' I announce with a kind of ponderous light-heartedness. My little joke to ease Jodi's discomfort. She'll think I'm just doing a guy's thing, keeping my emotions in check.

The building – as they say – has fallen into a state of disrepair. In fact, driving past a week or so after my return home, I was more than a bit shocked to see it. Such a waste of community enterprise. Not to mention money.

'I read that some sort of restoration is in the pipeline,' I remark off-handedly. 'It's kind of disgusting, don't you think, to see how it's been let go.'

'I don't understand…' Jodi says. 'Did he bring you here?'

'It was the opening,' I tell her. 'The ceremony. My mother brought me. She was always hanging around community functions and the like. Anywhere where she might get her picture in the local rag. Vincent… Mr Cornish…he was here with his sister. I think she was involved in getting the place built. I got bored listening to the dreary speeches. I went outside. He was round the back, having a smoke. Wasn't his scene either. We talked a bit. He told me he was an upholsterer. I don't remember what I talked about… School, I guess. I was thinking maybe I'd go to college when I left. It was all kind of easy-going and innocent. Then – just as I was about to go back in, as I thought my mother would be getting cranky – he says he has to come back later. Some job he'd been asked to do… I don't know. Anyway, why don't I come and keep him company? he says. Real friendly like. I might've been a bit naïve, but I wasn't dumb. I knew what he had in mind. He was gay, that was obvious. He fancied me, something wicked. I could see it in the way he looked at me. So I said – sure, why not? I thought I could look after myself. And I kind of liked him, you know. I guess I was a bit confused, sexually. I didn't think I was gay. But I was sort of interested in the idea that I might be…'

Jodi considers this. 'Didn't you have girlfriends?'

'No. I knew a lot of girls, but I didn't like any of them. Not like that, you know. Not like I wanted to go out with them, have sex. I used to look at stuff in magazines, pictures…like any normal guy. But the truth is, I could get just as turned on by some fabulous-looking surfer guy as by pictures of horny women, you know, doing porno stuff… I was a young guy with a young guy's interest in sex. I just wasn't sure where to channel it.'

Jodi is quiet for a moment. Then she says, 'I don't want you to tell me any more. I don't think I could bear to listen to it. I'm afraid…'

'Afraid of what?'

'I know it must've been an awful experience for you, Franz. But I can't help feeling…you're a little bit to blame. This man is a beast. But he read the signals you gave out. And he acted on them. Horribly, for you… But that's what happens. There. Now you think I'm cold and unsympathetic. And you've been so supportive of me.'

She won't look at me to tell me this. Forthrightness, it seems, has its limits. I can't help thinking how grotesque she looks, how spoiled by the bruising and swelling inflicted on her face by Trent's hard, measured slaps. How good it must have made him feel, letting fly, paying out all that anger and frustration and disgust.

'I respect your honesty,' I tell Jodi. 'You're right, I was a selfish little prick. I asked for it, and I got it.'

Jodi begins to sob. 'Now I really hate myself,' she moans. 'You are so understanding and forgiving. And all I can do is add more hurt to your pain.'

I resist the urge to comfort her. She fumbles for a tissue. Wipes her eyes and nose. Folds the damp rag between her fingers. Her hands now strike me as unusually large, great man-like paws. Her face is too ugly to kiss.

'I should take you home,' I say. 'You need to be by yourself. Get some things settled in your mind. It's Trent you need to think about. You and Trent. Not me.'

She nods miserably. 'Yes. And I have such a wretched headache coming on…'

By the time I get her home, she's oddly changed. She's had her little weep. She feels better for it. Conciliatory. She has that unfortunate moment of candour to make up for. Or maybe she hates the immediate prospect of her own company.

'Come inside for a little while, please, Franz. I'll make you coffee. Or something to eat. I know it's early, but let's have some lunch together. I've got some nice fresh bread. I'll make bruschetta.'

I worry about her headache. And if Trent should come home…

'My head's a little better,' she says. 'I'll take some tablets. Trent never comes home to lunch,' she reminds me, quite cool. 'Anyway, he thinks I'm at school. He's still obviously upset and angry with me, otherwise he'd have phoned me, wouldn't he? I've had my mobile on all morning.'

I leave the car in the street. We enter the house. Trent and Jodi's house, still. As I close the front door, I can almost breathe its hostility towards me.

'Would you like a beer or some wine?' Jodi offers. 'I feel awful keeping you from your work.'

'Today my day is for you,' I tell her expansively. 'I have no business that can't wait until tomorrow.'

I switch off my mobile, just in case. There are two bottles of beer in the fridge, presumably the remnants of Trent's six-pack from last night.

Jodi takes a packet of paracetamol from the cupboard. She swallows two tablets with sips of red wine from a cask. 'I know you shouldn't take pills with alcohol,' she says. 'But someone told me they actually work faster that way. Is that silly, do you think?'

'If it helps you relax…' I say. 'Two regular tablets won't kill you.'

She slices bread for the bruschetta. I tell her I need a pee. The door to my old room is closed, but I look in anyway. The bed is made up as I left it. The same ice-blue sheets, washed and newly pressed. A smell: the elusive scent of air freshener. Lingering in the doorway, I feel my eviction more keenly than when I left.

Returning to the kitchen, I top up Jodi's glass. There's the pungent aroma of garlic on crispy toasted bread.

'How do you feel now?' I ask.

'Much better, Franz, thank you. There's just the tiniest throb on the side of my temple. It'll go in a minute, I'm sure.'

We sit at the table and eat the bruschetta. I tell Jodi it's delicious. I tell her she makes the best bruschetta I've ever tasted. Again I say, though I know it distresses her, 'I wish it was the way it was. You, me and Trent, sitting around the table, eating and drinking and having a laugh.'

She pouts a little. Her swollen lip makes her mouth look kind of lopsided. 'Do you know what I find hard to understand, Franz?

Why you came back. It seems…well, a little perverse. I'm sure you must have lots of wonderful childhood memories, but… that awful man's abuse. That's all you really remember, isn't it. That's why you had to leave. If you had friends or family here, I could understand it…a little…but you haven't, have you. You don't have anyone…apart from me and Trent now…and that's gone bad.'

My lips feel greasy, so I wipe them with a kitchen towel. I take Trent's last beer from the fridge, top up Jodi's glass again. She's looking more relaxed now. The wine is doing her good.

I tell her my story.

'After we moved away, my parents split up. I lived with my mother until about six months ago. She'd had boyfriends, you know, guys she went out with, but it was nothing heavy. She needed companionship and sex, I could understand that. Then this one guy came on the scene…nightclub bouncer. He moved in, I had to move out. We didn't get on.'

'What d'you mean?' Jodi asks pointedly. 'You didn't get on. Did he hit you?'

'He didn't hit me. He watched me. Constantly. He was built like a bruiser. He was screwing my mother like crazy, you should've heard them at night. But when it was just me and him, he'd…look at me. Stare at me like I was something he wanted to possess. I tried staring back, you know, outstare him, but he just…kept on staring. I thought – he's trying to make me feel uncomfortable, force me to move out. And then, this one day, I'm watching TV, he's sitting behind me, Mum's out somewhere, and I can feel his eyes on the back of my head. I turn round, and he's got his dirty great cock out…tugging away at it…'

Jodi's glass is dry. She empties the rest of the cask into it. 'The disgusting animal,' she spits. She falls back onto her chair. 'What did you do?'

I hesitate.

'Suffice to say…there was a confrontation. It was very unpleasant. A little blood was spilled. Not mine. The authorities were involved. I had a conversation with this rather genial guy, sweater and specs type, who told me I had issues I had to resolve...'

'Issues...' Jodi stares at me through huge, wonderfully round glazed eyes. 'You mean...?'

'It's my cross,' I say. 'I attract certain types. Older guys... Older women, too. It's not my fault. Sometimes you resist...sometimes you don't. Mum's boyfriend was just too gross.'

'Oh, Franz...' she murmurs, beginning to sway a little.

'The guy you went with,' I say, 'who got you pregnant. He was older too, wasn't he?'

'Did I tell you that?'

'You kind of implied...'

She's having trouble focusing. 'Yes...he was...twenty something... I don't know... It wasn't that, though... It was... He used to do the gardens, you see...mowing and... He'd been coming for months... I had this silly crush on him, he kind of picked up on it... He couldn't help himself.'

'He raped you,' I say bluntly.

She shakes her head. Vigorously. 'No. No. You don't understand. He lived in Tramontane House...'

It takes me a moment to fix Tramontane House in my mind. A sheltered workshop for the intellectually disabled.

Jodi leans across the table towards me. I have a feeling she's about to tumble from her chair.

'Trent mustn't know... He mustn't ever, ever know... It'll kill him. It will so...devastate him...'

She lifts her glass, and then puts it down again, without taking a drink. 'Oh gosh... I feel quite strange...'

I help her to her feet. 'I think we should get you into bed,' I say.

'No...' She clings to me. 'Oh, Franz, what we've been through, you and me...'

We shuffle down the hall, Jodi rubbing shoulders with the wall. 'Oh gosh,' she says again, 'oh fuck... I'm so pissed...'

We come to a crashing stop against Trent and Jodi's bedroom door.

'I have to have a pee first… I'm bursting.'

She stumbles across the hall into the bathroom. The door shuts in my face. I go into the bedroom, turn the covers down on the bed. Plain ice-blue sheets, the same as the sheets on the lodger's bed. Franz's bed, as was.

Sitting on the side of the bed, I check out the bedside drawers: Trent's socks and underpants; neatly folded T-shirts; track pants; a blue sweater; vanity travel pack; a jar of Vaseline.

I move around the bed to Jodi's side. The bedside clock reads 1.47 p.m. Have we been drinking and talking so long? I count the hours of the afternoon before Trent will be home. Time enough, I would think. Time enough for some rejuvenating sleep. Or whatever.

I slide open the top drawer of the cabinet. An unsurprising jumble of underwear. A fiesta of colours, as gloriously varied as flowers at a carnival. I push them aside, let my fingers probe the bottom of the drawer. It's interesting, the letters or documents people like to keep safe in their underwear drawer. A snapshot of a smiling retard somehow seems unlikely…

Finding nothing, I push the drawer shut. I have my fingers on the second drawer when I hear the cistern in the bathroom flush.

Jodi enters a few moments later. She sits gingerly on the bed beside me. She's quite pale. 'You shouldn't be in here, Franz. Should you?'

'No.' I remain seated.

'I've been sick,' she says.

'Yuk. No kisses for you, then.'

She looks at me, as she did earlier, a little askance. I grin. Poor Jodi. Poor sick Jodi. I slip my arm around her waist. She rests her head on my shoulder. A little sigh, I hear. A little sigh of surrender. I tighten my grip. With my free hand, I feel her breast.

'Franz…'

Squeeze.

'Franz…you mustn't…'

She's hardly resisting. I take my hand from her breast and slide it between her legs, under her skirt. I touch. She's left her knickers off, saucy girl.

'No...please...'

I lean back, taking her with me. We lie together on the bed. I set my fingers to work.

She weeps.

I unzip my pants.

'Franz...'

It's okay. We shan't tell Trent. Our secret, Jodi. Like your little baby's retard dad.

I settle myself more comfortably. I have her skirt around her waist. I have her exposed.

She resists. 'Don't, Franz... Don't...'

Don't.

Don't tell me don't.

Dear Jodi.

Don't you ever tell me don't.

5

'We do really like it, don't we, Brad? But it is a little more than we were hoping to pay...'

Brad nods. He's the silent type. The thinker. The brooder. Full-time uni student. Something or other in the social sciences. She's the breadwinner, the money pants. Ms Personal Assistant to the Managing Director of Furlough Hill Plastics. They've only been married two months, but they're childhood sweethearts, so they have that air of domestic familiarity you get with older couples who've become a little bored with one another. It's Lisa who tells me this, of course. That they're childhood sweethearts et cetera. She's the one I deal with. It's her signature I want on the contract. They're slightly younger than me, though she has a kind of aged, grown-into face. Lisa. Brad and Lisa. Lisa and Brad.

The unit is ten years old, three good-sized bedrooms, L-shaped lounge/dining, newish kitchen, freshly painted throughout, single LUG, small private courtyard, manageable body corporate fees. Blah blah. It's a steal at $350,000. Property prices in lower Tramontane Park have been steadily improving for the past twelve months, I explain. There's no sign of them slowing, or levelling off. And I have two other prospective buyers keen to view…

Brad steps outside for a smoke. It's begun to drizzle.

'He'll have to give those up,' Lisa tells me confidentially. 'I feel a bitch about it, because it's his only indulgence. He hardly drinks. He spends most of the weekend studying. But on one wage…well, you know how it is.'

I follow her through the unit as she inspects it for the third time. She pauses in the smallest bedroom, the one with the frieze of teddy bears lining the walls.

'Study,' I suggest helpfully, 'unless…'

She gives a hoarse laugh. 'Hardly! God, no! Not before Brad finishes uni. Not then, probably, for a year or two. We want to be financially secure – really secure, before we start a family. I expect by then we'll be looking for a bigger place anyway.' She brushes past me, back into the empty lounge.

I can see Brad, despite the drizzle, examining an oil stain the previous owner's bomb of a car left on the drive.

'I really don't know…' Lisa sighs. 'I think we'll just have to rent a little longer.'

'It is unusually large compared to other units in Tramontane Park,' I remark, watching for Brad's return. 'You know what I would do if I were in your position? I'd rent out one of the bedrooms. Just for a year, say, help you with those initial payments. Someone quiet, single, steady income… Maybe you should have a chat with Brad.'

My mobile rings. I excuse myself, step out onto the rear courtyard, leaving Lisa to consider my suggestion while she does one final turn of the unit. I think I recognise the number even before I hear his voice. I hesitate just a second before answering. 'Hey, Trent. How's things?'

'Can we meet someplace…?' He sounds vaguely apologetic. 'I need to talk to someone… To you.'

'I don't know if we should, Trent,' I say after a brief moment. 'It's kind of… awkward between you and me.'

'I know. But… I'd still like to… It's about Jodi. She's told me something. It's driving me crazy.'

I leave my card with Lisa. I like Lisa. I think we'd get on real fine. I'm not so sure about Brad, but maybe he's the sort of guy who warms slowly. Lisa says I'll be hearing from her.

Trent is waiting for me in Post Office Square. He checks his watch. 'You got time for a beer? Or do you have to be someplace?'

'I'm done for the day,' I tell him. 'Shouldn't you be at work?'

'I didn't go in. Jodi's so weird. She won't talk to me.'

We go to the Freemasons again. It's the middle of the afternoon, but it feels like evening. The drizzle is getting heavier.

Trent pays for the beers and we sit in a sheltered corner of the beer garden. There's no one else around. It's raining steadily now.

Trent lights a cigarette. 'Jodi had a baby,' he says. 'Years ago. She never told me.'

I poach one of his smokes. He doesn't appear to notice.

'How d'you know?'

'The other night. After you and me…here… We had this great row. She told me then. How could she do that? I thought we knew everything about each other. All these years and she never said a fucking word. Not a whisper.'

'Wow,' I say. 'That's some bombshell. So how come she's not talking now?'

He takes a nervous drag on his smoke. 'Tuesday night it all came out. It got heavy. Jeez, I was fucked up… Yesterday morning we were still kind of at a standoff, you know. I was real pissed off with her, still. I could see she was as miserable as shit, but I just couldn't…approach her. I went to work. I don't know what she did. I don't think she went to school. When I got home, she was in bed. Just lying there, wide awake.

94

Staring at nothing. Didn't even acknowledge my presence. It was like she was in some kind of trance. I thought she'd taken something…'

He's shivering. It has gone off a little cold, but I guess it's not that. Poor Jodi. She seemed fine when I left her. Not fine, but okay. A bit downbeat. It was just sex. She knew I wasn't going to tell. I never dreamed she might consider taking something. I can see why Trent might think that. But not for the reason he thinks.

'Last night was just…' He crushes the butt of his cigarette into an ashtray. 'I don't know. It was like she wasn't there. She wouldn't get out of bed. I had a crap night's sleep. I must've got off about four. Then, this morning, when I woke up, she's not there. Boy, did I freak out. She was in the bathroom. She'd locked the door. I yelled out. I said – if she didn't answer, I was gunna call the cops. That's the only time she's spoken to me. She said she was having a bath. She sounded…kind of okay, but… I don't know. Almost lunch time before she came out. Just kept refilling the bath. Stayed there till she'd used up all the hot water. She looked like she'd been in a sauna. Skin…like salmon. D'you know what she's doing now? Watching TV. All those crap afternoon shows. She's never watched them before. Wouldn't eat anything. She looks dreadful. You'd think she's got some disease. I just don't understand. The baby…and my reaction…it was pretty explosive, but now…it's like she's gone into some kind of shock.'

Our glasses are empty. Trent contemplates his as if it held the secret to his rediscovered happiness.

'Let's have another beer.'

He lights a second cigarette while I get the beers in. His mood seems to have darkened by the time I return. I wonder if it's the rain. It's a depressing sort of day.

'I'd like to kill the bastard,' he says.

I nod. I know who he means.

'She was only thirteen. Can you believe that? She didn't know what she was doing.'

'What about the guy?' I say. 'Did she tell you who he was?'

'Some kid who mowed their lawns… Said he was in some care programme, you know, for homeless kids and the like. Did a runner, didn't he, soon as he found out what he'd done…'

I watch him for a moment. Then I say, 'Kids and young guys from Tramontane House used to do mowing and stuff. That's what I've heard.'

'Wouldn't be one of them,' he says flatly. 'They're all fucking mentals.'

'From someplace else, then,' I say. 'I guess.'

'I mean,' he says, 'I just can't believe she'd do it with a guy who wasn't the full quid. It's too stupid.'

'Yeah,' I say. 'Still…thirteen…you do some pretty dumb things when you're thirteen. Maybe you should ask her. When things have settled down between you. Talk it over. Hey?'

He considers this. Then he says, 'D'you know what I think? I think that's why she can't get pregnant. It's psychological. It's kind of mental resistance because of what happened. It's shame.'

'I've read about cases like that,' I say. 'But you know, now she's confronted it, now it's sort of in the open between you, maybe it'll be okay.'

'You're an optimist, Franz,' Trent says with a small, surprising bark of laughter. 'Never say die, eh!' He becomes serious again. 'You could be right, though.'

He calls me Franz. It hasn't bothered me before. It's amused me. Maybe it was their ignorance that amused me, I don't know. Today it kind of irritates me a bit. It was Trent who called me Franz in the first place. It was Trent's joke. Jodi just picked up on it. You'd have thought she'd have known better.

'You know, it's not right calling me Franz,' I say, not unpleasantly. 'You should look it up.'

Trent blinks once or twice. 'Look what up?'

'Schumann,' I say. 'My surname. Schumann was Robert. Franz was Schubert. Different composer. I think he died of syphilis, or something.'

'Syphilis,' Trent repeats. As if this was the whole point of my correction. 'Shit, eh!' He falls silent. I guess he's still thinking about those mentals at Tramontane House.

My mobile rings. An unfamiliar number. Lisa and Brad. Well, Lisa.

'Hi,' I say, keeping my voice tight.

'The unit,' Lisa says. 'We'll take it. Brad and me. Brad really likes it, and we've done our sums. I think we'll be okay. We have to talk to the bank, of course.'

'Uh-huh,' I say. 'That's okay.'

'When can we meet?'

'I'm not sure…' I tell her. 'I'll have to call you back.'

Trent is watching me closely.

'Have I rung at a bad time?' Lisa asks, anxious.

'Sort of. It doesn't matter. I'll arrange something.'

'Good,' Lisa says. 'Sorry. For the bad timing.'

'It's not your fault,' I say. 'How would you know?'

'You'll be in touch, then,' Lisa says. 'Tomorrow?'

'Sure,' I say. 'As soon as I can.'

'Good,' Lisa says again. 'Oh…and…'

'What?'

'Your suggestion. Brad thinks it's a good idea.'

I close the call. Slip the phone into my pocket.

'Who was that?' Trent wants to know.

'A client,' I tell him.

'Yeah?'

'Yeah. About a unit. Looks like a sale.'

'Where?'

'Tramontane Park. Federation Street.'

'Don't bullshit with me,' Trent says. 'That was Jodi.'

'Why would Jodi phone me?' I ask, more in a mode of inquiry than defence.

'You tell me,' Trent says threateningly. He reaches out his hand. 'Give me your mobile. I want to check your numbers.'

'You're beginning to piss me off, Trent,' I say. 'Why don't you go home?'

'Your mobile,' Trent insists, his hand wavering a little.

'Look,' I say, 'it wasn't Jodi. Okay? If you must know, it was a guy I knew years ago. When I was growing up here.'

'You lived here before?' Trent says, sounding vaguely peeved. 'You never said. We always thought you came from Melbourne, or someplace.'

'I grew up in Tramontane Park,' I tell him. 'We – me, my parents – we moved away when I was sixteen. I came back because I had some issues I had to deal with.'

'With this guy?'

I nod.

Trent settles back into his seat. 'So…what's the story?'

'It's not really any of your business, Trent,' I say. 'It's personal. It's not easy to talk about.'

Trent stares at me for a few seconds. I can imagine a million thoughts buzzing around inside his head. Which one to hold onto…?

'Are you trying to tell me you're gay?'

'I'm trying not to tell you I was abused,' I say. It comes out somehow kind of droll.

Trent looks sceptical. 'This guy got a name?'

'Vincent Cornish,' I say, without a moment's hesitation. 'He's an upholsterer. Now let's drop it. Okay?'

'Cornish…' Trent says. 'I've seen his van around.'

'He lives in Tramontane Park,' I tell him. 'Ridge Road. Big block, backs onto scrub. The house is a dump, but the land will be worth a bit.'

Trent sniggers. 'Mr Real Estate Consultant.' He gives me a long hard look. He's not convinced. Not entirely. 'So what is it between you two?'

'What do you mean?' I ask.

'You said you'd come back to deal with it. What he did to you. How're you planning on dealing with it?'

'I don't know,' I say.

'Don't reckon he'd have been too pleased hearing from you.'

'No. He wasn't. I'm trying to set up a meeting,' I say. 'To talk.'

'That's very civil of you, Franz,' Trent says, slipping back into his old manner as if all his venting over Jodi was suddenly forgotten. 'What d'you expect to achieve?'

I shrug. 'Maybe it's just unfinished business,' I say. 'You know…'

What goes through his mind at this instant, I don't know. But something changes between us just then. I interest him in some way that I didn't before. Or maybe I've just touched a nerve. There are a myriad ways in the world to do someone harm. A lie here, a betrayal there. That's before you get into the heavy stuff. We all lose our innocence sooner or later. Isn't that so? Better early, I always think, than late. It steels you against whatever hurt there is still to come. I could argue this with Trent, but it doesn't come up.

So, don't ask me how, but here I am driving my little Getz across the river to Tramontane Park, with Trent sitting beside me. The light's gone from the afternoon, but the rain has cleared out. I can see stars in the sky over The Heights. They don't seem real, somehow; they seem more like those luminous stick-on stars I see sometimes decorating some kid's bedroom ceiling in a house his folks have put up for sale.

It'll be good meeting Vincent again. I've phoned a few times, but he's usually not at home. The one or two times he has picked up the phone I've found it difficult to speak. I have to face him. I'm kind of relieved I've got Trent with me. Maybe this is what I needed, a little backup for my confrontation. I don't really like the word confrontation. It seems unduly negative. After all, there are no issues that can't be dealt with amicably as long as all parties approach their differences with open minds. My counsellor told me that. My sweater and specs man. A spirit of reconciliation, he said. Forgiveness even when there is nothing to forgive. The truth is, you can harbour a grudge so long the reason for your resentment – the insult, the offence – becomes unsure. A little cloudy. Prey to doubt. All the more reason to resolve disputes quickly, don't you think?

6

The lights were out. We didn't think he was home. But the back door was unlocked, so we went in.

First thing Trent says is, 'Smell that? Cat stink.'

I might've guessed he shared Jodi's distaste for cats. There's enough light coming through the kitchen window to get a general sense of where everything is. It's so quiet you'd hear a mouse squeak. Except there's this big tomcat, suddenly there on the table, stepping over dirty dishes. Meow, big tomcat goes. I scratch his ear; he likes that.

Then something really weird happens. The light goes on. I think Trent must have flicked the switch, but he's nowhere near it. I remember then, driving up Ridge Road, how dark it was. There was no light anywhere. The whole street was blacked out like there'd been some kind of power failure.

Then, just to really freak us out, Vincent appears. Kind of stumbles into the kitchen like he'd been hiding behind the door, or something. It's so comical, I almost laugh. Vincent recognises me, straight off. It's been ten years, but I haven't changed so much. It's not like I'm sporting a beard or a fashion haircut. I'm standing there stroking his cat. Vincent is so goggle-eyed seeing me, he maybe doesn't see Trent who is standing just behind him. Next to the stove.

'Hey, Vincent,' I say, real genial like. 'How're you keeping?' And I wink at Trent.

This is when Vincent becomes aware of Trent. Vincent turns, sharpish. Trent tries to take a step back, but he's already up against the stove. There's that sort of mental flash then when you think, this is it. This is the moment I'm going to remember for the rest of my life. There's a real adrenalin rush. Trent has his hand on the handle of a small cast-iron skillet. He raises the skillet and takes a swing at Vincent. It catches him square on the jaw. Vincent's head snaps back and he drops to the floor. Trent looks at Vincent. The tomcat leaps off the table and shoots out the door. Vincent is groaning. He's pissed his pants. Trent still has a hold of the skillet. He doesn't look at me. It's like

I'm not there. He stands over Vincent and brings the skillet down hard. Cracks his skull with it. Two, three, four times he brings the skillet down on Vincent's head. Pulverises it.

I sing out. 'Go, boy!' I sing. I can't help it. I'm so caught up in the moment.

Not that Trent needs any encouraging. If he got a buzz out of giving Jodi a smack, I think, he's gotta be really jumping now…

Garrison Town

Scenes from the Home Front: Brisbane October 1942

The captain drove her home. She refused to go to a hotel. She let him feel between her legs, but it wasn't what he wanted. It wasn't what he'd paid for, but he was too polite to complain. She liked that about the Yanks: so polite, so charming. So generous.

The first Yank she'd gone out with, a lieutenant, had his own car and driver. She still had the little bottle of perfume he gave her. Never pushed a drink on her she didn't want. Everything was ma'am this and ma'am that.

'Why, ain't that the prettiest little cottage?' he says when they pull up at the Beck house.

It was early, so they took a ride on down the street until they stopped in the shadow of the powerhouse.

'Take a walk, driver,' the lieutenant says, and she's alone with him.

He smelt nice, he looked good enough to eat, but she didn't like it because she felt cheated by all that yes ma'am, no ma'am malarkey.

'You watch yourself,' she told him just before he kissed her. 'I'm not an easy sort of girl.'

'You just tell me when to stop, honey,' he says and already his hand is under her skirt and up over her knee.

He was good as his word too, but none too happy about it. Even in the dark she could see the smirk on the driver's face when he got called back so quick. At least she got to keep the bottle of perfume.

She let the captain escort her up the steps to the front door. Her father's house, she explained: she was separated from her husband. Pulling him into the dark of the porch, she kissed him hard on the mouth. 'You want to see me again?'

'Sure, baby.'

He didn't mean it. She was too much trouble for him, when he had so many willing local girls to charm and seduce. She worried that it would get back to Theo. She would never convince him there was nothing to it, just cocktails in Lennon's, free nylons and smokes and a chaste night at the flicks. The truth was, there had been too many men, already. Too many cashed-up, sex-hungry Yanks since that first hands-off date with the lieutenant. It was not what she intended, leaving Theo. It was the war with its potent coupling of fear and opportunity. Such uncertain times, such unnatural freedom… It surprised her that she fell into it so easily.

Former Detective Sergeant Beck knew his daughter was seeing American servicemen. If he hadn't been so sick, he might've cared more. He wasn't sorry he was off the force. It wasn't like the old days. The Americans taking over the city just seemed to be pushing his face against it. He didn't like their smart-arse comments, their white teeth or the cream they put on their hair. It irked him that errant GIs and Yankee sailor boys had to be turned over to the marshal provosts for prosecution almost as much as it irked him to hear Brisbane referred to as Little America. It disgusted him that so many local girls were ready to drop their drawers at the flash of one of those pearly white smiles. Every time he saw some big-shot top-brass cove drive past in a shiny black limousine like he was the governor of one of those tinpot South American dictatorships, he spat in the gutter.

Now most mornings he spent an hour or two yarning with his mate Vic, who owned the garage and pumps at the end of the street. He wished he didn't have Iris hanging around the house, chain-smoking through the *Women's Weekly* or *Truth* or long baths. Every day the same since she left Simm. After tea she puts on a clean dress and underwear, paints her lips, fixes her hair and walks up the street to catch the tram into the city. Another night, another cashed-up captain or lieutenant, looking for a little company and anything else he might coax out of her. Whoring herself for the sort of luxuries her husband could get her, if he had a mind to. Had to be the sex. Why else leave the bed of a well-heeled doctor?

The girl was gone when Louis woke. Her name escaped him for the moment. His first thought was to find his pants and check that his wallet was still buttoned inside the back pocket. Rolling off the bed, his toe clipped an empty bottle. Oh, sweet jivin' mama…

Where the heck had he left his guitar…? It was a big old Stella, cost him five bucks in a Jew-run music store on Maxwell Street. Hawked it halfway round the world and he loses it in a two-bit whorehouse in some British colonial outpost. Before the war, between jobs, he'd play on street corners like those old blues men from South Carolina and Mississippi. Some days his takings equalled his present army pay. He owed that guitar. Dropping his head between his knees, he peered under the bed. Glory Hallelujah! Stored for safekeeping.

Raising his head made the room spin. Leaning gingerly forward, he grabbed his pants from the back of the chair. A reassuring bulge to the back pocket, the button still fastened. Good girl. Black like him, not that it made any difference. Just another sweet-talking whore. No more than sixteen, he reckoned, pretty enough still, except for her teeth. He'd noticed that with the Aussie blacks: lousy teeth.

Rose. That was her name. Like some high society girl in one of those English movies. The moment they're through the door she's all over him like a monkey.

'You like black girls?'

'Sure, baby.'

'Black girls better than white girls?'

Would it have shamed him to say no? Right now he wanted no truck with all that black shit white shit. He was just a guy getting some pussy.

Later, she said, 'You play cowboy songs?'

'Yeah, I play cowboy songs.'

'My brothers play cowboy songs,' she said. 'Murri cowboy songs.'

'What's Murri?' he asked.

'We're Murri. Black people are Murri.' She put a bottle to his lips and let him take a gulp of warm flat beer. 'Your people got a black name?'

He wiped his mouth. 'We're just niggers,' he said.

Born a nigger, die a nigger, he reflected. Being a soldier didn't make a bean of difference. Not to the army. The provos were the worst. Nigger haters to a man, that was Louis's experience. Beat a man just for stepping over the colour line. For blacks, in this piss ant garrison town, north of the river was no-man's-land. Venture over the bridge and you were as good as dead, if the provos caught you. No questions asked, just another dead nigger straying where he had no business.

It was different out of town. Out in the suburbs, at the dances, just walking the streets, a black GI could get treated real nice. Helping white ladies stow their shopping in their automobiles, just smiling and being on your best manners. You weren't no nigger then. You got asked home to tea by big-boned schoolgirls, busting out of their uniforms, wanting to show you off to their brothers and sisters. Their mommas too. He just had to know his place. Not to step over the line. There was a colour line here, same as the Victoria Bridge, though it wasn't going to get him shot if he forgot himself. Back Stateside, if he'd dared date some nice white lady's daughter, he could expect to have the dogs set on him.

Rose didn't stick around to hear him play cowboy songs. Louis must have slept like a babe, not to hear her go. And didn't lift his wallet, he kind of marvelled at that. He pulled on his shorts and singlet. He noticed it then, what was missing. Why he'd had that feeling of being more naked than naked. He turned the room over, tearing the filthy linen from the bed in a vain search to find it. That damn bitch, that goddamn black bitch whore. Souvenired his dog tags.

For months, Dr Simm had been complaining to the authorities about the vacant lot behind his practice on the corner of Brunswick Street and Merthyr Road. It was strewn with rubble from the schoolhouse that had burned down a year ago, overgrown with weeds and infested with vermin. Torn posters from a broken hoarding compounded the eyesore. He was moderately gratified, though somewhat mystified, turning the corner a few minutes after nine that morning, to see a police patrol car parked across the sidewalk. A sergeant beckoned him to approach. The man's face was familiar, though not especially friendly. At the back of the lot, partly obscured by a vandalised billboard, an American army jeep was parked alongside a black sedan.

'Mr Penny, isn't it?'

'Sergeant Penny, sir.'

Theo observed the scene on the lot. A short distance from the vehicles an American sailor sat slumped against a brick wall, his head in his hands. A uniformed policeman and two marshal provost officers stood over him. 'What have we here, Sergeant?'

'Dead tart.'

'Really?'

'Take a look?'

'Yes,' Theo said. 'I think I should.'

The pasty-faced woman slumped forward on the back seat of a black sedan appeared to have choked on her own vomit. There was an empty liquor bottle beside her and a greasy limp prophylactic draped over the dead woman's shoe. Her knickers were twisted around one ankle.

'These times…' Theo murmured, withdrawing his head from the scene.

The sergeant was probably right, the girl was a prostitute, but she could just as easily be some soldier's fiancée or wife. It disturbed him a little that he felt nothing for her. These days he kept his head up and his mind on his job. While the world around him fell to pieces, it seemed. With the American forces came sophistication and mayhem in equal measures, he had observed. It was futile to judge or conjure up fear of the deep abyss they were all about to fall into. The abyss was the war itself. Before the Japs bombed Darwin, some element of sanity prevailed. The threat and the danger was somewhere else. And then, after those bombs fell, everything changed. A macabre demonic circus had come to town. Ministers fulminated from their pulpits, and good luck to them. The denounced sat in Theo's surgery, waiting for contraceptive advice. Young girls he'd treated for acne and menstrual problems a year or so back had become garishly painted lounge lizzies, hanging around hotel bars night after night, waiting to be picked up. And as for their mothers…

He watched the senior provost officer approach. The MP drew the sergeant aside, though not out of Theo's hearing. It seemed, Theo thought, calculated to offend.

'We'll take our boy.'

Penny nodded towards the car. 'What about her?'

'She's yours.'

'Your boy anything to say for himself?'

'He's intoxicated.'

Penny accompanied Theo back to the sidewalk.

'Friggin' Yanks, 'scuse my French.'

Theo smiled. The man's knowing stare bothered him. He sensed that it had nothing to do with his disdain for Americans.

'How's Mrs Simm, Doc?'

'Mrs Simm…?'

'You got a new girl. Receptionist. Thought Mrs Simm might be poorly…'

Theo kept his smile. He was grateful for the arrival of a Black Maria. From the lavatory window at the rear of the practice, he watched the orderlies remove the prostitute's body from the American sailor's hired car.

Louis set out, retracing his steps from the night before. Blue sky, hot and cloudless, the meanest breeze on his face. October: late fall back home, springtime down under. He was still having trouble getting his head around that. He proceeded at a steady pace east along Grey Street. This narrow stretch between the rail track and the river was familiar territory. Bars, low-rent rooming houses and greasy spoon cafés: reminiscent in no small way of the South Chicago quarter where he mostly grew up. Card games, illicit booze, fly bookmakers, cheap whores… He'd spent more time here on leave since he'd come ashore in July than any place else in the city. Like most US army coloured boys. Some nights, some bars, coloured faces were the only ones you'd see. You'd think you were back down Mississippi way. Everyone carried blades. Louis carried a three blade jackknife, which he'd had to pull more than a few times. There was always trouble between white boys and coloureds and the coloureds and provosts. Just up the road, in the basement of a big old red-brick building, the provosts kept a lock-up, temporary accommodation Louis so far had stayed away from. Losing his dog tags could change that. Army property to the baton-wielding provosts. To Louis it was his beating heart, his mind and soul that had nothing to do with the shape of his face or the colour of his skin. He pressed on, across the street, turning the corner into the narrow filth-strewn lane that led to the wharfs.

Beck doubted he'd live out the war. Some mornings he could smell it the instant he woke: decrepitude. The stink of infirmity, old age and decay. He got a pension, for what it was worth, but it was the long empty days that made him miserable. The job had been pretty much all he'd known since Nora died. And before… Not that he'd ever thought himself a career copper. He'd made detective sergeant, he'd been content with that. Truth was, the discovery of the dicky heart suited him at the time. Citizens still thieved, murdered and beat up their spouses in wartime, but the old ways of doing things had changed. Not so much in the process as in the sense that nothing was ever quite what it seemed. The old certainties had gone. The photographer bludgeoned to death in his Queen Street studio probably owed a loan shark money. Or was blackmailing a city councillor with crook connections. Or then maybe he was a Jap spy assassinated by army intelligence. The job was rife with such crazy speculations. Or not so crazy. The thing was, you just couldn't do your job without feeling watchful eyes over your shoulder, monitoring your every move, in case you missed something. Or saw something you shouldn't have. You weren't even sure your boss was your boss any more.

That's all he thought it was at the time: a touch of paranoia. He'd been fretting all morning, and he couldn't think why. Cold one minute, sweating the next. Clammy hands, his head spinning as if he'd had a heavy night on the grog. And then that ache, spreading across his chest until his neck, jaw, arms, shoulders, every sinew of his body seemed to be in contraction. He wasn't a God-bothering man, not Beck. But he knew a sign when it was the sort that brought you face to face with your own mortality.

The only blacks Iris had seen before the Yanks came to town were the Abos who hung around the parks and alleys of South Brisbane. You didn't mix with them. They kept with their own people, except some of the girls who tarted themselves around the bars and factories at night. The men drank and brawled. You wouldn't know they existed unless one of them got knifed and killed and it got in the newspaper. The Yank blacks were nothing like them. Wild-eyed Rastuses, her father had said they were when he first saw them on the city streets. That's how they looked in the movies.

She saw Louis one Sunday about a month back when she was going to the Trocadero with her sometime friend Gloria who worked in the bar at Lennon's and had dated more Yanks than Iris could count.

'Look at that gorgeous buck Negro,' Gloria said. 'Don't he think he's the big shot, but.'

Louis was sitting on a crate outside a café, playing a guitar.

Iris was looking good that day, new dress from Finneys, lipstick and stockings her father's mate Vic had taken in lieu of a repair bill on a truck.

'Hey, babe,' the Negro said, 'don't you look a picture?'

She gave him her home telephone number, telling him to ring in the late morning when her father made it his business to be out of the house.

He called about a week later when she'd all but stopped hoping he might. It was just on midday.

Her father picked up the phone as he was coming through the door. 'Some Yank for you,' he told her. He never asked questions he didn't want to know the answer to. 'Sounds like a real hometown boy,' he noted sarcastically. He never said black. Wouldn't have even thought it.

If the day ever came when you could see who you were talking to down the telephone line, Iris thought, a girl would have to pick her dates carefully.

The Digger knew the girl. 'Don't trust the Abos, mate,' he told Louis. 'They'll thieve the fillings out of your teeth while you're asleep.' He winked. 'You blokes are okay. Civilised in the ways of the white man. Got a smoke?'

Louis broke open a fresh pack of Camels. The Digger was about nineteen, unkempt and dirty. When Louis came upon him he was sitting on the kerb, lacing his boots. He wanted to hear Louis play his guitar.

'Jimmie Rodgers,' he enthused. 'Jeez, I love the way he does that yodelling. You yodel? Don't know that I ever heard a Negro yodel.'

'Niggers holler,' Louis told him.

The Digger took a long drag on his cigarette. 'I just love these Yankee smokes,' he said.

Louis nodded. 'Where'd you see Rose?'

The Digger knew Rose from the red hat she sometimes wore. 'My mate been with her,' he told Louis. 'Hot little girlie, he reckoned. Don't go with the street tarts myself. I got a sweetheart back home in Rocky. She's enough for me.'

He had a boyish pockmarked face with a day's growth of downy fair hair on his upper lip. Rocky could have been the other side of the continent, for all Louis knew. To his ears, all Australians sounded the same.

The Digger introduced himself as Jacko Finn. He followed Louis down Stanley Street the way a stray dog will tail a fellow who has patted its head instead of giving its butt a kick. He told Louis Rose and two or three other black tarts operated out of a cottage down near the dry dock. He didn't know whether they lived there or if it was just their 'place of business'. The expression caused him to snigger. Louis thought he was a hayseed. Every few yards he'd stop to tighten the knot on his bootlaces.

Turning the corner back onto Grey Street, they passed a café just opening its doors for business. The proprietor's name, printed above the door, was Nowak. Louis hadn't seen a Polack name since he'd left Chicago.

'You want some brekkie, Louis?' Jacko asked. 'I know this cove. He'll have a couple of nice lamb chops for us. You and me, we're mates, right?'

Louis considered the dull ache cramping his gut. It wasn't hunger for a greasy-spoon lamb chop. Balls-scratching cook and a gob of spit in the pan to check that it was hot enough to fry. This godforsaken place, he thought. His soul sang for home.

Try as he might, Theo could not erase Penny's smirking face from his mind. He had noted the same look on certain of his more regular patients in recent weeks, those time wasters with boils on their necks or bunions protruding through the split seams of their cheap shoes. He didn't deserve this. Hadn't he given Iris a good life? Happiness? Happiness was a two-bedroom apartment in Balfour House, was it not? Happiness was an account at Finneys, a motor car in the garage, dinner parties, cocktails and gossipy afternoons with doctors' wives. And love and sex, it went without saying… How could he not give her happiness?

He said nothing when she left. He thought a few weeks with her father would give her time to reflect. It was the times... Everything was the times, affecting the populace like some mind changing drug. He waited for her to come back to him, renewed and loving. He heard instead that she was seen riding in hired cars with allied serviceman, her arm around their thick necks, her face painted like a street tart's. What could she want from these flash, uniformed loudmouths, except sex? Wasn't that the sentiment expressed in Sergeant Penny's contemptuous leer? The situation he had been caught in that morning could not have been more grotesquely suggestive. Penny knew it, half the neighbourhood knew it. How deliciously likely that the sailor's girl choking on gin and God knows what could have been precious Dr Simm's wife.

Another Digger had joined them, a red-headed rough-skinned guy, squeezing in the narrow booth beside Jacko to share his lamb chop. He didn't look at Louis. 'Cripes, Jacko,' he said, 'you don't have to sit with Yankee coons.'

'Louis is me mate,' Jacko said.

'Since when?'

'Since half an hour ago.'

The Digger's name was Blue on account of his red hair. He told Louis he didn't mean no offence, calling him coon. Louis laughed.

'Louis lost his dog tags,' Jacko said. 'Abo tart pinched 'em. We're gunna find the bitch, ain't we, Louis? Get 'em back.'

'Give her a poke, did you?' Blue asked Louis.

Louis said nothing. Blue's talk could be as honey-coated as he could make it, it didn't fool Louis one bit.

'Be best when you boys move on,' Blue said. 'Get stuck into the Japs instead of fooling with our Abos, stirring them up. Cripes, they'll be wanting the vote next. Bad enough we had to give it to the sheilas, eh Jacko?'

. Jacko had pulled a handkerchief from his pocket to wipe his greasy lips. 'Bugger politics,' he said. 'Let's go get your dog tags, Louis.'

Blue kept his seat. He stared at Louis. 'Yous boys want me along?'

Jacko shook his head. 'She'll be right, mate. I know where we'll find the tart.'

Blue was staring at Louis as if he hadn't heard.

'No,' Louis said.

He moved quickly, sliding his butt out of the diner before Blue could make his retort, which Louis could see he had a mind to. He'd left the Stella in the Polack's care, behind the serving counter. The Polack was wiping glasses with a dirty rag.

'Give me my guitar,' Louis said.

The Polack, cussing some Polack oath, slid the Stella over the counter top. Even in the gloomy yellow half-light of the café, Louis could see splatter of breakfast fat over the guitar's polished top. The Polack shrugged. He wiped his rag across the strings. If he spits, Louis thought, I'll knock his lousy Polack teeth out.

'You paying?' the Polack asked.

Louis laughed. 'So you can charge me double?'

'You don't pay, I call the MPs,' the Polack said. He tapped a grubby square of paper taped to the wall. 'I got the number. Here in five minutes.'

Louis rested the Stella against the front of the counter. A fly buzzed in his head. When he felt a touch at his elbow it was like a baton striking him, making him flinch as if it had caused him real pain. He knew it was Blue, and he knew he was going to regret what he was about to do, but he did it anyway. In one slick move, because he was practised at it, he pulled the jack knife from his pocket and pressed the open blade against the Digger's throat.

Beck's heart was beating fast when he got to Vic's garage. He would have gone straight home from his check-up, if Iris hadn't been there, lounging around half naked, her nose in a magazine, smoking those Yankee Doodle cigarettes, making him feel like a visitor in his own house.

Vic was coming down the street in the Dodge pickup when Beck got there. Making his round of bootleg suppliers of spare parts, Beck guessed. Bootleg was a word Vic had picked up from the Yanks. He was freer with it than he would have been if Beck had still been in the job. Jackals, bloodsuckers or canny operators, Vic called his suppliers, depending on his frame of mind. The Yanks were fair game, whatever the situation. Vic was full of envy for those traders who had premises close to the American bases, having heard stories about huge wads of greenbacks packed into biscuit tins and buried under dog kennels or kids' swings in suburban backyards. His eldest daughter Amy was employed mending Yankee uniforms and got to eat in the American Red Cross canteen in the city. Most days Beck called on his friend he took home something for lunch or supper, tinned salmon or Nestlés cream or American chocolate. Vic's business wasn't doing so well, that was the fact of it. Six months ago, when Beck started his regular visits, he noticed the bare hooks on the wall where gaskets and hoses and rubber belts and such paraphernalia should have hung. Vic had employed a mechanic back then, but had to let him go and do the work himself instead of hanging out in the pubs and bookies, his natural habitat, drumming up business. A local lad came in to do the donkey work, sweeping the floors, stripping and cleaning small engine parts, but Beck hadn't seen him in a while.

They adjourned to Vic's small back office to drink tea. The narrow space was hot and stuffy from being closed up for an hour or more. Beck sat in silence while Vic, sweating and oozing out of his tight overalls, lit the gas.

'You don't look so good, Walter,' Vic said. 'You need to take it easy, mate. Walking in this heat with that delicate ticker of yours.'

'Nothing wrong with my ticker,' Beck lied. He watched the flickering gas for a second. 'I'm rooting fit.'

Vic nodded. 'That girl of yours taking good care of you, eh?'

'Keeping me in smokes,' Beck said. He lit up, waiting for his tea. 'I look at her these days and I wonder who she is. Can't talk to her. She's too old to belt.' He took a long calming drag on his cigarette. 'She's her husband's problem, any rate.' He loosened his tie and shirt buttons.

Vic looked uneasy. 'You want me to run you home, Walter?'

'It's five minutes,' Beck said. 'I can walk it.'

He wasn't so sure that he could. The long walk down James Street from the surgery had left him feeling hot and listless. He could feel his chest tightening as he watched Vic bring the steaming tea to the table. He wanted to weep because there was no sugar. What good was a daughter working at the Red Cross canteen if she couldn't get a little illicit sugar?

Vic squeezed into the chair across the cluttered desk. He took one of Beck's cigarettes and lit it absently. 'You know what you need, Walter?' he said. 'You need a pick-me-up.'

He beckoned Beck to follow him into the workshop. Closing the garage doors against prying eyes, he drew Beck to the rear of the Dodge pickup. A grey tarpaulin was stretched across the goods he'd picked up on his rounds that morning. Beck had a good idea what Vic was going to show him. A redundant business doesn't pay butcher's bills or feed growing daughters.

Loosening a corner rope, Vic dragged a cardboard case to the back of the truck. He hesitated, his hand under the lid. 'Know what wartimes are, Walter? They're good times for heroics, and good times for enterprise. There's something for everyone.' He plucked a bottle of bourbon from the case. 'American ain't Irish, but don't look a gift horse et cetera, et cetera.' He pushed the bottle into Beck's hand.

Beck accepted it without protest, as he'd accepted tinned salmon and Nestlés cream from Vic's daughter, and packs of Camels and Lucky Strikes from Iris. Some years ago, he shot dead a thief who flashed a knife at him. A little corrupt receiving in wartime hardly measured up.

A sullen-looking girl of about sixteen, a grubby apron hanging loosely from her waist, answered the bell. Theo announced himself brusquely. The house, solidly built of red brick and stone, was dark and cool.

The girl directed him to an over-furnished front room. He could hear a girl's voice raised in anger in another part of the house. A door slammed. Presently Mrs Douglas entered. She was a small, expensively dressed woman of forty, pale-skinned as if she'd spent too long out of the sun. He wondered if she were anaemic. She apologised for calling him out, when she knew how busy his practice was, and the frightful cost of petrol. Theo smiled.

'It's my daughter…' Mrs Douglas said. She lowered her eyes.

The maid brought tea. Theo listened to the mantel clock's measured tick. The maid closed the door.

'Joy,' Mrs Douglas informed him. 'My eldest.'

The angry girl, Theo thought. She didn't sound sick.

'She's pregnant,' Mrs Douglas said.

Theo sipped his tea, which was too hot and sweet for his taste. 'How old is she?'

'Seventeen. Girls…and this dreadful business…'

He supposed she meant the war. Her husband was a naval officer; Theo was vague about the rank. A large painting of a battleship, guns blazing, hung over the mantelpiece, above the ticking clock.

'I'll examine her,' Theo said.

'Yes. She's less than two months…'

Theo stared at the woman's small bony ankles and tiny feet. Iris could never wear shoes like that. They'd look ridiculous on her. She'd never cared much for expensive clothes, anyway. She was a utilitarian dresser. Practical. He liked that about her, comfort over fashion. Of course, a slim, well-heeled naval officer's wife could carry off just about anything.

'It would be better if she didn't have it,' Mrs Douglas said.

'I imagine,' Theo said.

He'd last seen the girl some months back after she'd slipped and sprained her ankle, alighting from a punt on the river. He remembered her tittering laugh and knowing look as he examined the sprain. He had a lovely gentle touch, she told him. She'd raised the hem of her skirt considerably higher than was necessary. Her mother was sitting in reception, reading a novel she'd brought.

'And the boy?' Theo asked.

'The boy?'

'The father. Is he aware…?'

She lit a cigarette, ignoring him for the moment. A boyfriend, a nice lad from a good school, outraged but understanding and supportive parents… This wasn't it. The deliciously named Joy had been spreading her favours much further afield. The girl was probably lucky not to have contracted venereal disease. Papers and medical journals arrived on his desk almost daily revealing figures and accounts of sexual abandon that would make a good man cry. Professional tarts were less of a problem than the good-time girls, the enthusiastic amateurs like Mrs Douglas's knocked-up daughter. Professional girls were regularly rounded up and subjected to compulsory medical checks. A colleague of his had taken a position at the Wattlebrae Infectious Diseases Hospital. He told Theo about girls, still infected, jumping out of the window to root with American servicemen in the hospital grounds. Most were tarts, but many were wives whose servicemen husbands were overseas, fighting the good fight. One good-time girl, a teacher of unsuspecting young college ladies, had infected a dozen men with gonorrhoea before being forcibly detained for treatment.

Theo said nothing of this. If the girl had VD, he would have to report it. The mother had probably not even considered the pox.

She stubbed her cigarette on a small silver ashtray. 'How difficult would it be to get a termination?' she asked.

Her directness caught him by surprise. He listened to the little mantel clock strike two before murmuring that he might be able to arrange a discreet referral.

'As soon as possible,' she said.

'Of course.' He smiled.

She did not respond.

It was pointless speculating where she got her information. Such women always knew what they needed to know. A few words over afternoon tea or a card game... The urgency, he suspected, had less to do with social embarrassment or her daughter's health than her husband's unexpected return. It was no business of his how she might account for the necessary fee. Such procedures – in or out of wartime – never came cheap. He jotted a figure on a slip of notepaper, which she read without comment. A fair sum, he thought, in the circumstances. Backyard abortions were for shop girls and impoverished Catholic wives.

Hunger helped Louis run: an empty, grumbling belly. A full gut would have slowed him down. He could handle the Stella hanging over his shoulder. He'd lost count of the times he'd had to take off from street playing just because some cop or loud-mouthed white boy took offence at his choice of guitar picking. He'd lost Jacko streets back when the mob had started after them. Louis didn't have to hear Blue hollering for his black nigger ass to know it was the Digger leading the pack. Louis had never run so hard in his life. Hell, thieved dog tags wasn't worth getting his throat cut. Only the Jews in Europe got it worse than the coloureds in America, Louis had always thought. For that, he had the daily news to enlighten him. The daily news had never enlightened him about the habits of the Australian native. Sometimes Louis felt his life was like one of those bad dreams you wake from only to find yourself caught in another just as bad. Like he was running from one demon into the claws of another. Louis knew what it meant. It meant there was no escaping your fate. But it never stopped him running. A little black mouse running on a wheel. It was what his Daddy told him. 'You always running, boy, and never getting nowhere.'

Iris went out to the street when she heard aircraft, but there was nothing to see. It frightened her how aircraft so far away could make so much noise. It brought home to her the reality of wartime, more so than ration coupons and air raid shelters and identity cards. Or the streets filled with uniformed men and military trucks and cars trailing smoke from gas producing charcoal burners. All this seemed like some comic-like make-believe world. She thought how everything was so frightful early in the year. The air seemed charged with fear and anxiety. You couldn't pick up a newspaper without reading some terrible report on the front page. You never got the Japs out of your head, the savage things they were doing, their hateful unstoppable advance. Then the Yanks came and the Japs didn't seem to be doing so well, and then the talk in the street and in the homes and the workplaces was about nylons and cheap spuds and two-timing lovers and what sort of woman would trade sex for a bag of onions. It was strange and exciting but no longer scary. At least, not so that it would keep you awake at night. Only the airplanes unnerved her, their rumbling engines making the china shake in the cabinet, and the news front pictures they impressed on her mind of falling bombs and burning cities.

Nin's Father

Nin's father was a retired army officer. He returned to the small Darling Downs community after the war and bought a half share in a motor repair business with his cousin. The cousin was a genius on the shop floor but drank heavily. One day in 1950 he fell into a flooded storm drain on the way home from the pub and was drowned. Thereafter, Nin's father ran the business on his own.

He was an astute man, hired good staff, and the business prospered. The people in the town liked and respected him because he had spent the last year of the war in a Japanese prisoner of war camp. They called him the duke, an ironic reference to his English wife who sounded like the actress Edith Evans in a movie someone had seen about the British ruling class.

Nin's father was a tall stringy man with a slight limp. He would never say what caused the limp, though everyone knew it resulted from his experience as a POW. Another outcome of the year spent in captivity was a deep religious conviction. 'Suffering made me believe,' he would tell people. 'Not my own – which was nothing – but seeing others.' He was a popular reader of biblical texts at evening classes held at the School of Arts. Later, he travelled to the more isolated communities in the outlying districts and read the Sunday service.

There were two children: Nin, the elder, and a son who died of leukaemia at the age of seven. For a long time after the death, Nin's father couldn't bear to hear his son's name mentioned. He insisted his wife dispose of all the boy's clothes and toys, even his simple drawings and paintings. He wanted nothing in the house to remind him of his son's existence. Wisely, his wife hid the photographs that included the boy. For this he was thankful later, though it was a long time before he could properly look at them.

The boy's room, a boxed-in section of the veranda, he stripped bare, then furnished with a desk, bookcases and two easy chairs. It became his retreat, where he could write his sermons and select his reading texts away from the household chatter of his wife and daughter.

The death of his son did nothing to diminish the father's faith, but it changed him in other ways. He became remote and difficult to talk to. When he laughed, someone said, he sounded like a travelling salesman laughing at a smutty joke.

One day, when Nin was returning from school, she heard her parents arguing in the kitchen. She went to the back window to listen. She didn't know what the argument was about but her mother's voice was brittle and complaining. It seemed she had been weeping. She told her husband she couldn't bear to be touched by him ever again; it was like being mauled by a stranger.

Nin could see her father's shadow through the curtain. For a long while, he didn't move or say anything. Then her mother began sobbing again and he went away and shut himself in his room.

When she was sixteen, Nin became friendly with a young Indian woman called Lila. Lila's husband, Mr Dass, was employed as a cleaner at the motor repair business that Nin's father owned. The business by this time employed more than a dozen men. Nin's father knew each by his first name with the exception of Mr Dass. Mr Dass was only ever Mr Dass.

Lila was twenty-one the first time she came to Nin's house. Mr Dass was much older and people who saw them together often mistook them for father and daughter. They had a young son whose name Nin had long forgotten. Later they had another son whose name was Prakash. Years after, Nin's mother sent a newspaper cutting showing a tall athletic-looking Prakash standing with his mother at a graduation ceremony. There was no mention of Mr Dass.

Lila was a bright studious young woman who had learned to type before she got married. She wasn't very pretty but she had a nice figure which Nin admired. Nin was dumpy at sixteen and hated herself.

One Sunday afternoon, just after lunch, Lila came to the house. Nin answered the door. Lila was going to do some typing for Nin's father. He had been asked by the bishop to write a little history of the church and the town and the families who had lived and farmed there for almost a hundred years. He had refused at first, thinking there were others better able, but the bishop was persuasive. So he talked to the old-timers, made notes from the parish records, and once or twice drove into Toowoomba to read the old newspapers in the public library. The little book began to take shape.

When Mr Dass heard of the work, he went to Nin's father and offered to have it typed for him, free of charge. It was necessary, Mr Dass said, for Lila to keep her hand in. And she had her own typewriter, a little portable machine in a simulated leather case.

That first afternoon, Lila spent about three hours typing up notes and rough drafts and helping Nin's father sort through the photographs that were to illustrate the book. Afterwards she sat on the veranda with Nin and drank a glass of lemonade. Nin remembered the day with a particular clarity. It was September, unseasonably warm after a dry winter, and the garden was filled with the heady smell of native flowers in early bloom.

Before she went home, Lila told Nin she hoped they would see more of each other. Lila didn't have many friends. She and Mr Dass and the baby had come from the coast about a year before and were still trying to settle in.

Each Sunday afternoon thereafter, Lila came to the house to help Nin's father with his book. They always repaired to the study that had been the boy's room, and Nin's father closed the door. He didn't want Lila distracted by Nin loitering on the veranda, pretending to read a novel. When the days grew hot, he brought a large pedestal fan from the workshop and set it up behind the door where it whirred away noisily and sent tremors across the floor and through the walls, causing the crockery along the kitchen shelves to rattle.

There were no proper windows to the study: the veranda had been boxed in with sheets of masonite and louvres of frosted glass. The louvres faced south to the neglected rear of the garden, the cats' hunting ground. The prospect was further obscured by a large corrugated-iron water tank, overgrown with grapevines. Nin could remember hiding under the tank stand when she was small and had misbehaved.

Lila always stayed a while after her visits, sometimes just for a few minutes, sometimes for an hour or more. Nin's mother occasionally asked her to stay for tea but Lila always declined. She liked just to walk in the wild back garden with her friend Nin.

One day, not long before Christmas, they stopped to pick a few mean grapes from around the water tank.

Lila was silent. Nin, her mouth full of shrivelled fruit, stepped up to the louvre window and peered into her father's empty study. The louvres were shut but there was a thin opening where the strips of glass and the frame didn't come together properly.

'You should ask Dad to open these up,' Nin said. 'It's so stuffy in that room unless the breeze comes up from the south.'

'He doesn't like to,' Lila said. 'He says there are snakes in the trees and they can come through the window.'

Nin stepped back, smirking at her father's whimsy.

Lila was nervously fingering the buttons of her dress. Then she said secretly, 'You could come and watch us if you wanted to. If you can see in.'

Nin's father liked to take a walk and stretch his legs after he and Lila had finished for the day.

Nin listened for the sound of his feet on the drive while she considered Lila's strange suggestion. 'Why should I do that?' she asked.

'He touches me,' Lila said. She rested her long dark fingers lightly across her chest. 'I want you to see.'

Nin blinked. She couldn't imagine her father's great paws caressing Lila's little pointy breasts. 'Does he unbutton your dress?' she asked matter-of-factly.

Lila shook her head. Her eyes had grown large and childlike with silent pleading. Nin felt suddenly afraid.

'You must tell Mr Dass what you see,' Lila said. 'My husband will know what to do.'

All week, Nin was troubled. She had strange dreams in which her father kept following her around the house, coming into her bedroom when she was reading and, once, opening the bathroom door when she was having a shower. She knew it was wrong, that it was Lila her father wanted, but Lila was never there. One night, Mr Dass appeared in her dreams, dressed in a neat blue suit, and carrying Lila's typewriter. When Nin unzipped the cover, a small green snake slithered out and curled itself around her ankle.

Nin saw little of her father that week, and was glad. She felt uncomfortable being in the room alone with him. She couldn't help looking at his hands, the hands she imagined sliding around Lila's tiny waist and fondling her through her dress.

She wondered if he said anything, made some little animal noise while he was touching her; Lila hadn't said. If it had been winter, Lila could have worn a thick sweater or a coat and said she was cold. If Lila had been born in India where it was hot every day and not at the coast near Coffs Harbour, she could have complained of the fan, saying it was giving her a chill.

Nin wondered what she would have done if she were in Lila's place.

'Why didn't you just tell him to stop it?' she had asked when they were standing by the tank stand.

'I did,' Lila said. 'He just laughed and said, "Silly girl."'

Nin waited feverishly for the long week to end.

Sometimes she looked at her mother and pitied her. If her mother caught her watching, she would smile and say, 'What's up, Dumps?' (Nin hated being called Dumps. Her mother seemed to think she was still a little girl.)

'What's up, Dumps?' her mother said again just before Lila arrived.

Nin, nervous and sulky, stared at her shoes, and said nothing.

Crouching by the tank stand, Nin got cramp. She had positioned herself earlier, before her father and Lila had begun work. She was afraid to move in case she was heard. It was cooler than usual, the sky overcast; there was no need in the study for the noisy fan.

Every time her father turned towards the window, Nin started, certain that her head bobbing quickly down and then up behind the frosted glass would catch his attention. Then a tiny lizard ran over her foot and she nearly cried out.

Lila was working at the typewriter, saying little. Nin's father moved about the room, sorting his papers, thinking out loud. Occasionally he stopped Lila at her work to explain something to her. Twice he came up behind her and put his hand on her shoulder, but nothing happened.

Nin's cramp grew painful. She wanted this silly game to end so that she could go away and rub her legs, and breathe properly again. She was ready to give up. And then, when the moment came, it seemed so natural she almost overlooked it. Her father, leaning over Lila's shoulder, had slipped his hand under her arm and was gently massaging her left breast. His face was oddly without expression, as if his head was quite ignorant of his hand's deviation.

Lila had stopped typing. She looked up, looked at the little crack between the louvre glass and the frame where Nin's round unblinking eye was witnessing everything.

Afterwards, Lila asked quickly, 'Did you see?'

'Yes,' Nin said, a little breathless.

'Then you must come and tell Mr Dass. Now, please.'

Nin hadn't prepared herself for this. It wasn't that she had forgotten what was expected of her, but she felt that just seeing was enough for one day. Lila was adamant. She wanted Mr Dass to know the disgusting thing his employer had done to her.

'I would confess it to him myself,' she told Nin as they walked slowly (but not slowly enough for Nin) across town, 'but Mr Dass may disbelieve me. I said to him, you see, I thought I should be paid a little something for my work, and that made him very angry. Mr Dass thinks highly of your father. He will believe you because you are his daughter.'

Nin wondered if Mr Dass would still think highly of her father when he had heard what she had to say – and if he no longer did, what worth would he put on her story? But Lila was untroubled by such conundrums. 'Mr Dass will know the truth,' she said. 'He will think, how could you imagine such a thing of your own father?'

When they arrived at the Dass house, Lila took her young son into the garden. Nin was invited into the sitting room and given a glass of lime cordial to slake her thirst. Her mouth was unutterably dry.

Mr Dass was polite but distant. He listened carefully to everything she told him, and then smiled. 'You are very naughty to tell such tales,' he said. 'What would your father say if he heard you? He would give you a good thrashing, I think.'

'But it's true!' Nin said hotly. 'I was watching!'

'It is titillating nonsense,' Mr Dass said. 'Young ladies' minds are full of it. It is these romantic books and magazines you read. I have told Lila, she has a young baby, she should behave like a woman, but all the time she talks like a silly schoolgirl.'

Mr Dass continued smiling. He had not raised his voice or moved his arms or his legs since Nin had begun telling her story. He kept his hands clasped loosely in his lap, and every now and again, just to emphasise some small point, he would lift his thumbs, stand them apart for a few seconds, and then bring them together again.

Unable to look Mr Dass in the eye, Nin concentrated on his stubby little thumbs instead.

'I am thinking,' Mr Dass went on, 'Lila has put you up to this. I cannot believe you would invent such a tale. I know Lila, she will do anything to get out of typewriting. She is idle and good for nothing except having babies.'

Nin crouched in her chair. She knew she was going to cry, and she didn't want Mr Dass to see.

Across the room, Mr Dass looked on a head hung in penitent shame. His voice, never sharp, softened appreciably. 'I will of course say nothing of this to your father. It is just a girlish prank.'

'I think I should go home now,' Nin said, rising.

'That is an excellent idea,' Mr Dass said evenly. He followed her a little way to the door.

As Nin was hurrying down the passage, he called after her, 'Will you tell Lila I am wanting her, please.'

Nin didn't wait to see Lila. She walked down the garden path with its rows of pretty flowers either side, and onto the street. But Lila had left the sanctuary of the garden and was looking out for her at the end of the block. She had the grizzling boy in her arms. Seeing Nin's screwed up face, her eyes grew round with fear.

'Oh, what happened?' she cried. 'Tell me what happened?'

'He smiled at me,' Nin sobbed, running past. 'He just smiled and smiled.'

Hares

You should have seen them, he said. Hares. Mob of them, big as wallabies. He pulled her close to the window, but the open ploughed field where he had seen the hares had given way to crops of vegetables and stretches of bright yellow rape seed. Bad timing, he said, meaning her decision at that moment to go to the toilet. It was disgusting, she told him. Someone peed on the seat. And it flushes straight onto the track. He laughed, not caring much. She stared out the window, watching for more hares, while the train lurched and swayed, rattling across the border into Slovakia.

They were both retired, comfortably off. She was the one who wanted to go. Before it was too late, she said. She was not old. Sixty-eight is not the time to be contemplating final things, she had told their friends. The truth was, she was in remission, felt strong and wanted to make the most of it. Their friends agreed. It was Maurice who took some convincing. She would watch him from the back veranda while he mowed the lawn or picked the last tomatoes, knowing he would come in late in the afternoon for his glass of beer and with a new argument against their going. Why Europe, he had said at first, why not New Zealand? You always said how ridiculous it was that New Zealand was so close and we had never been there. It was true, she had often expressed a desire to see the thermal springs at Rotorua. But New Zealand was not Europe. And there was not the sense of urgency then, when going to New Zealand one year could be put off because there was always the next year. Or the year after.

Who was it said, she asked him once, that being hanged in a fortnight concentrates the mind? He shuffled off to the computer to Google it. He took it so seriously, this dying business, more so than she, it seemed. At least they could talk about it. She had feared that it would be too much for him, that he would retreat into bewildered silence. Of course it was the practicalities they discussed; practicalities were his strong point. There were the wills to update, bequests to consider. Funeral arrangements. There were some good jokes over that. It kept the real things at bay, the painful, hurtful part. The part about fear and loss and helplessness. And love. If there had been children, it would have been different. Grandchildren, especially. Young people are so tiresomely free with their feelings.

Occasionally, when a bottle of wine was all but drained (she was not supposed to drink), she would note his unease, and sense a struggle inside him to say something that he could not say when he was sober. Was it her courage he wanted to speak of, her seemingly calm acceptance of her condition? Her agnosticism? (The sooner you die, the longer you're dead, some joker on TV quipped, giving her a laugh.) Were there infidelities he wanted to confess? She would have liked to think so. Something other than sex and death informed his discomfort; she could see. Something more like hurt and anger. Why are you doing this to me? he wanted to say. How will I live without you?

The closer they came to leaving, the more he fretted. She would tire easily, he said, lose her medication. He went over the small print of the travel insurance. He feared she would die suddenly in some unspeakable foreign place. The horror stories he had heard about overseas deaths and the rigmarole surrounding the return of bodies. She reassured him: have me cremated and posted home. So much cheaper.

Before they left, their friends threw them a party. Austria, they sighed. The Alps, Salzburg, Mozart. Vienna. It embarrassed them to feel so envious. She had always dreamed of visiting Vienna, she told them. It was Maurice's sister, Angela, who gave her a moment's pause. She aspired to see Venice, but knew she would never go. You should leave something wanting, she said. When you die. Some wish, some desire. Some dream unfulfilled. That's how life is.

She had travelled a little when she was younger. Asia mostly, though there had been a week in New Caledonia in 1968. This, of course, was before she met Maurice, who had never travelled outside Australia. Mostly they holidayed in north Queensland to escape the raw Tasmanian winters. Their friends came home with tales of river cruises, medieval castles, concerts in grand palaces and English pub walks. What was the food like? she would ask of a French provincial bus tour. Maurice would query the cost.

In Vienna, they booked into a small family hotel a little out of the city centre. Maurice said it would be a more authentic experience than staying at one of the major chain hotels; one Hilton was no different from another half a world away. In the event, he was right. Street cars clattered past the front entrance. The guests were mostly German or Swiss, or salesmen who exchanged business cards at the bar while she practised her German on the concierge. A transport pass bought at the Tabak across the road from the hotel allowed them to travel freely around the city. In the evenings, they walked a block to a pub where they ate pork sausages and sauerkraut and goulash soup. Maurice complained about the stink of cigarettes, irritated that people could still smoke where others were eating. He was given to saying, Back home you couldn't do this, or Can you imagine anyone doing this in Australia? until she told him to give it a rest. She had gone fully expecting him to hate every moment of the experience, and was determined not to let it get to her.

For the first couple of days, because the flight had tired her, they had stayed mostly around the hotel. The one excursion was to Schonbrunn Palace because it was only a short bus ride away. The day was unseasonably hot, the palace and grounds thick with camera-wielding tourists. They climbed stairs, shuffled with the throng from room to room, Maurice alternately grumbling because he was not allowed to take photographs and reading from the literature they had picked up at the entrance... Emperor Franz Joseph, who was born in the palace in 1830 and died here in 1916, replaced all the empire-style furnishings with those of rococo... Outside they drank lukewarm coffee in a crowded café and wrote postcards to their friends. Struggling to find the words to describe what she had experienced, she wrote the attendants are all stony-faced and Maurice is taking a photo of sparrows eating cake crumbs under the table…

At the end of the week, the exposure to the city's fabled riches had left her struggling to recall, in any meaningful way, what she had seen; she wished she had had the patience and energy to take notes. She had to remind herself that she was in Vienna, the anticipation and thrill of arrival of a week ago having given way to something mundane. Familiarity. Where to today? Maurice would ask. What about the Freud Museum? There's a museum dedicated to *The Third Man*, did you know? He wanted to ride the Ferris Wheel at the Prater. An American couple shared the cabin with them. Isn't that something? the woman marvelled. On a calm, clear day, the panoramic view of the city from the top of the wheel was breathtaking. The man shrugged, lifted a camcorder to his eye. Sure, baby, but it's not Paris.

Maurice photographed everything, each shot meticulously recorded in a notebook he had bought at the airport. She had observed, as the week progressed, that there was less of a whine to his complaints, though he still had something to say about the local beers, if not the old women in the street with their defecating dogs or the tardiness of the hotel housekeeping staff. She was surprised, given his disdain back home for public transport, at the readiness with which he took to riding the streetcars. Clutching his knapsack and chattering non-stop, he was like a small boy being taken on a special excursion. On Kartnerstrasse, one afternoon, he disappeared into a basement store and returned wearing a black fedora. You look ridiculous, she told him. She could not understand the change in him. He had begun to enjoy himself while she weakened to the pull of home and what was waiting for her.

It was Maurice's idea that they take the intercity shuttle to Bratislava. It was a few days before they were due to leave, and he felt they had 'done' Vienna. He wanted to see something of the old east, the Europe that had been closed to the free world after the Second World War until the fall of communism in the late eighties. Before leaving Australia, he had confessed to knowing next to nothing about European history. All you read about, he said, is financial crises, political scandals and ethnic butchery. It was his last breath of resistance to their going. She told him to think on the trip as a late education. Now his head was filled with dates, statistics, potted histories and references gleaned from a myriad pamphlets and information sheets. Enough material, he was thinking, to inform a Rotary talk after their return to Launceston.

It was about half an hour into the journey that he saw the hares. There was that childish delight in the new and unexpected again. Except that this time it prompted memories of his childhood, growing up in a small farming community in the north-west. He fell quiet after that, his comments confined mostly to the surprising frequency of wind farms and to the crops he recognised growing in the fertile soil of the agricultural plain stretching across the Austro/Slovakian border. She sensed that something of the energy that had driven him to take such delight in the experience of Vienna had burned out, and that, like her, he was preparing himself for the return home and – as far as it was practicable – the resumption of their normal lives. What that meant for him, she could only guess at. What she did know, what she had come to realise, was that, however helpless he might feel in the face of it, the wasting months she faced ahead would be all the more unbearable if she had to journey them alone.

Arriving in Bratislava, his spirits revived. The city was smaller than Vienna, the old town, though again crowded with visitors, seeming less a cultural artefact than the more famous city across the border. Maurice thought it much like Melbourne, noting the bustling narrow streets and alleys with their student-filled bars and cafés. Everywhere there were brightly coloured banners touting some sporting tournament the city was host to. This, Maurice read, while they sat drinking beer, was the historical heart of the city, the old-world Hapsburg baroque. That vision of the communist era that had piqued his curiosity, the Eastern Bloc concrete with blank apartment buildings and potholed streets, could only be explored by taxi or street car to the outer suburbs. Instead, after lunch, they dozed on a city bus tour. A castle was visited, foreign embassies pointed out and a monument, too high on a hill for her to climb the steep path, photographed. On his return, Maurice described rows of gravestones, explaining that the monument commemorated the Russian soldiers who had died liberating the city during the Second World War. In Europe, he said, the dead never leave you, do they. It seemed to her a very un-Maurice thing to say. Whatever photographs he had taken, she noted that he was no longer keeping a record of them.

Minutes after leaving Bratislava Central, he fell asleep. The section of carriage they were in was empty, apart from an elderly woman sitting opposite them who was accompanied by a small boy, most likely her grandson. The boy flipped through a picture book while the woman watched the passing scenery, turning occasionally to say something in German to the boy. Maurice slept through the ticket check on the Slovakian side of the border and was still asleep when the train passed the open fields she recognised as the place where he had seen the hares. For some utterly stupid reason, she suspected that it would be the hares – or, more pointedly, that she had missed seeing them because she was in the toilet – that would linger in her memory while the jewels of Vienna would need Maurice's meticulously recorded photographs to give them some sense of propinquity. Perhaps Angela was right; Vienna would have been more meaningful to her if she had never visited.

With this dispiriting thought in her head, she left Maurice sleeping while she went again to the toilet, which thankfully was relatively unsoiled compared with the morning journey. On her return, she was surprised to see the boy standing in the aisle with a grave expression on his face, and his grandmother sitting where she had sat, next to Maurice. Maurice was slumped forward, his head seemingly resting on the windowsill. Reaching for her hand, the grandmother placed it on Maurice's, which was familiarly warm and calloused. The woman's expression resembled her grandson's. *Tot*, she said sharply. *Tot*. And then, because she was not understood, in English. Dead.

The Methuselah Gardens

It is only at breakfast that my mother does not speak. She is, I think, a little intimidated by the neatness of the hotel dining room and by the other guests all talking – rather too loudly – in a language she doesn't understand. I suspect too that she wants to smoke. There are ashtrays on the tables but they are small and white and spotlessly clean. No one else in the room is smoking – nor has smoked, as far as I can remember, in the three days that we have been here.

I can tell by the way she is holding her cup that she is nervous. There is something a little affected about it, unnatural, and her hand shakes, though she is careful that not a drop of the strong dark coffee is spilt. When she glances at her watch and then at the entrance from the lobby, I know that it is eight-thirty, the time the English couple come down to breakfast.

My mother has never travelled outside Australia before. It is a revelation to her. She is discovering an interest in things that would never have interested her in Australia. On the train from Munich, she interrupts my thoughts constantly, reading anecdotes from a book about Mozart that she has bought in London. She stares at the scenery and every lake we pass, each tiny ribbon of water, is an occasion to hum the opening bars from *The Blue Danube* with painful imprecision. Her head is filled with the possibilities of arrival.

The Hotel Rimini stands in a quiet side street of the ninth district of Vienna. It is close to the city centre and a block away from Freud's consulting rooms, which now form a museum. It was while we were visiting the museum yesterday that we passed the English couple on the stairs, speaking to them briefly for the first time. My mother calls them our other half, the woman being about my own age, her companion closer to my mother's. The other patrons of the Rimini – a small family hotel – I judge from their dress and demeanour to be business people. They come down to breakfast early and are always gone before nine. Our conversation with them is restricted to a polite '*Morgen!*' as we enter the room. Their own brisk chatter is scarcely interrupted. My mother sits at the table, folds out her napkin and begins her silent meal. She breaks a piece of bread, butters it, spreads a little jam and then chews on it thoughtfully. I wonder if she is thinking of the bacon and eggs she cooked for my father every morning for nearly forty years, but I never ask. If I speak softly, my mother, who is a little deaf, will never hear. To speak up is to proclaim myself, to hear my own voice come back to me sounding more foreign than that of the German-speakers at the neighbouring tables. I begin to understand my mother's native silence.

When the English couple enter, they pause a moment to murmur their 'Morgens', nod cursorily in our direction and then settle themselves at their usual table close to the door. The man walks with a limp. I can't say I'd noticed it before yesterday when we met them at the Freud museum; he'd needed his companion's hand then to help him down the stairs. Inside the museum, my mother had looked to see if they'd signed the visitors' book but there had been no entries since the day before. Naturally her suspicions were aroused: she thinks there is something illicit about their relationship; in short, that they are lovers. But watching them at their breakfast I am struck by how alike they are, how, when they touch, it is open and unselfconscious, how their eyes meet at a safe distance across the table. They speak desultorily in whispers. Occasionally he will lean forward, turn his head to hear her more clearly. I suspect that, like my mother, he is a little deaf. He pours milk into his cereal, stirs his second cup of coffee, breaks another piece of bread. The woman eats like a sparrow.

The woman interests me. Before yesterday, I admit, I had hardly noticed her. From a distance she seemed all hard lines and angles. It's true, she's tall and ungainly like a schoolgirl surprised by a sudden spurt of growth. Her face has the haunted look of the undernourished. I could imagine someone making love to her with a sort of cold fury, and hearing her bones crack. And then, passing her on the stairs, close enough to touch, I caught the faintest whiff of scent. It could've been the perfume she used, the smell of her clothes; its very elusiveness was enough to arouse my senses. The air in the stairwell was chilled, almost icy, yet as we paused to exchange a few words I thought I saw tiny beads of perspiration form along her upper lip. Continuing up the stairs, I thought how those tiny beads of sweat might collect in other parts of her body, under her arms and breasts, between her thighs; how her body would shine after lovemaking (what nonsense was that about broken bones…?).

My mother – I trust – sees nothing of this. She thinks that since the break-up of my marriage I have little interest in women. It's years since I was living at home. Now that she has me, she wants to keep me there, keep me from leaving her on her own. My mother is in mourning, though she works hard not to show it. My father died a year ago, slowly but uncomplainingly of a large malignant tumour embedded in his brain. I was expecting my mother simply to get on with her life. It was she, after all, who had been the driving force of the marriage, she with her committees and charity work. My father was a quiet, solitary man. My father had an interest in botany.

I try not to think of the woman when I'm with my mother. It's something I've noticed before, how she seems to know exactly what I'm thinking, even as I think it. It's as if the smallest gesture, the briefest flicker of an eyelid, can give me away. Sometimes I feel that even silence is a trap, that silence has a texture that can change as my thoughts change, and that my mother knows me too well not to understand the nature and the meaning of those changes. This morning, as we finish our breakfast, I focus my thoughts on the woman's companion.

He is taller than my father was, but stockier; you might say, pugnacious-looking. I am curious about the cause of his limp. Is he some underworld figure, I wonder facetiously, who has fallen foul of a rival mob and had his kneecap shattered as a lesson in territorial rights? His clothes fit him comfortably; there is no suggestion of the neat tuck or the hidden adjustment. His hair is short, neatly parted. It is this very air of respectability that makes me suspect that he is not entirely what he seems. (It would appear that I have become infected with something of my mother's imaginative response to the new and exotic.) In Sydney, I think, he would be a well-known racing identity, or a criminal lawyer, or a company director, someone with an interest in imports/exports...

And quite composed. It strikes me at last what it is about this couple that sets one apart from the other when so much else connects them. It is particularly noticeable now that they have finished their breakfast. He leans back in his chair, lights a cigarette (the first I have seen him smoke). He closes his eyes, purses his lips contemplatively. His hand, resting on the table, is perfectly still.

The woman plays nervously with her napkin. The smoke from her companion's cigarette drifts slowly across the room, caught by a draught from an open window. There is a lull in the chatter and the woman's agitation grows. In my mind, I am calming her, soothing her, stroking her gently as if she were a cat. My mother stirs suddenly, folds her napkin and rests it neatly across her plate.

The conversation in the room remains muted; the mood of disapproval is quite palpable, though I can only guess at what is being said. Within a few minutes, most of the other guests have left (it is almost nine o'clock anyway). A waitress begins clearing the tables.

With the other guests gone, the woman begins to relax. She says something in a low voice to her companion which makes him laugh out loud. He puts on a great display of stubbing the butt of his cigarette in the little white ashtray. He knows we are watching him; he has been aware of it since they sat down to breakfast. It occurs to me that his indifference to others' sensibilities may go beyond getting under the skins of prissy foreigners: it was the woman, his companion, after all, who had been the most visibly distressed. Yesterday, at the museum, she had seemed elevated in our eyes by his need of her to help him down the stairs. I remember how he had kept his eyes averted as we passed, how his response to my mother's cordial greeting had seemed afterwards unnecessarily curt, almost begrudging. It was as if we had caught him in some shameful act, not indecent exactly, but injurious to his pride, his sense of well-being. I understand now why they never use the hotel stairs, but will wait interminably for the lift to return from the upper floors even though their room – like ours – is only one flight up. I understand too that the pleasure he took in his cigarette was not in the smoking but in the way it drew attention to his companion's diffidence, her fear of scrutiny. It occurs to me also that giving offence to our German-speaking neighbours was probably incidental; this little piece of theatre on the nature of vulnerability had been purely for the benefit of my mother and myself.

Nudging me with her knee, my mother indicates that it is time we were leaving. Today she wants to look at the shops on the Kartnerstrasse and take a photograph of the horse-drawn carriages standing outside St Stephen's Cathedral. As we approach the door, the English couple too are preparing to leave. The woman pushes back her chair. She keeps her head lowered, brushing out her skirt with a slow sweeping motion that strikes me (as she has hardly eaten anything) as largely reflex. Her companion stands with surprising ease. It is only because I have watched him, have begun to learn something about him, that I can see how deliberate and controlled this seemingly smooth movement is. He stands a moment, a little unsteady on his feet, and then steps confidently around the table. For the first time, he looks me squarely in the face. His eyes are small and dark but there is a playfulness about them I find rather attractive. His mouth, pursed in a little smile, leaves an impression that is quite openly ironic.

After lunch, my mother retires to her room for an hour or so to rest. Her stamina, I have to say, is undiminished. It is the idea of travel, I think, that has begun to tire her, the lure of the unfamiliar. I suspect that she is more than a little homesick. This morning, shopping for souvenirs, she talked for the first time of going home. It wasn't said with any great sense of longing or urgency, yet I could see that something about her had changed. I think it is simply this: she has finished mourning my father's death.

Downstairs in the lobby, I notice the English woman waiting near the reception. She is looking at some postcards on a revolving stand. She is dressed as she was at breakfast except that over her arm is the heavy winter jacket she wore yesterday when visiting the museum. She takes a card from the stand and stares at the picture as if trying to locate it within her recent travels. I pass behind her, without speaking, and pretend an interest in a newspaper someone has left on the reception desk. Almost at once, the manager approaches, swinging one of the room keys from his finger as if it were a toy. He tells me I may take the newspaper if I want it, if I wish to read it. '*Vielen dank*!' I say. With some deliberation, I fold the newspaper and put it under my arm. The manager's eyes are filled with amused curiosity. He knows my German is thoroughly inadequate to read a local newspaper.

Moving away from the desk, I notice that the English woman has left the postcard stand and is making her way across the lobby to the hotel entrance. I walk quickly after her. Outside, she pauses at the top of the steps and slips into her jacket. She turns as I come up behind her. For a second, I think she is laughing, that she is expecting me, that her only surprise is that I have caught up with her so soon. Her hand flies instinctively to cover her mouth; her eyes are wide and searching and I think I see in them something of the manager's amused curiosity.

For the first time, I notice that she is taller than me, by half a head at least. I wonder how this might influence our lovemaking (my wife barely reached my shoulders). I take a pace or two down the steps and look up at her. For some reason, I feel this gives me a certain advantage. Yet it's as if I've lost her attention already, as if she's not even aware that I've slipped from her sight. She stands transfixed, staring back through the hotel door into the lobby. (It seems inconceivable that she should be admiring her reflection in the glass.) A little too loudly, perhaps, I apologise for having startled her. She notices me then (that it is me, not some comic apparition), almost running down the steps past me into the street. I think she's going to walk on without speaking but after a short distance she stops and looks back. She seems anxious to get away from the hotel. I hurry to join her though it is beginning to rain and I have left my coat in my room. As we continue walking, she tells me that her father (yes, her father) is reading and that she had a sudden craving for coffee and a piece of rich chocolate cake. We walk to the end of the street and wait for a streetcar to pass before crossing the busy road.

The rain becomes heavier and I cover my head with the newspaper. The woman strides on ahead, her hands thrust deep into the pockets of her warm winter jacket. She is wearing comfortable-looking walking shoes and thick black stockings which have become splashed with dirt from the wet pavement. Glancing ahead, I see that she is bearing down on a small huddled group taking shelter under a café awning. She is like a mortar shell striking home: the group not so much parts to let her through as disintegrates, human fragments flying off in directions as myriad and random as if they had been pieces of shrapnel.

Inside the café, she removes her jacket and hangs it on a hook behind the door. There are three or four other people in the room including a stout woman with a small dog on an extendable leash. As I close the door, the dog approaches, cautiously, to sniff at our shoes. The leash extends, and then continues to extend as the dog, responding to its owner's bark of command, returns by the more intricate route around the legs of the tables and chairs. The English woman watches this spectacle for a moment and then indicates a table near the window. In the street, the rain is coming down in sheets.

No sooner are we seated than someone comes to take our orders. My companion speaks clearly in English and uses her fingers to indicate two coffees and two pieces of chocolate cake. The proprietor tears a numbered sheet from his notebook and leaves it on the table. While we wait, the English woman stares out of the window as if I am not even here. I take the opportunity to observe her closely, noting the long straight nose, the firm jaw, high cheekbones. In profile, she loses that gaunt emaciated look that I found so unattractive earlier. Her eyes are large and unblinking. She is aware of my close scrutiny and yet doesn't seem to mind at all. I can't believe that this is the timid woman I saw eating breakfast with her father this morning.

The coffee arrives with the pieces of cake and two small glasses of water. She pays the proprietor with a clean uncrumpled banknote and leaves the change on the table. We drink the water quickly and then start on the cake. While we are eating, she begins telling me about herself with a familiarity I find quite alarming. It is as if we are old friends, meeting for the first time after an absence of many years. I learn that she is a former mistress of a private girls' school and that she has given up her work to look after her father, a retired naval officer. She calls him the captain, though it is not clear if this had been his rank or if it is simply a family nickname. I mention his limp and she explains that about four years ago her parents were driving to London from the Cotswolds when their car was involved in a collision with a dairy truck. Her mother was killed instantly; her father's left leg was so badly crushed it had to be amputated. I am tempted to try and amuse her with the thought I had earlier that he was a major underworld figure who'd had his kneecap smashed, but something warns me against it. Her voice is soft and controlled but not altogether sure as if the story she is telling is in fact someone else's, half-recalled or not entirely understood. I watch as she scrapes up the last crumbs of her cake, remembering the sparrow's appetite she'd had at breakfast.

When I ask how long she and her father have been in Vienna, I sense a change in her manner, a slight tenseness as if in bringing her story so quickly up to the present I have been in some way pre-emptive. Because she doesn't answer, I begin telling her something of myself. She listens courteously but with little apparent interest until I mention my mother. She's not at all indifferent about my mother. Her father, she murmurs, thinks my mother has the face of an angel.

I have never thought of my mother as angelic. When I was a child, it was she who used to beat me because my father hadn't the stomach for it. When she grew old, something of the fire went out of her which saved her, I think, from becoming hard and embittered. In old age, my mother is still quite beautiful, something she finds strange and rather cruel. The English woman smiles when I say this and I wonder if she understands what I mean. I tell her about the tiny park across the road from where my mother lives. Every morning, a plump matronly woman brings a group of old people from the nearby retirement village to walk between the narrow beds of flowers and native shrubs. My mother calls the park the Methuselah Gardens because it is only the old people who regularly use it. A boy on a skateboard or a young mother walking her children is a rare sight. My mother is afraid that in not too many years she too will be walking in the Methuselah Gardens, a little freakish old lady with a mannequin's figure and the face of a porcelain doll.

The English woman is stirring her coffee. She's not looking at me but at the rain in the street and the people hurrying past in their raincoats and struggling with their umbrellas. I wonder if she's even been listening to me. She asks if I've ever had a dream in which I didn't appear and is surprised when I say I don't know. Finishing her coffee, she leaves the table and hunts through the pockets of her jacket hanging behind the door for a packet of cigarettes. I see her remove what I think at first is a little paperback book, taking it from one pocket and securing it in another. The cover looks familiar and I realise as she is returning to the table that it is not a book at all but a stack of postcards that she has taken from the stand at the hotel.

When she smokes, she reminds me of my mother. Perhaps it's the way all women smoke these days, a little guiltily, thinking of their hearts, their lungs, lumps in the breast. (One thought tends to lead to another.) She asks if my mother has taken a lover since my father's death. The question seems not so much indelicate as absurd. Her father, she tells me, for six months has been making love to a woman of forty-five who is employed to help with the cleaning. Every afternoon, before she leaves, she assists the captain upstairs to his bedroom. They undress and while he unstraps his artificial limb she turns back the covers of the bed. After she has gone (it never takes long), he sits in the kitchen and drinks a glass of sherry. One day, while she is waiting to be paid her wages, the woman confides that her husband thinks the work is too much for her because she is too tired at night to make love to him. When the captain hears this, he's delighted. Then the woman takes a few days' holiday and he becomes morose and restless. He's unhappy when there's no woman around him, at a loose end. Each afternoon, he stumps around the house after his daughter, like a panting dog.

After she has told me this, I think she is going to weep. I wish the rain would ease so that we can leave. I want to hear the woman with the dog say thickly, 'Goot afternoon!' as I open the door (I hope she keeps her hand on the dog's collar). I want to smell the damp of the English woman's jacket, discover that she has thirteen postcards of the Museum of Fine Arts hidden in her pocket. Tonight, I believe, somewhere in the heart of Vienna, the captain will charm my mother over dinner. My mother is not easily charmed, so there will be coffee and liqueurs before a taxi is called to return them to the hotel. My mother will stumble into bed a little drunk.

In his own room, the captain will find his daughter asleep. He will marvel at the stillness of her body, smell, perhaps, the semen draining from between her legs. As her breath dies, he will see that it is her eyes that move restlessly beneath their parchment lids: this dreamer, dreaming her dreams of invisibility.

Balkan Soup

1

'All good?'

'All good,' Amy said. 'She's a bit pissed, getting it sprung on her, but she's fine. She loves kids.'

'Nice sister,' Nic said. 'When we get back, we go to Tasmania, pick up bubba. Me and Leah, we get to know each other.'

'Sure,' Amy said. 'I told her that.'

She'd left Nic in the bar while she went outside for a smoke and to phone Leah. She didn't want him hearing her side of the conversation if it turned fractious. In the event, she thought it had gone pretty smoothly. After texting the flight details, she'd turned her phone off and finished her smoke before returning to her vodka and tonic.

It was an hour since they'd put Lucy on the plane to Launceston; another three before their flight to Singapore. She checked her documents for something to do. Passport, boarding card, flight itinerary: Brisbane to Singapore, change for Frankfurt, change again for Bucharest. Nic had gone to the bar to buy peanuts. Sitting around waiting made him restless and hungry. With Amy, it was something else. She'd never been outside Australia before, not even to Bali, and everyone she knew had been to Bali. There was a buzz in the international terminal that excited her. She liked the noise and bustle; it comforted her. It made her forget the sight of Lucy trotting off with the Virgin flight attendant. She'd watched for the girl to look back, but wasn't surprised when she didn't.

'Aren't you a cutie?' the attendant had said. 'Give me a smile, sweetie.'

Lucy looked a peach in her pink dress, red sandals and her hair tied back with a green ribbon. She carried a change of clothes and her colouring books in a red and yellow backpack. If the weather turned cold, Leah would have to buy her a coat and gloves.

Nic returned to the table. 'You want peanuts?'

She shook her head. Until four days ago she'd been selling cosmetics at Myers. Romania was about as far away from Australia as she could imagine. She watched Nic crunching on his peanuts, his fingers tapping the table to some pounding backbeat in his head. He was lean and swarthy, with small dark eyes and lank brown hair that curled over his collar. Her Gypsy lover. She only called him that to tease him, or get under his skin when he was in a mood. Gypsies were thieves and layabouts, he'd told her. They lived in slums and made their money dealing drugs and fleecing mug tourists. She didn't know anything about Romania other than what Nic told her. They were going to stay with his brother and sister-in-law who had an apartment near the city centre and a small business selling mobile phones. She'd seen photos of the apartment; it seemed cramped and over-furnished compared to her unit in Wynnum. There was a second bedroom and no kids, so she reckoned she'd cope.

The truth was, they were only going because Nic's work visa was about to expire and he had to reapply out of the country. She saw it as an opportunity for a little adventure, to experience something rare and exotic. And Nic was paying: the airfares, the restaurants and the excursions he would arrange to show her his beautiful country. A month, he reckoned, to get his visa sorted, and then they'd return. She had an open ticket, but she didn't know until this morning that Nic's was one-way. Immigration rules, he told her. He'd book as soon as he got his visa re-stamped. It didn't make any difference, but she wished she'd known.

'Get me another vodka tonic,' she said. 'Please.'

'On the plane we drink for free,' he said.

'You want me to pay?'

He shrugged and loped back to the bar. Switching her phone on, she checked for messages and then quickly turned it off again. Four missed calls from Leah. Nice sister... Nic didn't get it; that she could have a sister living in the same country and not see her in five years. Leah had gone to Tasmania around the time Amy got pregnant. It was only supposed to be for a couple of weeks, then she hooked up with some guitar-picking charmer she met in a pub and stayed on. Now she worked tables while her guy sang the blues for beer money. They lived out of town in some run-down farm cottage. Cows and stuff, Lucy would like that, Amy had thought. Leah could hardly say no, seeing how Lucy was already on the plane when Amy phoned.

'A couple of weeks,' Amy said. 'She's a real quiet kid, she'll be no trouble.'

In Romania, Nic said, family was more important than anything. He grew up sharing a room with his brother and an apartment with his parents and his mother's parents. His father's parents were steelworkers who lived in some industrial hub outside Bucharest. All dead now, except his older brother, who had been his closest friend and protector when they were scrawny kids fighting their turf in a rough neighbourhood.

Amy didn't say, but the only fighting she and Leah did was with each other. She was a little jealous of Nic's rough and tumble childhood, largely because he relived it with such unaccountable pleasure. Weren't they ruled by communists then? Wasn't everything grey and drab, nothing to eat except potatoes and cabbages? He laughed at her ignorance, but she was too impatient for a history lesson. Memories of her own childhood were compartmentalised in the do-not-revisit part of her brain. She never liked looking back. She liked to say that her life started when she left school, the year she turned seventeen; the year her parents were killed in a fiery car crash on the Gold Coast. It sounded offhand, the way she told it to Nic. She had to say, it was ten years ago; she grew up fast, took control of her life. There was no money; it had all gone on a failed carpet cleaning venture just before the crash. Leah went to uni for a couple of years, worked bars to pay the rent. Amy had the looks for more glamorous jobs and well-heeled boyfriends. Weekends, she partied, smoked dope and got drunk.

'You have Lucy when you get drunk,' Nic had said. 'Bad girl.'

A note of disapproval; she hadn't expected that. She recalled it, with just the meanest twitch of unease, as they watched Lucy trot off with the Virgin attendant.

2

Nic's brother met them at the airport. He didn't look much like Nic, short and stocky with a thin black moustache that made her think of London spivs in old black and white movies. Outside the terminal, the brothers hugged and danced like kids, yabbering in Romanian.

The day was cold and grey, the ground wet from recent showers. George piled the suitcases into a van and drove them into the city. Everything looked as drab and grey as the overcast sky, the occasional roadside stall selling bunches of flowers, the only flash of colour. Walls and buildings were scrawled with graffiti, dogs roamed aimlessly and she lost count of the number of carts she saw hauled by malnourished donkeys. Closer to the city, parks and advertising hoardings raised her spirits a little. The street where George and his wife had their business was narrow and choked with traffic. There were fashion shops either side and a restaurant on the second floor.

'You come and meet Elena,' George told Amy. 'She's dying to meet you.'

George's wife was as slim as a store mannequin, pale-skinned, and had the bluest eyes Amy had ever seen. She hugged Amy like she was meeting a long lost cousin. 'You like shopping, Amy?' she asked. 'You and me, we'll go shopping. The boys can go to the casino and lose money.'

Amy didn't know about the casino. She knew Nic liked to play the tables at Jupiter's on the Gold Coast. George said they should go to the restaurant upstairs to eat. An assistant would mind the shop. Amy looked at the gear they were selling. Nokia, Samsung, Motorola. Familiarity reassured her.

They went upstairs to the restaurant, which was near full and noisy.

All the guys seemed to have the same thin moustaches and dressed in snappy business suits. The women were loud and brash.

Elena stayed a while then went back down to the shop. 'Tomorrow I take the day off,' she told Amy. 'We go shopping.'

Nic talked non-stop, English mostly at first, then Romanian the more beer he drank. Amy got slowly drunk on red wine.

Late afternoon she stumbled down the stairs with Nic to the street. A taxi took them to George and Elena's apartment, close enough to walk if they'd been sober and didn't have the suitcases. The apartment seemed smaller than she remembered from the photograph. Nic brewed coffee and began a long story about football games he and George had played as teenagers. Amy felt sick. She stripped to her underwear and crawled into a lumpy bed.

It was dark when she woke. For a moment, she had no idea where she was. She could hear the low murmur of conversation through the wall and Nic's familiar soft chuckle. Her head thumped like she'd been on a weekend bender. She lay still, drifting in and out of sleep.

At some point, she felt Nic curling up against her, his breath rank with beer. 'I want to go home,' she whispered.

'You miss bubba,' he said.

She nodded. In truth, she hadn't thought about Lucy all day.

3

After the first few days, Nic began leaving his brother's apartment early and she wouldn't see him until late in the afternoon. He said he had old friends he wanted to look up and was re-establishing contacts for his Gold Coast jewellery business. She'd thought he might have wanted to introduce his Australian girlfriend to his mates, but he said they spoke little or no English and she'd be bored.

'Nicci's friends only like to drink and talk sport,' Elena told her. 'Let him go. Me and you, Amy, we have good fun together.'

Elena had taken time off from the shop. At first, Amy thought it was just to keep her company, something Nic had asked her to do, or simply as a gesture of Romanian politeness. But after a day of shopping and a round of cafés and bars, with Elena's constant chatter and laughter in her ear, she realised that Nic's blue-eyed sister-in-law had taken something of a shine to her. Close girlfriends were not really Amy's thing; she liked the company of men, whether as lovers or just good mates. Her one special friendship had been at school, and that had turned ugly when she discovered the girl was gay. Nothing gay about Elena, she thought, noting how she flirted with waiters, barmen and any male shop assistant who might knock a few lei off a price tag. Mostly too she paid for lunch and drinks, which Amy appreciated as she could see her money running out within a few weeks if she had to pay her way. Nic had promised her some money, but he was proving as stingy as he was absent.

'We'll put it on George's tab,' Elena would say, fishing another credit card from her purse.

Maybe it's just swagger, Amy thought; showing the Aussie girl how successful they were as entrepreneurial small business owners. Bucharest wasn't quite what she had expected, though exactly what she had expected, she couldn't say. The city was both exotic and familiar, as she had discovered entering the Ionescus' shop that first day. The language and the currency flummoxed her, but the bustle and noise of the streets could have been Brisbane on a busy Saturday.

After a couple of days, with Nic still doing his own thing, she began to feel the endless trek around Bucharest's trendy and not-so-trendy commercial hotspots a bit wearing. Then the purchase of a leather purse was soured when a pickpocket lifted it from her bag a bare hour after she'd bought it. To her eternal relief, she'd not had time to put any of her cash or cards in it. Elena shrugged, blamed it on the Gypsies, and dragged her back to the shop so that she could buy her another one. By then she could see that Amy had had enough of shops and cafés.

'Tomorrow we visit the People's Palace,' she said. 'Second biggest building in the world, you know. Big ugly monument to that bastard

Ceausescu.' She made a spitting gesture. 'Nic tell you something about Romanian history, Amy? Politics, culture? Or you just read books about Transylvanian vampires?'

Amy didn't read books about anything much. History, politics, culture; not something the guys she'd been out with had shown any interest in. She knew she was shallow. Travel, she realised, was never going to broaden her mind, just feed a sense of difference and alienation. Already, not much more than a week since she'd left Australia, and she was painfully homesick. It didn't help that she was seeing so little of Nic. Some days he didn't get back to the apartment until after midnight. If he was hooking up with old lovers, he was still coming to bed wanting sex before rolling over to sleep. And it was such bad, perfunctory sex because the apartment walls were so thin, and because there seemed such little love in it, just brute need. He could see that she was unhappy, insisting that another few days, a week maybe, and they'd have more time together. At least it made him part with some money.

'Buy something nice for little bubba,' he said. 'Something nice from her Uncle Nicci.'

Lucy had been on her mind a bit lately. Maybe it was because she was homesick. Elena too had become curious about the child Amy had left behind. It surprised her that Amy had no photograph to show.

'Nicci loves children,' she said. 'George...' She made a face. 'It's all the business and making money with George at the moment. Children can come later.'

She wasn't going to argue with George's position, but Amy had noted the way she looked at mothers in the street with their small children in tow.

'You have a baby with Nicci,' Elena said. 'If you want to keep him.'

Amy laughed. They were sitting in a café again, drinking strong coffee. 'It's not that simple.'

Elena shrugged. 'Sex is simple. Having babies is not so hard.'

'I never wanted Lucy,' Amy confessed. It sounded cold, but that was how it was. 'It was one of those relationships – you know, too much drinking, lots of careless sex. I liked the guy, I thought we'd be good together. A kid just kind of figured in there.'

'Like with Nicci,' Elena said. 'But not so good.'

'He fucked off,' Amy said. 'Week before I went into labour. Never saw the bastard again.'

Elena lit a cigarette. 'Nicci would not do that.'

'Nicci would need to commit,' Amy said. 'He'd need to stay in Australia and he'd need to make a lot of money.' And no screwing around and no pissing off for days with his mates or business buddies, she thought. She took a drag of Elena's smoke. 'Anyway, I don't want any more kids.'

They left the café and walked up Calea Victoriei, a busy congested street of hotels, department stores and fashion shops. Amy kept a tight hold of her bag, wary of pickpockets. They entered one of the older department stores and took the stairs to the basement. Amongst the medley of small specialist stores there were a number of Turkish bazaar stands where the day before she had bought some brightly coloured scarves for Lilith, who minded Lucy when she was at work. She hadn't thought particularly about taking something home for Lucy. The girl was too young to care where it came from, and nothing much seemed to interest her anyway apart from colouring books. It was only because Nic had told her to buy something that she browsed amongst the stalls of kids' clothes. A simple dress caught her eye, red with green trim, colours that featured strongly in Lucy's bunch of crayons.

She'd promised Elena that, the moment she got home, she would send a photograph of the girl. 'She's a real cutie,' she said. 'My sister's good with kids. She won't be missing me a bit.'

She wondered briefly how Leah was dealing with Lucy's frustrating bouts of silence. Once, she went almost three weeks without saying a word.

4

The night Leah phoned, she was sleeping alone. Earlier, Nic had taken her to eat at a gloomy, foul-smelling restaurant that served mostly local food, after which he met up with George to play the tables at the casino. Amy caught a cab back to the apartment, where she shared two bottles of wine with Elena before going to bed with a raging headache. It seemed to have become a feature of her stay in Bucharest: hangovers and persistent headaches. If it wasn't for the amount of booze she was drinking, she'd have said she had a brain tumour. Leah's call caught her coming out of a deep sleep.

'Hey,' Amy said. She took a long breath. 'How're you doing?'

'How d'you think?' She sounded cranky.

'Lucy,' Amy said. 'How's my kid doing?'

'She doesn't speak.'

'Sure she does.'

'Nearly two weeks, Amy. She hasn't said a word.'

'She will. She takes time to warm to people.'

'That is such a crock of shit,' Leah said. 'She doesn't communicate. Not verbally, not emotionally. When she's not running me ragged, it's like I'm not here. Like I don't exist for her. I'm smoking myself crazy just watching her. You should've given me a heads up, Amy.'

'Yeah,' Amy said. 'Sorry. She's not hard, you know. You've just got to get used to her.'

Leah was silent for a moment. Like she realised she was making too much of a fuss. Like she should just get on with it. 'When are you coming home?' she said.

Amy was silent. 'I'll let you know.'

'A week? Two weeks?'

'Nic's got some stuff going on,' Amy said. 'You know, networking. Business contacts. It's good here, Leah. It was kinda weird at first. I don't get the money, leis and shit, but a lot of people speak English. Everyone's really nice to me. You know me, I can take a bit of that.' She was silent for a long moment, as if it were a joke wanting a chuckle.

Then she said, 'My visa's good for three months.'

'I can't,' Leah said. 'Not three months. It'll fuck my job. Mitch… Everything. Social will have to take her.'

'No way,' Amy said.

'Mitch would've done it a week ago.'

'Fuck, Leah. She's your niece.'

Leah hung up.

She had known it would come, sooner or later, but she wasn't expecting the threat to dump Lucy on the Social. She fired off a rash, angry text in response, then made herself some coffee and toast and waited for her head to clear.

Around five, Elena came out of her room looking for her smokes. 'I thought Nicci was home,' she said. 'I heard you talking.'

'My sister,' Amy said. 'She hasn't a clue what time it is here, stupid cow.'

'Everything good back home?'

'Sure,' Amy said. 'Everything's hunky-dory.'

Elena looked blank, but said nothing. She lit a cigarette.

'She's not coping too good with my kid,' Amy said presently. 'She's a bit retarded, you know. Lucy. She doesn't talk a lot. It can kind of spook you if you you're not used to it. I should've left her with Lilith.'

'Lilith,' Elena said. 'The lady you bought the scarves for.'

'She minds Lucy while I'm at work,' Amy said. 'I can't take her to kindie. Kids pick on her because she won't talk to them, busybodies asking dumb questions. It's not like she's properly mental. She's just wired a bit different.'

'A genius child, maybe,' Elena said generously. 'Does she have some special gift?'

Amy thought of Lucy with her colouring books, but it was nothing she hadn't seen with other kids. 'Lilith reckons she'll need special teaching,' she said. 'School will be a fucking nightmare.'

She took her cup and rinsed it under the tap. From the window, she could see a large dog in the side alley, turning over bags of rubbish for food scraps. She had never seen so many dogs as she'd seen in Bucharest. Elena called them *maidanezi*, street dogs that had roamed and bred across the city since the times when the communist government turned people out of their houses and forced them into collective housing. They always struck Amy as lethargic mutts, lazing in gutters or apartment entrances or just perambulating the streets like vagrants. She had seen small groups congregating near water fountains in city parks. Some were tagged, ones that had been picked up by the authorities, given a health check and let loose again. Lucy would be in her element here, Amy had thought, knowing the girl's love of chasing neighbours' pets down the streets, even into their yards. Elena said the *maidanezi* were mostly harmless, but warned her against feeding or patting them. No one wanted them culled or put down, she said, but when they packed, they became dangerous. People got bitten, some had died. A Japanese tourist bled out from a severed artery. There was a report, Elena said, a year or so back of a four-year-old boy eaten alive in a city park.

'This Lilith,' Elena said, when Amy had come back to the table. 'She's a good minder?'

'She's good with Lucy,' Amy said. 'She knows how to handle her.'

'So why leave her with your sister? She has children?'

'No,' Amy said. 'Not that she's owned up to.'

Elena laughed. A good joke. Then she said, 'Family, you know. Sometimes they disappoint you. Look at George. I tell him: you stay out all night, no sex for a month. So he fucks some street girl on the way home.'

Amy was a little shocked to hear this. Maybe it was another joke; it was hard to tell from Elena's mordant expression.

'Not Nicci,' Elena said. 'Nicci's a good guy. I should've married Nicci, but George asked me.'

'Leah's guy's a muso,' Amy said. 'He's an arse. If I don't go home soon, he'll dump Lucy on the Social. I'll have to go through hoops to get her back and then I'll have some pasty-faced social worker on the doorstep every five minutes checking us out.' She took one of Elena's cigarettes without thinking, and lit up. 'I should've left her with Lilith.

She'd have taken her, but she wanted a shit load of money up front. She never said until the day before we left, and it really got my back up. Nic said he'd pay, but there's a principle, you know? It's like blackmail, pulling a stunt like that.'

'You bought her those lovely scarves,' Elena said.

'Who else am I going to put Lucy with?' She knows I won't put her in the kindie. It's why I'm so pissed. I thought I knew her.'

'Your sister,' Elena said. 'You think you know her?'

'We were like this, when we were kids,' Amy said. She crossed her fingers. 'We shared a lot of shit. Then we drifted a bit at high school. Different classes. And sex, you know. I've had guys sniffing around me since I was eleven. Leah's a bit of a dog. Nothing to look at, always saying something dumb. Guys weren't interested much. She went to uni, so I guess she used her smarts to make up for it.' She smoked a moment in silence. 'People change, don't they? People change people. I reckon I'll be a better person for meeting Nic, I don't mind saying it. He's a top guy, he's been a saint with Lucy. This guy Leah's hooked up with… I must have been out of my brain, sending my kid to live with some low-life, guitar-picking dropout.'

5

Nic introduced her to Sandu Grigorus, his new business partner. It was lunchtime and they were eating in the restaurant above the Ionescus' shop. Sandu seemed like just about every other young Romanian guy Amy had met, swarthy and kind of roguishly good-looking, but thankfully missing the obligatory spiv's moustache. He was somewhere in his late twenties, with a slight American twang to his near perfect English. She thought maybe he'd picked it up from watching Hollywood blockbusters, but it turned out he'd lived in Chicago for about five years and had come back to Bucharest for a cousin's wedding. He was too young to be another of Nic's old schoolmates, but there was some history between them, most of which she picked up in throwaway comments and sudden lapses into Romanian, which usually finished with the sort of conspiratorial chuckle you get from a private joke. She didn't particularly want to hear what kind of business deal they were hatching; she'd heard enough to know it involved jewellery and Nic's proposed expanded business on the Gold Coast.

She hadn't realised until just before they left that Nic already had a silent partner in Australia, some Greek guy called Vasilis, who she'd heard Nic speaking to a few times on the phone. Vasilis was into land and property; he owned the block where Nic had his business and was holding the lease open until he returned. Listening to Nic talk about business bored her, so she never took much of it in. She didn't think to consider how plausible something might seem. Nic had plans and they were big, which was all good, as far as she was concerned.

Then she started to hear stuff from Elena, who'd heard it from George, which didn't seem to gel with what Nic had been telling her. She didn't like to confront him, and only got a shrug and a dismissive laugh when she did.

'Don't listen to Elena,' he said. 'What would Elena know? I never told George that.'

Listening to him now, rattling on to Sandu about how much money he was making in Australia, all she could hear was the sales pitch. After two years selling cosmetics at Myers, she knew how likely the pitch was to match the product. Sandu was a good listener, but he wasn't getting too excited by what he was hearing. Maybe he'd heard it all before, Nic tending to bang on a bit when an idea took him. They'd been talking mostly in Romanian, which made her feel excluded. She'd already drunk a bit, but when Nic went downstairs for a smoke, Sandu offered to fill her wine glass. It was the first time he'd paid her much attention.

'Nicco tells me you have a child,' he said.

'Lucy,' she said. 'She's staying with my sister.'

'She's pretty?'

Amy smiled. 'Yeah. A real cutie.'

'You should've brought her,' he said. 'Show her off.'

'She's five.'

Sandu nodded. 'I have a little girl,' he said. 'April. She lives with her mother.'

'In Chicago.'

'Uh-huh.' He took his phone from his pocket and showed her a photograph. 'You have a picture?'

'Afraid not.'

'Too bad,' he said.

'Why? You like small kids?'

'Of course. Doesn't everyone?'

Amy laughed. Sandu slipped his phone back into his pocket and she noted his long dark fingers, each one bearing an ostentatious gold or silver signet ring.

'Your wife,' she said. 'She didn't want to come to Bucharest?'

He shifted his gaze slightly, away from her. She thought he looked a bit sour.

'She's not my wife,' he said. 'She's the girl's mother.'

After Nic returned, they talked some more business and then Sandu left. Nic picked up the tab.

'Smart boy, Sandu,' he said. 'Me and him together, we'll make a lot of money.'

Sandu had been working the jewellery trade in Chicago and was going back after his cousin's wedding. How this fitted in with Nic's business interests, Amy couldn't imagine. Maybe he just wanted a sign over his shop: Nic Ionescu and Partners Jewellery: Chicago, Bucharest, Gold Coast. She guessed it would look pretty impressive.

They spent the afternoon trawling the department stores on Calea Victoriei, looking for a dress for her to wear to the wedding. The day was warm and close, and much as she liked having expensive clothes bought for her, she was glad to get back to the apartment. Elena and George were both still at the shop. She could see Nic had a hankering to get her into bed, but she wasn't in the mood for sex. She told him to make coffee while she took a shower.

When she came back into the kitchen, the coffee was simmering on the stove, but Nic had gone. She had thought the shower would freshen her, but she felt dull-headed and a little nauseous. All the years she'd lived in Queensland's subtropics, she should have been used to the heat. Maybe it was different in this part of the world, she thought; more oppressive, the air polluted with shit from heavy industry.

She hadn't seen much of Romania beyond Bucharest, but what she had seen depressed her. Great stretches of farmland that made her think of the southern tablelands, shit roads once you got off the highway and villages that looked like some mediaeval movie set. The people appeared lean, ragged and hungry. Donkey carts loaded with farm produce or junk furniture didn't seem so quaint after she'd seen a dozen of them. The contrast with the smart, glitzy centre of Bucharest couldn't have been more striking. She thought Nic would be embarrassed showing her this poverty, but he wanted her to see what he'd come from. Romania was still in transition, he said; the old ways couldn't be swept away in an afternoon. He took on a kind of preachy tone when he was trying to push a point home to her, and it was beginning to get on her nerves. She was tired of hearing that Romania's future lay with entrepreneurial types like himself.

A week ago, one warm, hazy day, he took her to Ruse in Bulgaria. It meant crossing the Danube from Giurgiu, a port city built on mudflats and marshes. The river was flat, wide and dun-coloured, even with the sun on it. Long, industrial barges moved slowly up the river, outrun by the odd brightly coloured sailing skiff. She photographed picture after picture, knowing she would probably never look at them again.

Elena had told her that the most picturesque parts of the country were towards the east and the Black Sea, or north into the Carpathian mountains. Nic had promised to take her to Bran, Transylvanian home of the legendary Vlad the Impaler, something worth photographing, she had thought, but he'd lost interest. This time of year, he said, the castle would be crawling with sightseers.

Half the vehicles they passed on the highway to Giurgiu seemed to be either trucks or tourist buses. Nic told her Ruse was sometimes called Little Vienna for its architecture, so she took more photographs and then they had lunch in a noisy crowded bar. Afterwards, it was the Gypsy camp on the fringe of the city she remembered, the stringy teenagers throwing stones, and the dogs, everywhere the dogs, just as there were around the streets of Bucharest. She couldn't help venting about it as they drove back, and Nic accused her of seeing only the ugliness, saying she should stop being so superior. It was the first pointed criticism he'd made of her, and it hurt. She felt sick and bored and unappreciated and wanted to go home.

The next day, Nic was all charm and generosity, but it was a while before she stopped feeling anxious. It was the same when Leah threatened to turn Lucy over to the Social. Back then, subsequent texts had reassured her; Leah had come good, Lucy was most likely talking, and Mitch was just a harmless prick. Now, a week after Ruse, she was still feeling the pull: being on her home turf again, seeing her mates and having her kid back. Nic walking out on her because she refused him a fuck simply reinforced her feeling that it was time to go. And yet she stayed.

6

Sandu had taken rooms in a small hotel near the railway station. He had no family in Bucharest, apart from his cousin Gabriela, who was marrying a well-healed Audi dealer. He had friends he could have stayed with, he told Amy, but he didn't want them vetting the women he took to his bed. He said this almost as an aside as they were sharing a smoke on the roof garden of the Ionescus' apartment block.

It was a still, warm night, too sultry to sit inside. Nic and George were a few metres away, arguing over Romanian politics; Elena had gone downstairs for another bottle of wine.

'You should come to lunch,' Sandu said. 'There's an excellent restaurant across the street.' He turned his gaze for a second to Nic, and murmured, 'Your lover neglects you.'

159

'Not always,' Amy said. 'But I'm good for lunch.'

Sandu smiled. 'I'd say tomorrow. But I have to go to Varna.'

'Where's that?'

'Bulgaria. On the coast. A beautiful city, very cosmopolitan.' He smoked reflectively for a moment. 'What d'you think? A little business in the morning, and then we go to Micu's. You'll like the *tarator*, a Bulgarian specialty.'

'What is it?'

'Cold soup. Or liquid salad. There's much debate.'

'I think I'll pass,' Amy said.

'No, no. On a hot day, it's the perfect dish. Yoghurt, cucumbers, garlic, nuts, dill… Very cold. You'll love it.'

'It's a long way to go for a bowl of soup,' Amy said.

'There are other attractions. You like gold?'

'Sure. What girl doesn't?'

'I will show you gold to die for,' Sandu said. 'In the archaeological museum. Three thousand years old. Exquisite pieces of jewellery. Excavated from the Necropolis only forty or fifty years ago. Now they are a wonder of the world.'

'Necropolis,' Amy said. 'A graveyard. Gold chains around old bones.'

'But very beautiful.'

Amy finished her cigarette. 'Nic won't come,' she said. 'He's going to Brasov.'

Sandu shrugged carelessly. He would have known that. 'Another day, then.'

'I didn't say I was going with him,' Amy said.

7

Sandu turned up just on eight, after Elena and George had gone to work. Nic was on the phone, talking to his contact in Brasov. He paused to exchange a few words with Sandu, some joke in Romanian, Amy thought, as they both laughed.

'Be good,' he told Amy, and put the phone back to his ear.

His offhandedness irritated and hurt her. It was as if he were being deliberately provocative. She followed Sandu out to his car, a late model Audi he'd borrowed from his cousin's fiancé. 'What was the joke?' she asked him. 'You and Nic, chuckling like schoolkids.'

Sandu sat a moment, listening to the purr of the Audi motor. 'He told me, "You fuck Amy, I'll find out and I'll kill you."' And he laughed again.

She had slept badly and dozed for most of the two-hour drive to Varna. The landscape, what she saw of it, seemed much the same as around Bucharest: stretches of mostly flat farmland, small villages, and the highway a steady stream of trucks and tourist buses. Twice she woke with the sensation that she was being touched, but each time he had his hand on the wheel, a freshly lit cigarette hanging from the side of his mouth.

'Good sleep?' he asked her once, and told her she snored like a donkey.

Familiarity was unravelling something of his charm. She'd wanted to ask him about his relationship with Nic, but it was her life he was interested in, the messy business of love and sex, work and having a kid with an absent father. If she opened up, it was because she'd always been one to talk about herself, and because anyway, she reasoned, she wouldn't have been telling him anything he hadn't heard already from Nic. All the same, it was something of a relief to see the sign to Varna, particularly as she was busting for a pee.

A wide boulevard brought them into the centre of the city. Sandu miraculously found a parking spot in a side street choked with parked cars and took her into the rear entrance of a small jeweller's shop. A thin, bald-headed man was introduced as Miro and then she was shown a toilet at the back of the premises. Sandu and the jeweller had gone upstairs to talk and a fresh-faced girl of about eighteen or nineteen had been left to mind the shop.

Speaking in a halting English, she told Amy that if she were to walk down the street past the concert hall she would be in the shopping precinct. Beyond that was the park and beaches. 'I will tell your friend you will be by the information stand in one hour,' she told Amy. 'Here you will be bored. Miro talks and talks like an old woman.'

The day had turned quite hot and she wished she had brought a hat. It hadn't occurred to her either, until she was in the busy shopping precinct that the only money she had was Romanian. She passed a mini-mart and used her MasterCard to buy a straw hat, cigarettes and a can of Coke. The shopping didn't seem so very different from Bucharest: the same chain fashion stores, gift shops, bars and restaurants. Then there was McDonalds and the usual fast food joints. She found the information stand at the corner of an open pedestrian square. Beyond that was the gardens and the sea. The Black Sea, she told herself, rifling through her bag for her camera: a place as rare and distant in her imagination as the mountains of the moon.

Feeling the heat, she walked back across the square and sat on a bench next to a pair of giggling schoolgirls. It was almost an hour since she'd left the jeweller's shop and every few minutes she looked over her shoulder for Sandu coming to meet up with her. The hour passed and she weighed up the option of waiting or walking back up the boulevard. She was about to get up when she was distracted by a man in black clothes and a black top hat walking across the square. He had a long, dark gloomy face and walked with a kind of swagger. There was some sort of pack strapped to his shoulder, and until she noted his white socks all she could think of was a chimney sweep, stepping out of a TV period drama. The moment he saw her camera, he changed direction and came towards her. He stopped a few metres away and stood stock still till she had her picture.

'Thank you,' she said.

He stepped closer and held out his hand.

She shook her head. 'No money,' she said. 'Sorry.'

He jabbered something in Bulgarian and took another step towards her, his hand still raised. Now she started to panic. The schoolgirls who had been sitting on the bench with her had moved away. Other people crossing the square walked on without looking.

She shook her head again. 'No money,' she said. 'No fucking Bulgarian money. Go away.'

He lowered his hand for a second and laughed. 'Money,' he said. 'Yes.' The hand came out again, but he stayed his distance.

She glanced around, half afraid to look away. All she could think was: Sandu. Where the fuck is Sandu?

He took another step towards her. She could see the pockmarks on his face and a red welt under his chin where he might have nicked himself shaving.

'Money,' he said. 'For picture.'

She pulled her wallet from her bag and emptied all the coins she had into his outstretched hand. 'Romanian shit,' she said. 'It's all I've got.'

He moved the coins around his palm, totting up their value. 'Money,' he said. 'Very good.' Then he bowed, so that she could see the tear in the top of his hat, and walked off.

'Gypsies,' Sandu said. 'One per cent of the population, ninety per cent of the bad press.'

They were eating in Micu's, a small restaurant in a side street about a block back from the shopping boulevard. Despite the heat, Amy was hungry for rare steak and a full-bodied red wine. She'd noted that *tarator* was not on the menu.

'It was humiliating,' she said. 'I was looking for you and you were late.'

He shrugged. 'It's business. And Miro likes to talk.'

Her anger was making her drink. Sandu had only half filled his own glass and had barely touched it. Drink driving was a serious offence in Bulgaria, he told her. And he didn't want to prang his cousin's fiancé's shiny blue Audi.

He checked his watch. 'We should go soon. There will be tourists at the museum and everyone wants to see the Thracian gold.'

'As long as there are no Gypsies,' Amy said.

He sighed. The talk of Gypsies was beginning to tire him. He excused himself and went to the toilet.

Amy finished her wine and drank a little water. She felt light-headed from the heat and alcohol, her senses attuned to the sounds and smells around her. The restaurant was dull-lit, a half dozen tables squeezed into the cramped space. There wasn't a seat that wasn't taken and the hubbub of exotic, impenetrable chatter exhilarated her.

Earlier, she had been struck by a lad sitting in the corner sharing a dish of some stew or other with his girl. He had long, unruly dark hair and just the impression of a moustache and fuzz on his chin. There were textbooks on the floor at the girl's feet, so she guessed they were students. The girl, pale-looking, even in the restaurant gloom, was feeding the boy with her spoon while he broke pieces of bread, which they ate between them. There was a water bottle on the table and she imagined they were too poor to buy wine. They had finished their meal when Sandu left the table, and were leaning back in their chairs, gazing silently across the table at each other. Because of the bad light, particularly in the corner where they were sitting, it was not until Sandu was returning that she noticed the boy had slipped out of his shoes and was probing under the girl's short skirt with his foot. Watching made her feel like a voyeur, but she was helpless to look away. She felt, in that instant, a sudden longing for the carelessness of teenage love. She felt drunk with an even deeper sense of exhilaration, and she felt hungry for sex.

8

After Varna, she became Sandu's lover. Maybe if Nic had returned to Bucharest that night, as she'd expected, it would have been different. If it wasn't too late already. Leaving Micu's restaurant, Sandu took her to a small hotel that he'd clearly been to before and booked a room for the afternoon. He closed the door, pulled her close and put his hand between her legs.

'Remember what Nic told you,' she said. 'You sure you want to do this?'

He hesitated a second and then lifted her as if she were a child and dropped her on the bed.

Driving back to Bucharest, she'd fretted that Nic would know, would read something in her behaviour that would give her away. She never was very good at hiding her betrayals. And then around eight, just as they were entering Bucharest's outer suburbs, he phoned to say he was staying on in Brasov for a few days. He'd met an old schoolmate and wanted to spend some time catching up. She could hear music and chatter in the background and guessed he was in a restaurant.

'Tell George it's Rudi,' Nic said. 'George will remember Rudi. They liked to fight.' He wanted to know if she was entranced by the Thracian Gold and she told him the queues were horrendous, so they went to the beach.

When she hung up, she said, 'Always the old mate bullshit. Let's go to your place.'

Sandu dropped her back at the Ionescus' flat around eight in the morning, just as George and Elena were leaving for work. She slept until four in the afternoon, when Sandu phoned.

'Come to the casino with me,' he said. 'I'm feeling lucky.' He told her he liked to play blackjack, he didn't have the face for a poker player.

For an hour, she watched him win a little, lose a little, until the cards finally turned his way.

'It's you who brings me luck,' he said. 'You know what? Tonight we make love here. Beautiful suite. Big bed, nice sheets.'

She spent the evening willing more of her luck on him and getting slowly drunk on cocktails. For a month, she thought, she'd endured a kind of squalid sex in the Ionescus' shitty flat and pokey hotel rooms; she deserved a little pampering. She hadn't fucked in a classy five star hotel since Nic took her to Jupiter's on the Gold Coast.

How much Sandu won, he wouldn't say, but around midnight they took the lift to the fourteenth floor.

A phone call just after seven in the morning woke her. She felt hung-over and dry. Sandu was in the shower. She thought it was Nic calling, but it was Elena.

'Where are you?' she said. 'Two nights you haven't come home.'

'I'm with Sandu,' Amy said. 'You don't have to worry.'

'Why should I worry?' Elena said sourly. 'Who you fuck is your business.'

'We're not fucking,' Amy said. 'If Nic gave a shit about me, I wouldn't need Sandu for company.'

Elena was silent for a moment. Then she said, 'If you want, I don't have to go to work. We'll spend the day together. You and me.'

Amy sighed. 'You know, Elena. I'm good right now.'

'Last night maybe was good,' Elena said. She sounded sour again. 'You're a long way from home, Amy. You'd better know who your friends are.'

After his shower, Sandu disappeared for a couple of hours.

Amy dozed for a while, then called room service and asked for breakfast to be brought to the room. 'And paracetamol,' she said. 'A pack.'

Despite the headache, she felt hungry. A pock-faced Asian guy brought a trolley and laid the table with a crisp white tablecloth. She took two paracetamol with juice and then ate cereal and poached eggs with salmon and a slice of buttered toast and jam. The coffee had gone cold, but she poured a cup and swallowed two more tablets. Sandu still hadn't returned, so she took a shower. When she came out of the bathroom, he was sitting on the bed, crunching on a slice of cold toast.

'Get dressed,' he said. 'There's someone I want you to meet.'

Riding down in the lift, she said, 'Elena called me. She knows we're fucking.'

'Of course she does. She will tell George, and George will tell Nicci.'

'I don't want a fight,' Amy said. 'I'm not a schoolgirl.'

'No,' he said. 'You're right. Boys fight over their women. And Gypsies. Gypsies fight over everything.'

She watched his face as he said this and it struck her that she was being played. 'If Nic put you up to this,' she said, 'I won't be happy.'

He shrugged a little. 'I think since Varna you have been happy,' he said.

The lift stopped at the second floor and filled with loud Germans with their suitcases. A small pasty-faced boy was squeezed between Amy and Sandu. Amy stared at the top of the boy's cropped head until the lift doors opened onto the lobby and the Germans scrambled out.

'Who is it you want me to meet?' she asked Sandu. 'Not another fucking jeweller.'

'My cousin,' Sandu said. 'Gabriela. She should be here now.'

A tall, austere-looking woman in a blue suit was sitting at the bar, drinking coffee. She laughed when she saw Sandu and kissed him on the cheek. Amy she observed curiously, her eyes widening as if some surprise had been sprung on her. 'Is this…?'

'No, no,' Sandu said. 'This is Amy. Nicci's friend. Nicci is in Brasov for a few days.'

'Ah,' Gabriela said. 'So you did not bring her.' She took Amy's hand and squeezed gently. 'You are the Australian girl. Let's have a drink.'

Sandu ordered cocktails and they moved to a table in the corner. It was a bit early for Amy to be drinking and she still felt hung-over. She puzzled over why Gabriela should say Sandu hadn't brought her until she realised it was Sandu's Chicago lover she was referring to. His daughter's mother, Sandu had called her, giving Amy the impression that the relationship had ended, something Gabriela clearly wasn't aware of. Maybe that was a conversation for a private moment, Amy thought. She sipped her cocktail while the cousins small talked about Gabriela's fiancé and the wedding. Gabriela's poise and expensive clothes suggested some smart executive job or cosmetics rep. Amy had met a few in her time and they were all Gabrielas of a sort. If it wasn't for the impending wedding, she would have said call girl; she knew how they liked to hang around casinos and private clubs.

When they'd finished their small talk, Sandu told Amy that Gabriela had been in Odessa for the past few weeks, visiting her father, who was too sick to come to Bucharest for the wedding. 'Gabriela's father is Ukrainian,' Sandu explained. 'We are cousins on our mothers' side.'

It was said with a touch of knowingness, which made Amy wonder if she was meant to read something into it. She wanted to say, Romanian, Ukrainian, it was all of a muchness to her, but feared it would simply expose her as ignorant. She swallowed the last of her drink and excused herself to go to the toilet.

When she returned, Gabriela was sitting alone. A barman hovered over the table with fresh cocktails and a plate of canapés.

'A phone call,' Gabriela said. 'With Sandu, it's always business.'

'He's coming back?' Amy said.

'Of course.' She indicated the plate of canapés. 'Eat.'

'I've just had breakfast,' Amy said. She sipped her cocktail. 'I can take a few of these.'

Gabriela smiled. 'I thought you looked a little unwell earlier.'

'You mean hung-over,' Amy said. 'I'm good now.'

'Australia,' Gabriela said, after a moment. 'You have casinos there?'

'We sure do. You like to play?'

'It's my work. I'm a croupier.'

'Oh,' Amy said. 'Here?'

'Here. Germany, France, England. Maybe one day Australia.'

'I could write you a reference,' Amy said. 'If it helped.'

'Yes,' Gabriela said. 'We should keep in touch.' She glanced at her watch and sighed a little. 'If I have to go, you will be all right? Sandu can talk on the phone for hours.'

'I didn't know the jewellery game was so full on,' Amy said. 'Nic's the same. Always chasing up some contact or other. To be honest, it bores me witless. But I do like diamonds.'

Gabriela smiled again. She held out her hand so Amy could admire her engagement ring. 'You like?'

'That's some stone,' Amy said. She thought it ostentatiously huge and wildly expensive for sure. 'Did Sandu get it for you? Or are there big quids to be made flogging Audis to cashed-up Bucurestis?'

Gabriela withdrew her hand and put a finger to her lips. Caught in the light from the bar, the stone sparkled and danced.

9

The day had warmed up and become humid. Amy had no appetite for lunch and after two cocktails her headache had returned. She wanted to sleep, but as neither the Ionescus' flat nor Sandu's hotel room was air conditioned, she stayed in town. Sandu left her outside a department store and gave her money to buy a swimsuit. He said he would pick her up in an hour and take her to a local pool.

Gabriela had left by the time he'd returned to the bar. Amy couldn't make up her mind whether she liked the cousin or not. She had a sense that there was more to Sandu, Gabriela and Nic than just being cousins and friends. She remembered the look Sandu gave her in the lift, making her think she was being played. If Nic was not with an old schoolmate in Brasov, he was probably with another woman. She'd not been in Bucharest more than a few days before she'd felt he was tiring of her, regretting that he'd asked her to come. She was seeing a computer sales guy when she met Nic, so maybe it was the contest he liked, taking her from another lover. She'd thought they clicked, that he'd be the guy to stick with, particularly as he was so good with Lucy. Something changed after they'd moved into George and Elena's flat, and it wasn't just the crap sex because of the thin walls. Sex anyway with Nic was never anything special. Sandu was more fun in bed, but then he was younger, clearly more practised, and weren't new lovers always more fun? All the same, if she had been played, being passed from one lover to another like some teenage beach party slut was pretty low. Better to think Sandu an opportunist and Nic too trusting, whatever he might have said to Sandu the morning he took her to Varna. Which didn't put her in too good a light, she realised, but then she always had been easy prey to good-looking guys.

She bought a swimsuit she liked and then went to a café and drank tea with paracetamol until Sandu picked her up. Her head had finally cleared, and despite the oppressive heat she felt rejuvenated. Sandu sat with his phone and a can of Coke while she did laps of the pool and then he took her to a restaurant for an early dinner. After skipping lunch, she was hungry and without the headache she was ready to drink.

The restaurant was a small, gloomy bar in a back street not far from George and Elena's flat. There were three or four other diners, their conversation drowned out by pulsating Gypsy music coming from a sound system behind the bar. Sandu ordered two beers and a starter of bread and soup, some meaty broth that tasted of over-salted pork and garlic. She asked him if he'd got Gabriela's engagement ring for her, and he gave her a thin, somewhat furtive smile. He was less talkative than usual, a touch withdrawn, and she wondered if some business deal had gone south.

A lean, sandy-haired man came in and went up to the bar. Sandu said he was an old acquaintance of his and went over to speak to him. A waiter came to take away the soup bowls. Amy went to the toilet and when she returned the sandy-haired man was leaving. He gave her a sharp look as they passed. She noted the intense blueness of his eyes, bluer even than Elena's. He was dressed untidily in a loose-fitting grey suit with a white open collar shirt.

'He looked a bit shady,' Amy said, resuming her seat.

The waiter came to the table. Sandu ordered a bottle of wine.

'He used to work for me,' Sandu said. 'In a consultative capacity.'

The phrase amused Amy. It was like he'd just discovered it and wanted to impress her. And then she thought it was maybe something else. 'You seem to know a lot of people here,' she said. 'I thought you'd been living in Chicago for years.'

'I like to keep in touch,' Sandu said. 'The business, you know. Bucharest is good, now. There is money on the street. I'm thinking, maybe it is time to come back.'

'Why did you leave?'

'I went to work for my uncle. His father migrated to America after the war. He was a jeweller too. As was my father and grandfather.'

'In the blood, then,' Amy said.

Sandu smiled. She didn't ask how the daughter and her mother came into it. The waiter came with the wine.

'Are you going into business with Nic?' Amy asked.

'Is that what he told you?'

'He said you were smart. He's a bit of a fan, if you ask me.'

Sandu's smile was a touch smug, she thought.

'I try to be useful to him,' he said.

'How does that work?'

He stared at her a moment before pulling a sheath of papers from his jacket pocket. She thought it was some manufacturer's or dealer's catalogue, pages of sparkling gems and exquisite jewellery. He said it was all stolen stuff. House break-ins, jewellery shops, even bank vaults.

'Millions of dollars' worth,' he told her, 'all needing a buyer.'

She almost laughed. 'Nic's never handled hooky gear,' she said. 'He's straight up and down.'

Sandu nodded. 'So in Australia he deals with people he trusts. Here it is a little more complicated. A little more dangerous.'

She felt a murmur of irritation at his knowingness. And then something else, that made her pulse quicken.

He pushed the papers back into his jacket pocket. She was sure it was the sandy-haired man who had given them to him. She would have liked a closer look, a quick skim through to see if Gabriela's ostentatiously expensive engagement ring was featured in its pages.

A storm broke as they were leaving the restaurant and they had to run to get out of the sheeting rain. The change cleared the air, but the rain persisted into the evening. Sandu's room was hot and close, so they sat by the open window for a while smoking a couple of joints he'd picked up sometime during the day. The dope relaxed her, made her feel good about herself. Another week, she thought, and I'll go home. The wedding was in four days, so after the wedding. Gabriela would want her to be there; didn't she say they should stay in touch? Who would take her, that was the question. It would have to be Sandu.

There was no way now she could go with Nic; there was no point going back to the Ionescus' flat, except to pick up her gear.

She thought about the conversation she'd had with Sandu in the restaurant. Maybe she was dumb to stay with him, if he was into something dodgy. She hadn't liked the look of the sandy-haired man, but then any legit jeweller would likely have a list of hooky gear. She didn't need to over-think it. The dope helped there. She glanced around the poky little hotel room with its cheap furniture and stained, unravelling carpet. She didn't mind it so much, as long as she was there with Sandu. Maybe she minded the lumpy bed and the lingering whiff of soiled clothes, but it was only for another week. She dragged on her joint and sighed a little. It was all good.

Sandu was watching her. 'What are you thinking?' he said.

Butting her joint on the sill, she opened her legs and drew her skirt up. 'I'm thinking you should come and fuck me,' she said.

Sometime in the night she woke, sticky with sweat and a dull ache in her head. The drapes were still open, the room dimly lit by the street lights. She pushed the sheet to her waist and turned over to catch a bit of breeze on her back. It took her a few seconds to realise that Sandu was not in the bed beside her. She pulled herself up. She saw him, then, the shape of him, hunched on the chair in the dark corner of the room. He was tying his shoelaces.

'What are you doing?'

'I have to go out,' he said evenly. 'Go back to sleep.'

She'd been dreaming a few moments before. In her dream, his phone was ringing.

'What time is it?'

'I don't know. Two. Three.' He stood up. 'An hour, maybe. I'll be back.' He went to the window, standing a little to one side, looking down onto the street. 'It's business.'

Always business with Sandu…

He came and sat on the bed beside her, leaned over, kissed her. His hand cupped her breast. 'An hour,' he said. 'Maybe a little longer.'

She waited for the door to close. Slipping from the bed, she pulled on her shirt and went to the window. A fine drizzle was falling, the narrow street below dull lit and choked with parked cars. She watched for him to exit the hotel front entrance. He stood a moment, looking up and down the street. Someone was picking him up. She didn't like that. Then he stepped off the sidewalk and crossed the street. She saw then, half obscured under a shop awning, a man was waiting for him. She thought it might have been the sandy-haired man, but he was thickset, the peak of a cap hiding his face. He stood with Sandu a moment, the two of them talking. Their voices drifted up to her, low and heated. She moved a little to one side of the window; she didn't want to be caught watching.

The men continued arguing for some minutes, the level of heat rising and falling, like the drone of heavy trucks on the distant boulevard. Suddenly the voices fell silent. Sandu turned and stepped off the sidewalk. She watched him walk between two parked cars and then fall face down in the street. The thickset man, she saw, was walking quickly away. The gunshot had barely registered.

10

George came to pick her up. He knew the hotel. He said there was a service entrance that opened onto a side street; he'd meet her there. She didn't know who called the police. They arrived just as she finished dressing. A half dozen people were standing around Sandu's body. She recognised the guy from the hotel desk; the others were just stickybeaks from neighbouring tenements. She took the stairs, not wanting to activate the lift. Another wailing siren she guessed was the paramedics arriving. The side street was unlit, choked with parked cars. There was no sign of George. She didn't know which way he'd come; she was nervous about missing him if she moved away from the hotel. There were stars out and a quarter moon, but the street and cars were still wet. Frank Sinatra was crooning somewhere; some of the tenement windows were lit.

A car turned into the far end of the street and drove slowly between the parked vehicles. She stepped back into the service entrance until she was certain it was George.

When she got into the car, he said, 'You sure it was Sandu?'

She nodded, too tense to speak.

They drove out of the side street and away from the hotel. When she looked through the rear window, all she could see was flashing lights, slipping into the distance.

Back at the flat, Elena was on the phone to Nic.

'I can't talk,' Amy said. 'I need a drink.'

Elena hung up. 'He's coming straight back,' she said. She opened a bottle of wine.

George lit cigarettes. The flat smelled of fried fish. Amy opened a window.

'It was horrible,' she said. 'I saw it. I saw him fall. The guy just walked off.'

'Did he see you?' George said.

'No. I don't think so. They were arguing. And then…' She took a deep drag on her cigarette. 'It was just a pop. Like a balloon bursting.' She'd begun to shake.

Elena took the glass from her and made her stand. She held her for a few seconds. 'You didn't have to see that,' she said. It sounded cold, like an accusation.

Amy sat down again. She'd stopped shaking.

'What about the hotel?' George said. 'Did anyone see you go in?'

'The guy on the desk,' Amy said. 'He gave me the once over. Like I was just some pick-up.'

'That's good,' George. 'Let them think that.'

Amy stared at him. 'Who?'

'The police. If they don't have your name, they won't find you. They won't even look.' He smoked a moment in silence. 'I think you should go home. As soon as Nicci gets back. He will arrange it.'

Amy said nothing. She was too numb to think about going home.

Elena came with the bottle to refill her glass. 'Take some pills and go to bed,' she said. 'I'll wake you when Nicci gets here.'

'I can't sleep,' Amy said. 'I'd need a shitload of pills to sleep. It'd kill me.'

George was checking something on his phone. He spoke to Elena in Romanian and she nodded.

'Too bad,' she said.

'What's he doing?' Amy said.

'He's looking to see what flights there are tomorrow. There's nothing today. Unless you want to go to Istanbul.'

'I don't care where I go,' Amy said. 'As long as I get out of here.'

Elena turned her cold gaze on her, but said nothing.

She blames me, Amy thought. She thinks it's my fault Sandu got shot. 'What did you say?' she said. 'When you phoned Nic.'

'What did I say?' The question seemed to offend her. 'What do you think I said? I said Sandu has been shot in the street outside his hotel. I said I knew because Amy told me. Because Amy saw it. She was there.' She drew on her cigarette and blew a long shot of smoke across the table. 'He wanted to know if you were all right.'

'He knew, didn't he?' Amy said. 'He knew about me and Sandu.'

Elena shrugged. 'He would have found out.'

'He knew,' Amy said, 'and he did it. He paid someone to shoot Sandu.'

Elena said nothing.

George looked up briefly. He glanced at Elena and went back to his phone. 'Nine-fifteen tomorrow morning,' he said. 'Air France to Paris.'

Amy looked at Elena. 'Say something, for fuck's sake.'

'You really are quite stupid, aren't you,' Elena said.

11

She went to bed, but couldn't sleep. She would have got up again, but didn't want to face Elena's withering gaze.

As soon as it got light, the sirens started. She'd got used to them before, but now they made her anxious. Twice she checked her bag to make sure she'd left nothing in Sandu's hotel room that might identify her. In Varna, she'd taken photos of the two of them, but they were still on her camera.

A bit after eight, she heard George leave the flat to go to work.

Elena brought her a mug of coffee. 'It's on the news,' she said. 'The police are saying nothing. They don't know. Maybe drugs, they think.'

Amy drank her coffee and took a shower. Drugs. Stolen jewels. Who would know? With Sandu, it's always business, Gabriela had said. Always on the phone. Nic too. She didn't want to think about it.

She dressed and went into the kitchen. She could hear Elena on the landing, talking with a neighbour. There was a sheet of paper on the table with flight times out of Bucharest for the next two days. She felt she was being pushed into leaving. If the police weren't looking for her, why did she have to go? Because of Nic. Because she'd cheated on him and made a fool of herself. Or because she'd dragged Sandu's dirty business into their lives? How would Nic come to her? she wondered. Angry and forgiving? Conflicted? Sympathetic for the horror she'd witnessed? Or just totally pissed?

She toasted some bread and took it into the bedroom. Elena came back into the flat and went to the bathroom. Take a pee, put on a face. Get ready for work. Amy felt a sudden pull for the ordinary and familiar. To hear English spoken with an Australian accent. To feel safe. She fished her camera from her bag and deleted the photos she'd taken of Sandu. It seemed more cold than calculating, but she didn't ever want reminding. The jewel thief (or was it drug dealer?) she hooked up with in Bucharest and saw shot dead in the street.

Elena came out of the bathroom and paused outside the door. 'Nicci's at Baneasa,' she said. 'Twenty minutes, maybe. You want me to stay?'

'No,' Amy said. 'You go to work.'

She waited until she heard the front door close and then texted Leah: coming home let u know times. She hesitated a second before adding: xx my kiddo for me. She pressed SEND and thought how good she felt.

12

After Elena left, she brewed herself fresh coffee and watched CNN while she waited for Nic to get back. Bombings, wild weather, political dirty business, it mostly washed over her, her mind fixed on the image of Sandu lying dead in the street.

The feeling of elation after texting Leah had morphed into renewed anxiety. She watched the door, her heart pumping a little faster every time she heard movement on the landing. If she muted the TV, the silence in the flat only unsettled her more. She shouldn't have let Elena leave for work before Nic arrived. She didn't like being alone; particularly, she didn't want to be alone when Nic came in. A smack, sympathy, kicked out into the street, she didn't know what to expect. He'd called her bad girl when she'd joked that she'd conceived Lucy while drunk. She'd thought then, there was a bit of the puritan in him. A part of her still wasn't convinced he hadn't arranged Sandu's killing, for all Elena's withering rebuke.

Switching the TV off, she went into the bedroom and dumped her suitcase on the bed. It was already half filled with a jumble of stuff she'd brought with her as well as gear she'd bought in Bucharest, most of it with Nic's money. His generosity in those early weeks had run a little dry since he'd introduced her to Sandu. The suspicion that she'd been played resurfaced, but better that, she thought, than being the cause of Sandu's cold-blooded killing.

She emptied the suitcase on the bed and began to repack. George had said there was an Air France flight to Paris in the morning. Or was it later? She couldn't remember. Before they left Australia, Nic had floated the idea of stopping over in Paris on their return: a couple of nights in an inner-city *pension*, baguettes and brioche for breakfast, afternoons cruising the Seine, late-night dancing in expensive clubs. The whole romantic shebang. She didn't know, but Bucharest had been called the Paris of the east, once. Before the war, Nic told her, before communism; but there was nothing like the real thing. She'd thought from this that he'd been to Paris before, but it was just a pitch. At the time she'd welcomed it because it meant they'd be returning to Australia together.

All the weeks they'd been in Bucharest, he'd said nothing about the status of his visa; and except in the early days, before the foreign became familiar and less unsettling to her, she'd barely thought about it herself. Now she didn't know or particularly care what his plans were. She could see no future with him, even if he returned to Australia, even if he forgave her for cheating on him.

Folding a pair of jeans she'd brought and never worn, she discovered the red dress with the green trim that she'd bought Lucy in the basement market a couple of weeks back. It was still wrapped in tissue paper, the edge stained with wine she'd spilled when showing it to Nic that evening.

'Very pretty,' Nic had said when she'd held it up for him. 'A little big, I think.'

It narked her a bit, that he should know Lucy's size better than the girl's mother.

It must have showed because Elena came over and gave her a hug. 'A little too big is good,' she said. 'She will grow into it.'

13

A police detective came to the door just as they were leaving for lunch. A short, gloomy man with the signature moustache and wearing a crumpled brown suit. Nic glanced at his ID and told her to go back into the flat. It seemed pointless to her as she couldn't understand what was being said, but maybe it was just his being interrogated he didn't want her to see. The murmur of conversation she heard through the door sounded cool and businesslike. She went into the bathroom and examined her cheek in the mirror. There was the faintest blush still under the make-up. A touch of the sun, it could have been, as if she'd fallen asleep sunbaking, her head turned to one side. He'd seemed more disappointed in her than angry, so she hadn't seen it coming. Maybe it was the face she presented, the stare, the pinched lips, the so-fucking-what look she'd perfected as a feral teenager. Half the time she didn't know she was doing it; it was just there, a defensive mask. He regretted it, the moment he let fly. It wasn't what he'd planned; she could tell that much. There were a few choice words, in Romanian to save her shame or humiliation. She felt it anyway. It seemed ludicrous then that she could have thought him responsible for Sandu's killing. He looked a bit sheepish when she told him what Sandu had said the morning he took her to Varna. Lads and their jokes. He knew what Sandu was like, that was the thing. He knew her a little better now, too, her weaknesses, her carelessness.

There was no argument when she told him George thought she should go home. He glanced at the flight times his brother had jotted down, and stuffed the slip of paper in his pocket. 'The police will come,' he said. 'Sandu is known to them.' He went into the bedroom and stripped to take a shower.

She would have gone to bed with him, if he'd wanted, but he showed no sign of wanting. He padded down the hall to the bathroom, not looking at her, shutting the door on her gaze.

After five minutes or so on the landing, he came back into the flat and told her the detective had gone. 'He wanted to know if I knew who the girl was Sandu had in his room,' he said. 'I said Sandu liked to fuck around. If there was no girl willing, he paid a prostitute. You have nothing to worry about. They are not looking for you.'

It was hard to tell if this was said to demean her, or if he was simply telling it as it was. She thought, if it was true, why the urgency for her to leave, but he didn't say he wanted her to stay. He drove her out of the city to eat at a restaurant she'd not been to before. He pointed out some of the buildings and monuments that were modelled on French originals, but on a dull, sunless day it all just looked drab and depressing. The restaurant was a chain franchise, busy with women and their noisy, unruly kids. She wondered if this was further punishment for her transgression: cheap eats and pulsating pop music. At least there was wine. He'd said little since they'd left the wide boulevards of the city, his odd glance in her direction curiously uninterested. This was what she would take back with her, she thought, this memorable last meal of chewy steak and insipid wine.

Mid-afternoon, they returned to the city. Nic drove up the narrow street to the apartment. The detective who had called earlier was standing at the entrance with a uniformed cop. Nic told her to stay in the car while he talked to them. She sat anxiously, biting her nails, the undigested steak churning in her stomach. After a moment, he came back to the car. The detective and uniformed cop were still waiting by the apartment entrance.

'You have to go with them,' Nic said. 'They want to talk to you.'

14

The room was airless, the single window opening onto a courtyard. The blinds were drawn when they entered, but the ceiling fan wouldn't work.

The detective flicked the switch four or five times, muttering in Romanian, and then drew the window blinds up. He lifted the sash casement and she felt the rush of cool air, scented with the stink of city traffic. 'Please,' the detective said, 'sit down.'

There was a wooden table, the sort you might find in a country kitchen, and four straight-backed chairs. A bookcase against the back wall held document files. Next to it hung a large framed photograph of a German shepherd dog.

Nic had told her she wasn't being arrested; they just wanted to talk to her. Someone had given them her name; they wouldn't say who. She thought they might let him sit with her. She might need something explained, she said. And she was scared. Nic spoke with the detective, who shook his head.

'I'll phone George,' he told her, 'in case we need a lawyer.'

She sat in the back of the detective's car while Nic followed her to the police station. The detective parked his car in the courtyard at the back of the station and took her in through a side entrance. He led her down a long corridor to the interview room. She was shaking when she sat down, her teeth chattering as if she were freezing cold. The detective said he would bring her a glass of water and coffee if she wanted it. His English was a little hesitant, but coherent. She was reassured a little by his slight air of indifference. A talk was all they wanted. Some information about Sandu, anything she could tell them, which wouldn't be much. Nic had said she'd probably be home in an hour. She'd need a drink, then, she thought desperately. A smoke and a drink. And a long, cleansing shower. When the detective returned with her water, there was another man with him, the sandy-haired man Sandu had met in the restaurant. She was struck again by the deep blueness of his eyes. He said his name was Detective Popescu. His colleague was Detective Lupu. Lupu placed a glass of murky water on the table. There was something floating in it: a fly, Amy realised. She felt sick.

Popescu asked her name and where she came from. She said Amy Hart and Australia, and then wondered if he meant where was she staying in Bucharest. And then she thought, they already know, stupid. Everything she said came out a little breathless, her mouth was so dry. She didn't want to look at the glass of water.

Lupu was writing in a notebook. He looked at her and said, 'Heart. Like…' putting his hand to his chest.

She spelt it out for him while Popescu opened a buff folder that he'd brought to the room with him. He seemed different from when she'd seen him in the restaurant, but she couldn't put a finger on it. Maybe it was just his manner, more policeman-like.

He slid a photograph from the folder and pushed it across the table to her. 'Sandu Grigorus,' he said. 'Shot last night outside the Hotel Banat.'

He spoke English with a strong accent that sounded comical to her ears. It lent weight to the weirdness of her situation. Surreal, she thought, it's surreal. Like she was a little high and it was all a bit of play-acting in her head. She gazed at Sandu's face looking up at her. He was younger, his hair longer, a thin, cocky Sandu smile. A party pic, not a police mug shot. Sandu had never been to jail, he couldn't have, he would never have been allowed into America. Not legally. She marvelled at the lucidity of her thinking. Not so stupid now.

Her mouth was still so dry. The silt in the glass of water had settled to the bottom, but the fly was still there. Popescu was staring at her. She realised he'd asked her something, and she had to make him repeat it. He wanted to know what she knew about Sandu Grigorus's murder. It was when he said murder, in that wacky B-grade movie accent, that it hit home what deep shit she was in.

15

For almost an hour, they quizzed her about her relationship with Sandu. She told them everything: Varna, the night at the casino, meeting his cousin, his shooting outside the Hotel Banat. She described his killer a dozen times, but the only detail she remembered with any clarity was the man's peaked cap.

It was Lupu who asked her why she was sleeping with Sandu if Nic was her boyfriend. 'You like to fuck around, Amy? You easy girl, eh. All Australian girls like you?'

She'd liked him earlier, when he'd seemed – not friendly, exactly, but a little more accommodating. Now she thought she'd never look at a dead fly floating on water without thinking of him.

Popescu wanted to know about Sandu's contacts, who she'd seen him with apart from Nic and Gabriela. She remembered Miro in Varna, but other than that, she said, it was all business over the phone. Lupu wrote it down while Popescu gazed at her through his unnaturally deep blue eyes. Was she supposed to mention him too? The sandy-haired man Sandu had spoken to only hours before he was gunned down. Seeing him enter the interview room earlier had just confused her. Did

Sandu know Popescu was a detective? A consultant of sorts, Sandu had said. That could mean anything. She feared now that whatever she said would only incriminate her in some way. Better, she thought, to say nothing. After all, she'd only seen him briefly in passing. If only it weren't for those startlingly blue eyes. Her mouth was so parched now she could barely speak.

Popescu could see her distress. 'You need a little time to think, Amy?' he said. 'A drink of water, yes?'

She stared helplessly at the glass of water.

Popescu nudged Lupu, indicating with a nod. 'Lupu likes insects in his water,' Popescu said.

It could have been true, Amy thought, for all his dour expression revealed. Lupu took the glass and left the room.

Popescu perused Lupu's notes for a moment. Then he said, 'What else can you give me, Amy?'

'I don't know,' Amy said.

'Well, you know Sandu Grigorus fenced stolen jewellery. You know what a fence is, Amy. It is an English word.'

'Yes,' Amy said. 'I know. I mean, I didn't know…what Sandu was doing.'

'And now he has been murdered. A few days after he meets you. Amy Hart from Australia. Cheating on her Romanian boyfriend.'

Amy said nothing. She felt powerless to explain. Whatever she said, she seemed implicated some way in Sandu's affairs. Couldn't she just say Lupu was right, it was only sex? A misadventure. What were they accusing her of?

Popescu glanced again at Lupu's notes and then pushed them aside. 'You see how it looks, Amy. To a suspicious detective. It could be – and I am leaning to this opinion – that you are an unfortunate innocent in all this. But we have to ask the questions, you understand.'

Amy nodded. She felt a little easier. 'I don't know what else I can tell you,' she said.

'There will be something,' Popescu said. 'A little detail you have forgotten that may be important.' He paused a moment. 'Your boyfriend...'

'Nic's strictly legit,' she said sharply. 'He and Sandu were just old mates. Nic would never get involved in anything dodgy. He'd screw his re-entry visa into Australia.'

'Maybe,' Popescu said. 'But you know, you associate with crooks...'

'Policemen associate with crooks, don't they?' It was out before she could think.

Popescu eased himself forward a little.

'Yesterday,' Amy said. 'You know I saw you. In the restaurant. He went up to the bar to talk to you. He said you used to work for him.' She remembered the phrase Sandu used that had so amused her. In a consultative capacity... She wasn't going to repeat it.

Popescu barely blinked. 'I know a lot of bad men,' he said. 'Sometimes they think I'm their friend, sometimes it is just an agreeable arrangement between interested parties. I have been a friend to Sandu Grigorus, and he has been a friend to me. Do you know why he went to America? Because he had made enemies. His business was the business of others before him. He was very young, you see, very ambitious. Every time he came home to Romania for a visit, I would tell him, stay in America. Be an honest jeweller. Here you will not be welcome. Others are doing what you were doing. And they are dangerous, violent men. They will kill you, I told him, if they think you have come back to do business here. But you know what I think? He was nostalgic for the old country. And he was a little arrogant. You would have noticed that in him, I think.'

'He came back for his cousin's wedding,' Amy said. 'That's all I know.'

Popescu shrugged. He cocked his head, alert for some noise in the corridor. Amy felt there was something more he wanted to say before Lupu returned.

'You have family in Australia, Amy,' he said. 'Brothers, sisters, children maybe?'

For some reason, Amy thought of Sandu's fatherless daughter in Chicago. 'I have a daughter,' she said. 'Lucy. She's five.'

'She will be missing her mother,' Popescu said.

'I guess.' She felt a sudden tightening of her chest. 'She's sick. You know…in the head a little.'

Popescu sighed. 'Then the sooner you are returned to her the better, don't you think?'

'Yes,' Amy said. She gave Popescu a hopeful look.

He was smiling. 'So,' he said. 'How do we make this go away?'

16

A French guy was sitting next to her for the flight to Frankfurt. He was about thirty, dark, like the Romanian guys, sporting a thin moustache and a couple of days' growth on his chin. His English was good. He'd been to Australia, a couple of months fruit picking to earn some cash and then a month diving off the Barrier Reef. He was a student then, but now he was repping for some international pharmaceutical company. He'd gone to Bucharest chasing a Romanian girl he'd met in Lyon, but she'd dumped him so he was hooking up with an old German girlfriend. He wanted to know if Amy was stopping over in Frankfurt; he hadn't told the girlfriend he was coming. She was tempted, but the hassle of getting her ticket changed set her against it. The tempting part was not the sex with a good-looking French guy so much as the need to put some space between Bucharest and Brisbane.

She still couldn't truly believe that she'd got away. She'd been terrified that Nic would not come up with the money to pay off Popescu. Maybe he got it from George, she didn't ask. Elena cold-shouldered her, but she was past caring what Elena thought of her. She was sure it was Elena who put the police onto her.

Leaving the police station, Popescu had followed them out to the car, which was parked a block away. He spoke privately to Nic while she waited in her seat. A few hours later, he went out with George while she stayed in her room, keeping her distance from Elena. When Nic returned, he told her he'd booked a flight to Frankfurt for her in the morning. He didn't say how much he'd paid Popescu to let her go, or whether he'd want her to pay it back. He didn't want to talk about the money part. He said he was sorry now that he'd introduced her to Sandu; that he knew he'd been fencing stolen jewellery before he went to America, but honestly believed his old mate had gone straight. It didn't make him feel any better about her screwing Sandu behind his back. Maybe he could forgive her in time, but George and Elena wanted her out of their flat. She avoided them in the morning, staying in her room until they'd gone to work.

Nic ordered a cab and took her to the airport. He said, 'Give my love to little bubba.'

She felt bad then for what she'd done to him. But then she thought: if he hadn't neglected her, she wouldn't have fallen prey to Sandu's charms. She didn't see why she should take all the blame. There was no talk of hooking up again when he came back to Australia. He still had his business on the Gold Coast. She didn't see how she could live with him without Sandu's presence haunting them like some tortured spirit.

At least now she felt safe. Now she was going home. Next week she'd be calling Lilith to look after Lucy while she went looking for a job. She needed the everyday, the ordinary, to get her life back on track. But what she needed too was a little time out, somewhere to lick her wounds and reorder her view of the world.

She gave the French guy her number in case his company sent him down under some day and he had a mind to refresh his diving skills off the Barrier Reef.

Coming in to land at Frankfurt airport, she watched the green fields rising to meet them and wished it was wetlands or rainforest, or better still the Gold Coast high rise looming into view. The French guy disappeared with a brusque adieu and she followed a line of chattering passengers to the transit lounge.

Lining up at a café bar for coffee, she checked her phone for messages. Nothing from Nic, which was no less than she was expecting, just a text from Leah.

The Sicilian Boy

A cold drizzle had set in when she left the house. Mooney was waiting in the car outside the front gates, the racing page of the newspaper open on his lap.

Valentin settled in her seat, wiped her glasses with a tissue, and lit a smoke. 'Benzos,' she said. 'Drawer full of them, enough to put an elephant to sleep. It's a wonder she's still breathing.'

Mooney put a pencil mark against a race fixture. There was a sour smell about him, as if he'd been up all night drinking.

Valentin turned her gaze back to the house. The Filipina housekeeper was on the porch, flapping dust from a cloth.

For a second, Valentin thought she was gesturing to her, but she turned and went back inside the house. 'Something doesn't fit,' she said. 'There's something they don't want to talk about. We'll have to get it out of the girl, when she's talking.'

She watched the house until the car window became too fogged to see. Timid sort, the old girl had said. Hardly spoke. Exemplary worker. References. Nursing certificate. That would explain the drawer load of benzos. She stared at Mooney's newspaper doodling for a moment. Mooney should have been in there, asking the questions. He was the DS. Twenty years in the job, he could've been inspector now. He just didn't give a shit any more.

She wound the window down a notch and dropped her smoke in the gutter. Through the drizzle, she saw that lights had gone on at the house, though it was barely four in the afternoon. Something didn't fit. Something they were holding back, if not the Filipina woman, then her employer. 'Poor Jane,' she'd said. 'Always struck me as a little pathetic. Not easy to like. I was letting her go in a few weeks, anyway. I can manage now with Felicia.' Felicia was the Filipina housekeeper.

The old girl, a thin, hawkish Scottish woman, was in her seventies. She'd hired Jane Coppin as her carer after suffering a stroke some months back. Maybe that was it, Valentin thought. Fear of being cut loose, no job. No support.

She wound the window up. 'Know what I think?' she told Mooney. 'There has to be a guy involved. Handyman, gardener, maybe. Fucked her and fucked off. Odds on she's knocked up.'

Mooney folded the newspaper and tossed it onto the back seat. He started the car. 'Keep it up, girl,' he said. 'We'll make a detective of you yet.'

Jane Coppin wasn't talking. Not about the benzos, not about wanting to kill herself. Valentin, perched on the edge of the bed, slipped her notebook back into her pocket.

The room was oppressively warm; outside, persistent late autumn rain beat against the window. A little chat, Mooney had said. Girl to girl. See if she opens up. It was the drawer load of benzos he was interested in. Who supplied them. Spurned lovers wanting to top themselves were for the shrink.

Valentin fished the notebook from her pocket and stared at the blank page. 'You got someplace to go?' she asked. 'When you get out of here.'

The meanest flicker of an eyelid. It was as if the bed had all but consumed her, the blanket tugged up to her chin, her freckled pasty face pressed into the pillow. Twenty-four. To Valentin, not much older herself, she seemed no more than a pubescent teenager. Parents dead, next of kin a married sister in Adelaide, according to hospital notes. It was all that could be teased out of her, once she was awake and lucid.

Maybe the old girl still had Coppin's references, Valentin thought. She flicked the page in her notebook. Flora McGregor, Casa Rosa. Hot property, Mooney reckoned: immaculate 1920s California bungalow, conservatory, manicured gardens. The whiff of old money. Not people who hire without careful vetting. As she slipped the notebook away, her mobile rang. Mooney. She left the room to take the call.

'Is she talking?' Mooney asked.

'Not to me.'

'Figures. Housekeeper just called in. You'll want to hear this.'

'There was a guy,' Valentin said. 'Didn't I say?'

'The old girl's grandson.'

'She never mentioned a grandson.'

'He lives there,' Mooney said. 'Delicate lad, by all accounts. Home schooled.'

Valentin glanced into the room. The girl lay as before, barely visible. 'How old?'

'Fourteen.'

The housekeeper, plump, fortyish, was ill at ease. A bead of sweat dripped from her long, pointed nose. A nose for people's dirty business, Valentin thought. She'd come with her husband, a stringy, grey-haired Caucasian sporting a dog collar. He wanted to sit in on the interview, but Mooney said no. God-botherers and Filipina brides. He couldn't hide his distaste. They waited while the housekeeper wiped her long nose with a tissue.

'Again for my colleague,' Mooney said. 'What you told me yesterday over the phone.'

'I do my job,' the housekeeper said. 'I don't pry. But I see things.'

'What did you see?' Mooney asked.

'Dominic – Mrs McGregor's grandson and that girl. Having sex.'

'Where?'

'In Mrs McGregor's studio.'

'The loft over the garage.'

'Mrs McGregor paints her pictures there. I am not allowed in. To clean.'

'So how did you see them having sex?'

'The window,' the housekeeper said. 'I saw them through the window.'

She started early that day. Five a.m. It was still dark. She was drinking tea in the kitchen when she heard footsteps on the stairs.

There were two attic rooms, one a small guest room, the other Miss Coppin's room. There were no guests at the house, so she knew it was Miss Coppin coming down the stairs. She was wearing her nightdress, the housekeeper said, who had come out of the kitchen to watch unobserved from the unlit hall. 'She is going to the toilet, I think, but no, so I follow her through the lounge and into the conservatory. There is a little light here because the moon is out and the sky is clear.' Miss Coppin has opened the conservatory door and gone into the garden. It is then that the housekeeper sees there is a light on in Mrs McGregor's studio. It is not a bright light, she says, just a little flickering light like from a candle. She watches Miss Coppin walk across the garden and then she looks up at the studio window again and there is Dominic with no shirt on, no undershirt, no nothing, as far as she can see. Miss Coppin has gone into the garage and Dominic is still at the window, but he is looking away because he hears Miss Coppin coming up the stairs. And then she is at the window, almost at the window, the housekeeper says, but she can see because Dominic is holding and kissing her, and then he pulls her nightdress over her head and then she doesn't see any more because they have gone away from the window.

'How long was she there?' Mooney asked. 'Did you see her return? Did you see Dominic?'

'Not Dominic. He sleeps sometimes in the studio. There is a sofa. Miss Coppin I see come back just before six a.m. Her feet are wet because of the dew. I am waiting for her by the stairs. "My goodness, girl," I say. "Have you been in the garden?" And she says, "Yes." She looks… I don't know. Like she has just woke up. And she says, "I was sleepwalking."'

'We talk to the boy,' Valentin said, after the housekeeper had gone. 'If he confirms it, we get Coppin in. Soon as she's discharged.'

'Can't talk to the kid without the old girl sitting in,' Mooney said. 'This one's for the DI. Do a search on Coppin. See if anything pops up.'

Valentin sat on the computer for twenty minutes, but there was nothing on Jane Coppin. Maybe before she was in Flora McGregor's employ she was someone else, she thought. New job, new name, old habits hidden. Did she know she was sprung, was that why she took the benzos? Did the old girl have her suspicions? She sensed it at the house, the two of them, McGregor and the housekeeper, holding something back. Why had the housekeeper come forward now? Mooney hadn't thought to ask. Was it at the minister's bidding? She must have told him. McGregor wouldn't have wanted it. Names in the newspaper. Bad enough having a dead employee to answer for. So many questions. Her mind was racing at the possibilities.

She looked for Mooney, but he was away from his desk. Lunchtime. She'd be sniffing beer and spearmint when he returned. Grabbing her coat and smokes, she left the station and drove across town to the hospital. Sex with a minor – statutory rape, if the boy was coerced. Timid sort, McGregor had said. Always the quiet ones… It pissed her, more than a little, that Mooney wanted it pushed upstairs. She got it, though: above his pay level. Way above hers, too, going it alone. But she wanted to hear Jane's side – if there was another side, if it wasn't all a figment of the housekeeper's imagination.

The girl was out of bed, sitting under the window, an iPod wired to her ear. She looked briefly at Valentin as she entered the room, then looked away.

Valentin closed the door and sat on the bed. The room was unbearably warm again. She loosened a button on her shirt. 'I don't want to know about the benzos,' she said. 'Not where you got them. I want to know why you took them.'

Jane had her face turned to the window, though there was nothing to see through the misted glass. She took the plug out of her ear. 'I didn't mean to do it,' she said. 'I don't sleep well. I took too many.'

'You walk in your sleep,' Valentin said.

The girl turned, sharply. 'Who told you that?'

'The housekeeper. Felicia. She came to the station this morning. She said she saw you in the garden. Sleepwalking.'

Jane turned away again, but there was nowhere to look. 'What else did she say?'

Valentin let the question dangle. She shouldn't have come. Mooney would go ape-shit if she compromised the case. A bare five weeks since she got her DC.'s badge. No one wanted a rogue detective on the team. But she had to know. 'The boy,' she said. 'Your employer's grandson. You had sex with him.'

'Dominic,' Jane said, after a pause. 'Yes.' Her breathing had tightened; she clenched and unclenched her pale bony fingers. Then she went very still. 'But it wasn't him.'

'She's delusional,' Valentin told Mooney, back at the station. 'Or pretending to be. Says she had sex four or five times with a young guy who looked like Dominic but whose name was Henry. Like he's got some kind of Jekyll and Hyde split personality. Presents as this sweet, innocent boy to hide his real nature, a precocious sexual predator. Except, the way she said it, it was like she believed he was a totally different guy altogether. Like inside Dominic there's this other guy Henry who's got a whole different persona and life story.'

Mooney didn't want to hear it. 'You expect me to take that shit upstairs? We'd both be back in uniform. Do a search on Coppin, I said. I don't recall telling you to go talk to her again. We need something concrete to give the DI, not the ravings of a suicidal tart with a fancy for teenage boys.'

'It's more than we had this morning,' Valentin said sourly. 'At least we know the housekeeper wasn't making it up.'

'Why would she?' Mooney said. 'What would be in it for her?'

Valentin was silent. He should've interviewed the girl himself, she thought. He should've been doing his job and not slipping out for a liquid lunch with his cronies. If she didn't push it, it was going upstairs and she'd be back to collating break and enter stats.

'Okay,' she said. 'What do we know? We know Coppin had sex with the boy. She's admitted it. If we can't talk to the boy, we should talk to his gran. I reckon Felicia told her what she'd seen and the old girl told her to keep it to herself. Jane would've been told to clear out, panicked because she thought she was going to get reported, and took the benzos. If the old girl backs up the housekeeper's allegation, you've got something solid to take to the DI.'

'Now you're using your head,' Mooney said. 'Exactly what I had in mind.'

'You have to understand,' Flora McGregor said. 'Dominic is not like other teenage boys. He's very insular, very withdrawn. I've had him since he was twelve, when his parents died. That awful car accident. He's had counselling, of course, but he's not really responded. He broods. Mr Tickner is good with him. His home tutor; he never settled in at school. Well, they don't, do they, not the deeply wounded like Dominic.'

It was hard to say what she made of the housekeeper's allegation. She had one of those austere, weathered faces that were hard to read.

Earlier she'd said, 'Felicia should have come to me with it. That'll be the pastor's doing.'

The pastor preached on the north side, an old suburb of warehouses and workingmen's cottages.

Valentin sensed Flora shared Mooney's distaste for the union. 'Maybe she thought you'd disbelieve her,' she said. 'It's a serious allegation.'

The housekeeper had gone home for the day. A bowl of fruit on a coffee table was the only offer of refreshment. Valentin peeled a banana while Mooney fidgeted. Sob stories about felon's lives made him impatient.

'You never suspected that Jane Coppin might be having sex with your grandson?' he said.

Flora sighed. 'To look at the girl…' She pulled herself out of her chair and fetched a framed photograph from a group on the sideboard. 'Like a Botticelli angel when he was a child. Still such a beautiful boy, don't you think?'

Valentin let her gaze linger.

Mooney said, 'You're avoiding the question.'

'It's an indelicate one,' Flora said, a little brusque. She returned the photograph to the sideboard. 'Is this why you think Jane tried to kill herself? Has she made some kind of confession?'

'She's yet to be formally interviewed,' Mooney admitted.

'So you only have Felicia's say-so.'

'Why would she make it up? Does she have a grievance?'

'Not with me. I've had her more than ten years. It's a question you should ask Jane.'

'We'd like to talk to Dominic,' Valentin said.

'I don't think so. Not before I've spoken to him.'

'We don't want to upset him,' Valentin said. 'If he denies it, that's the end of it.'

'I never much liked the girl,' Flora said. 'Jane. No presence. You know? Timid to the point of ethereal. I never once heard Dominic speak of her.'

'Is he home?'

'He's with Mr Tickner at the library. Come back tomorrow and maybe you can talk to him.' She ushered them out onto the porch. 'Felicia should have come to me,' she said, her hand at Mooney's elbow. Very disloyal, don't you think?'

Mooney drove back to the station.

Valentin lit a couple of smokes. 'I reckon Felicia's out of a job,' she said. 'What d'you make of Flora? She's a cagey one.'

'Not very cooperative,' Mooney said. 'Keeping something back.'

'She's protective of Dominic. What did you think? That photo. Butter wouldn't melt?'

'He needed a haircut.'

'You can see plain Jane falling for him.'

'Who fucked who?' Mooney said. 'That's the question. My money's on Coppin. That cock and bull about split personality. No Henry in there. Just a horny pretty-faced boy looking to lose his cherry. Easy picking for a little mouse like Coppin.'

'We should talk to the tutor. He might have had a sniff of something sus.'

'Tickner,' Mooney said. 'Only Tickner I know is a bookie. Wouldn't be him.'

A suspicious death kept Mooney with the DI most of the next day. Valentin spent the morning at her desk catching up on paperwork.

Lunchtime, she phoned the hospital to see how Jane Coppin was doing. She'd had a couple of visitors, a counsellor and a nun looking out for lost souls. It made Valentin think of Felicia's husband, the pastor. After phoning the McGregor house and getting no answer, she drove through sheeting rain to the north side.

Pastor Driffin's mission hall was at the end of a narrow cobbled lane, buttressed by a Moroccan steak house and a Vietnamese trader and payday lender. There was the whiff of paint and lacquer inside the hall, making Valentin think the cramped, gloomy space had once been an industrial workshop. She found the pastor in a small anteroom, reading to a skinny Asian girl of around thirteen or fourteen.

'Bhutanese,' he told Valentin after he'd sent the girl away. 'Many who come here are refugees with poor language skills. We do what we can.'

Valentin wondered if he'd met his Filipina wife through the mission, but didn't like to ask.

Driffin was still miffed at being kept out of the interview when she'd come to see Mooney. 'I would have spoken with Flora first,' he said, 'but Felicia thought she'd side with the girl if she denied it. And the boy was never going to admit to it.'

Valentin wanted Driffin's opinion of Dominic. She flipped the pages of her notebook. 'Insular, withdrawn. "He broods." Never got over his parents' death. Is that how you'd describe Dominic?'

'It's how Flora would describe Dominic,' Driffin said. He rummaged in a drawer for a packet of smokes. 'Have you spoken with him?'

'We're waiting for Flora's consent. I've seen his photograph.'

'What did you think?'

Valentin considered her response. 'I couldn't get past his take-me-to-bed eyes.'

Driffin seemed momentarily amused. He lit his smoke. 'His father was Italian, you know. Andreas Forenzio. Sicilian, actually. Came out as a lad in the sixties…'

Valentin jotted quickly as Driffin talked. The pastor's voice was soft and languid. There were long pauses as he drew on his smoke and slowly exhaled. In Valentin's mind's eye, she saw Andreas just turned seventeen, his parents returning to Sicily. He stays on, trains as a baker, marries Erin McGregor, whose mother Flora will become Dominic's guardian. They buy a modest home in a progressive suburb where Andrea continues to work as a baker. A son Vincenzo is born. Andreas takes Erin and Vincenzo to Sicily (his only return to his home country) where Dominic is conceived. Afterwards he is always playfully referred to within the family as 'the Sicilian boy', after his place of conception. And then tragedy; just after his seventeenth birthday, Vincenzo is stabbed to death in a brawl. Two years later, Andreas and Erin die in a fiery car smash after coming home late one night from a nightclub. Dominic is sent to live with Flora, his widowed grandmother…

Valentin reviewed her notes, an idiosyncratic shorthand of abbreviated words, dashes and exclamation marks. Names she wrote out in full and one underlined phrase. The Sicilian Boy. It made her think uncomfortably about what she'd said earlier.

'That remark about Dominic's photograph… I shouldn't have said it. It was unprofessional.'

Driffin stubbed his cigarette on a cracked saucer. 'I can't say I ever took to the boy,' he said. 'He's a little unhinged, if you ask me. Utterly self-absorbed. That's his nature, not his unfortunate circumstances. He's not changed measurably since Flora took him in. She has never sought spiritual guidance for him. Not from me, at any rate. Counselling apparently was of little help. He has no friends, that I'm aware of. Refuses to go to school. Peter Tickner, his home tutor, seems to be the only one he relates to. You should speak to him if you want a little more insight into the boy.'

Valentin slipped her notebook into her pocket. The Bhutanese girl had returned, hovering at the door with a takeaway coffee. She said the rain had stopped, the sun was shining. She'd been dancing in the puddles and her feet were wet.

'What did you make of Jane Coppin?' Valentin asked. 'Dominic obviously got close to her. Or she to him. D'you think she initiated the relationship, fed some need inside him for contact? Sex?'

Driffin said nothing for a moment. He took the coffee from the girl and told her to go into the hall to read. He closed the door. 'Flora told me something once, in an unguarded moment. She said Dominic adored his mother, and that his mother returned that adoration, even more intensely after Vincenzo's death. She said…she thought the relationship unhealthy.' He paused a moment to clarify his recollection. 'She may have said unnatural. In particular, it concerned her that her daughter would allow the boy to see her naked, right up to the year she died when Dominic had just turned twelve. Her reasoning, apparently, was that until the boy's voice broke he was an innocent.' He paused again, bringing his face close enough to Valentin's for her to smell the cigarette on his breath. 'You should get Flora to show you a photograph of Erin,' he said. 'She's more of a beauty, but she bears a marked resemblance to Jane Coppin.'

Valentin returned to the station to type up her notes. She did a search on the car smash that had killed Dominic's parents and found the bare details, but no photographs. It was a single-vehicle accident, late at night, speed and alcohol probable contributing factors. Andreas was driving. Vincenzo's death was more interesting. A top student with a couple of minor convictions for marijuana possession, he was knifed in a milk bar after an altercation with another local lad. The pair were known to each other, but not close friends. Both were carrying knives and according to the investigating detective's notes it was a 'dick fight', a couple of young bloods squaring off. The nineteen-year-old killer got eight years' detention.

A search on Flora McGregor revealed that she had a small reputation as a watercolourist, a 'naïve painter of no particular school', according to the brief bio. There was little personal information other than the date of her Scottish birth, her current state of residence and that she'd formally been an English teacher.

Finishing her notes, Valentin phoned Casa Rosa again, still getting no answer. The endless ringing made her uneasy. If no one was home, she would have expected an answering machine to kick in. According to Driffin, Felicia was still in Flora's employ (there'd been 'words' over the perceived disloyalty), but this late in the afternoon she'd have probably gone home. If Flora was ensconced in her studio with her paints and brushes, she guessed Dominic was out with Peter Tickner again. She made a mental note to get Flora's mobile number.

Mooney came in just as she was packing up to go home. He slumped into his chair, stretched his long legs under the desk.

Valentin sketched him in on her interview with Driffin and what she knew of the Forenzio family deaths. 'I can't get an answer from the McGregor house,' she told him. 'We should go back tomorrow. Early. If we don't get to talk to Dominic, we should get Flora or Felicia to show us a picture of his mother.'

Mooney opened his mouth but nothing came out. Working with the DI all day had exhausted him. He sent Valentin to the coffee machine while he called his bookie.

She stood at the tearoom window listening to the coffee dribbling into Mooney's cracked mug. Squally rain whipped against the glass. The weather had turned again. Halfway back to her desk, her phone rang, a number she didn't recognise.

It was Jane Coppin. 'They want me to talk to a counsellor,' she said. 'I don't know what to say. About Dominic. It'll just sound too weird. Or like I'm making it up. What should I do?'

Valentin took a detour into the Ladies. She checked that all the cubicle doors were open. 'I'll come and see you tonight,' she said. 'We can talk. Just you and me, like girlfriends. No cop stuff. I want to help you, Jane. I want to know the truth about Dominic.'

Back at the desk, Mooney grumbled about the time she took getting his coffee. He gave her a list of names he wanted her to check out in the morning, known associates of his suspicious death victim, a forty-something prostitute and drug addict, found at the bottom of the community stairs of the rooming house where she lived. Her neck was broken, cause unknown until they had the autopsy report.

'Maybe she got it falling down the stairs,' Mooney said, 'or pushed, or maybe some junked up punter snapped it for her.' There was a de facto too, subject of a restraining order, who'd slipped off the radar.

Valentin wanted to know what they were doing about Felicia Driffin's allegation against Jane Coppin. She could see it getting pushed onto the back burner, or dropped altogether.

Mooney took a mouthful of bitter coffee and spat it back into the mug. The Coppin case, he said brusquely, wasn't going anywhere until the boy had been interviewed, and the DI had it in hand. He told her to go home.

Twenty minutes after leaving the station, she pulled into the narrow overgrown drive of a red-brick house with a rounded bay window at the front. Inside, there were rooms off a long gloomy hallway and a large farmhouse-style kitchen at the back. The house was small, cramped and cluttered from years of shared residency with her mother Sal. There was a father, Hal, long gone from Valentin's life, a middle-aged hippy lost somewhere in the Gold Coast hinterland and rarely heard from. Sal never spoke of him, barely remembered him, except on the odd good days when she managed to stay off the vodka. Valentin found her propped in front of the TV, a joint dangling from her lips, a glass at her fingertips. She presented a coarse, pasty cheek to be kissed and Valentin noted the drooping eyelids and sour breath. The air in the room was dry and overheated, the TV loud enough to be heard in the street.

Valentin hung her coat in the hall and grabbed a beer from the fridge. Some kind of meat and onion stew was simmering on the stove, the sauce thick and caramelised from hours of slow cooking. She stood at the window and stared into the garden with its rampant late season herbs and ageing, unkempt lemon trees. The rain had eased again to a light drizzle, the evening light fading as she watched.

The DI had it in hand… She'd been mulling over Mooney's parting words since she'd left the station. What did it mean? The DI was going to take over the investigation? Or quietly drop it for lack of meaningful evidence? Mooney hadn't shown a shit of interest in what she'd discovered about the Forenzio family or Driffin's observation about Jane and Dominic's mother. If he was pissed off with her, it wasn't because she'd forgotten to sugar his coffee.

She killed the gas under the stew and took her beer into the front room. Sal had dozed off, her head slumped forward, the half smoked joint lying in her lap. Valentin put a light to the tip and slipped it between her lips. She grabbed the TV remote, muting the sound and flicking from channel to channel before turning the set off. She smelt it then, the familiar whiff of urine soiling the cushion under Sal's matchstick legs. She let the joint burn out and then went to her bedroom to change her clothes. If she left now, she'd be gone before Sal woke. She pulled on a pair of black boots and buttoned the red woollen coat she'd bought herself as a treat for making DC. She checked her face in the mirror, lowering her gaze at the point of eye contact. It was a little after six-thirty. She could grab a sandwich in the hospital café before going up to see Jane. In the hall, she paused at the front room door. She'd left her car keys on the table in the front room next to Sal's bottle of Smirnoff.

Sal was rousing as she entered. 'I've peed myself, sweetie,' she said. 'Give us a hand, there's a good girl.' She waited to be helped out of the chair.

'I'm going out,' Valentin said. She hated the icy indifference in her voice. 'You'll have to shower and change yourself.'

Sal slumped back into the chair, staring at some point over Valentin's shoulder. Again this shit, Valentin thought miserably. Unbuttoning her coat, she pulled Sal up from the chair and helped her out of her soiled pants and knickers. Half an hour to get her in and out of the shower and dressed again. She reheated the stew and tossed the pissed-on cushion onto the back porch. A job for the morning.

Jane wasn't picking up on her phone, so she left a message that she'd be there in an hour or so, texting the same info for good measure. Sal was sobered a little after the shower, wanting company. Valentin shared the stew and Sal's rambling chat and then put her back in front of the TV.

'I'll be gone a while,' she said. 'You can put yourself to bed.' She grabbed the vodka bottle before Sal could refresh her glass.

Outside it was cold and dry. A loose pattern of glittering stars had appeared in the night sky. Jane still wasn't picking up, but there was little point leaving a message. She'd be at the hospital in fifteen minutes.

It was after nine when she drove up. There was a squad car on the forecourt and a huddle of people under the bright entrance lights.

Valentin nodded to a uniformed constable, a plump rooky she sat with sometimes in the canteen. 'What's going on?' she asked.

'Jumper,' the constable said. 'From the roof garden. Some mental patient. You don't want to look.'

Jane Coppin's suicide closed the investigation as far as Mooney was concerned. She was simply finishing off what she started when she took the benzos. 'Guilty as charged, your honour,' he joked. He was in an unnaturally buoyant mood. Maybe he'd had a win on the horses, Valentin didn't ask. She felt anything but buoyant. She'd let Jane down, not being there for her when she'd promised. It was Sal's fault, but venting at her mother wasn't going to change anything. Neither would telling Mooney that she'd gone to the hospital, so she kept that to herself. But she couldn't stop brooding over the phone call, the fear and anxiety in the girl's voice. There were still questions to be answered; she wasn't ready to let it go.

'We know there was an affair,' she told Mooney. 'Whoever instigated it, Jane was always going to cop the blame. Shame. Guilt. She killed herself because she couldn't face the exposure. We owed her a hearing, if nothing else.'

Mooney wasn't having it. He'd spoken with the DI, who'd said there was no point questioning the boy now, if they couldn't get Coppin's response to the allegation. They'd done what they could with the information they had, in the time they had. 'Leave it for the coroner,' he said. 'That's the DI's view.' He poked through the mess of papers on Valentin's desk. 'What've you got on those names I gave you?'

Valentin spent the morning in front of her computer while Mooney went off with the DI again. Around ten, she took a break and phoned the McGregor house.

Felicia picked up. 'Mrs McGregor is in her studio,' she said. 'She is not to be disturbed.'

Valentin left a message to be called back and returned to her work. Flora wouldn't know. There'd been a local media report about an accidental death at the hospital, but no name given. Suicides were rarely reported until the coronial inquiry.

Lunchtime, she went across the road for a bite to eat and called the house again. 'I need to talk to Mrs McGregor,' she told the housekeeper. 'Jane Coppin is dead.'

There was a whispered oath in Felicia's mother tongue. Then she said, 'Dead? How come dead?'

Valentin wasn't prepared to say. She waited for Flora to come on the line. 'She jumped,' Valentin told her. 'From the roof garden.'

Flora said nothing.

'I need to talk to you,' Valentin said. 'Privately.'

'Come at two-thirty,' Flora said.

'Can I speak to Dominic?'

'We'll see. I don't want him upset.'

'I want to be there when he's told,' Valentin said.

A blustery wind whipped up leaves and litter as she drove. Mooney was right about the house: old money property in an old money inner-city suburb. If there was new money, it came from lawyers and corporate bosses, new tech entrepreneurs. The DI might make it, but a lowly DC. could only dream. Mooney's home, when he went there, was out in the sticks someplace, a fifties red-brick box he shared with a disappointed wife and four unruly kids.

Valentin parked in the street and stood a moment inside the gate, getting a sense of the house and grounds. It was the garage that interested her, with its studio loft over. She crunched up the gravel drive, obscured from the house by a row of dense hawthorn bushes. The garage was separate from the bungalow, built of the same stone and timber, wide enough to take two vehicles. The heavy timber doors would have been hung almost a hundred years ago, she guessed, when the house was built. There was little evidence of the loft above, other than a square window in the centre of the high pitched gable. Too small and not visible from the conservatory, so not the one referred to in Felicia's statement.

Stepping off the drive to get a better sense of the building, she saw that she was being observed. A man of about Driffin's age, lean and wiry with thinning white hair was standing under a tree, dragging on a cigarette. Brown jacket and pants, loose tie; not the gardener. Dominic's tutor, she guessed. Dropping the cigarette at his feet, he took a step towards her, and then stopped. His name was being called from somewhere behind the garage, a voice as clear and melodic as birdsong.

'Pe – ter… Pe – ter…'

A girl's voice, she thought instinctively. Or a boy's, barely broken.

She was back in the station by three. Felicia had answered the door, and then stepped aside, leaving Valentin to confront Flora McGregor's lawyer. There would be no interview with Flora and definitely no talking to Dominic. The allegation of sexual misconduct was withdrawn. Dominic had denied it and the housekeeper was no longer sure what she saw through the studio window. Jane Coppin was dead. The lawyer, a bearded grey-haired veteran of the local courts, warned Valentin against further contact with the family. The housekeeper shut the door in her face.

Mooney was still out with the DI. She went to the Ladies to freshen up. A bad night's sleep had left her looking drawn and sickly. Her cheeks were flushed from the bitter wind. There was the flush of humiliation too, from the dressing down the lawyer had given her. She shouldn't have been there; her DCI had been advised of the allegation withdrawal. She guessed the advice was still trickling down the chain of command.

Back at her desk, she started putting together the notes she'd gathered for Mooney on the suspicious death, but her mind wasn't on it. She kept hearing that birdlike call from behind the garage, the twin descending syllables singing the tutor's name. They never did get to talk to Peter Tickner. Wasn't it Driffin who'd said they should speak to Dominic's tutor if they wanted some insight into the boy? Whatever mental picture she'd had of him before, it wasn't the wiry, brown-coated guy she'd seen in the garden, stealing a smoke. If he hadn't been called away, she might have got some morsel of information out of him before the lawyer sent her packing. There was something imperative about that call, however birdlike. Called back to the nest, she thought, out of danger. She remembered the purposeful pace as he strode away.

Clearing the mess of notes from her keyboard, she punched his name into her computer. Nothing on him in the police database, but a web search turned up Peter Tickner as author of a local newspaper feature on crimes and suspicious deaths associated with city properties. She scanned the article to the penultimate paragraph where she read that sometime around 1920 Henry (Harry) Bull, a self-made man made rich brewing beer, married Julia Mendez, an Argentine beauty he'd met while travelling in South America. He built a house for her, an expansive California bungalow, hid it behind high stone walls and called it Duckworth. They had one son, Henry (called Little Henry), who died suddenly when he was fourteen. His mother's death the year before, which affected him deeply, was reportedly due to a cocaine overdose. The link between the two deaths was the subject of much rumour and gossip, but no court case ensued. Talk of the suicide of a third person in the house circulated for a number of years. Henry Bull sold Duckworth soon after the boy's death. The property changed hands a number of times before it was bought by the renown painter Flora McGregor in the late nineties. She renamed the house Casa Rosa after the home of her Scottish childhood.

Sal was asleep when she got home, snoring like a dog in front of the bellowing TV. Valentin lit the gas heater in the kitchen, opened a can of soup and sat with a beer while she tried to make sense of what she'd read. Two Henrys: Henry the brewer and – the one who interested her – Little Henry, mysteriously dead at fourteen a year after his mother's coke overdose. This surely was the Henry of Jane Coppin's fevered imagination. Jane thought (or had been led to think) she was having sex with a teenage lad who died eighty years ago. So what was this, some warped sex game gone wrong? And whose crazy idea was it? Never Jane's, given her mental state, unless it was getting caught by Felicia that unbalanced her. Dominic, then. Tickner would have to be involved; who else would Dominic have got the story from? And who was the third person in the house back then, rumoured to have suicided? She needed to dig deeper. If Tickner didn't invent the story, there had to be more archived information than his bare account in the local rag.

Turning the gas off from under the soup, she went into the front room to check on her mother. Sal was still dead to the world, head rolled to one side, mouth gaping. There'd always been booze, as long as Valentin could remember. What little she could recollect of her father was of him and Sal, high on pot and cheap wine, crooning folk songs to Hal's strummed guitar. Until she was seven or eight, they all lived in a commune in the hills above Byron Bay. She had no idea what Hal brought to the commune in the way of skills or trade, but for most of Valentin's wandering childhood and adolescence Sal earned a decent crust reading palms and tarot cards. All so much hokum to Valentin, though it was never anything but Sal's firm conviction that she had the gift. Part of her shtick was putting herself into a trance and channelling the dead for an endless stream of credulous grieving punters. Was this Dominic's game, Valentin wondered, channelling long dead Little Henry for a naïve, sexually frustrated Jane? Driffin reckoned Dominic's unnatural attraction to Jane was her likeness to his mother. What if it was the same illicit attraction subject of much rumour and gossip connecting the deaths at Duckworth all those long years ago?

In the morning, she phoned in sick. A touch of flu, she said; she had a doctor's appointment for eleven. Too many cigarettes had left her with a croaky voice and a tight chest, but otherwise she felt fine. She phoned Mooney, who told her the DI would be needing a word with her when she came in. The complaint to the DCI from Flora McGregor's lawyer was trickling down the chain of command.

She tried telling him about Tickner's newspaper feature article, but he didn't want to hear it.

'You're starting to sound as crazy as Coppin,' he said. 'Drop it. Don't matter what was going on, with Coppin dead there's nothing to investigate.'

She croaked something unintelligible and hung up. She knew he was right; she was jeopardising her career pursuing it when she'd been warned off, but she couldn't let go. Something about the case had got into her blood. She wasn't doing it for Jane any more. She was doing it because she had to know.

Showered and stoked with strong coffee, she left the house. The day was cold and overcast, bleakly wintery. It was a Thursday, and Thursdays, Jane had told her, were always a day out for Dominic. Sometimes it was the baths, sometimes the art gallery, and just occasionally, if it was an appropriate movie, a morning at the flicks. If she was going to get close to Dominic, it would have to be away from the house.

Approaching Casa Rosa, she pulled her little Fiat to the side of the road and switched off the engine. She remembered the description Tickner had given in his article. If nothing else much had changed, the high wall that Henry Bull built around the house had at some point disappeared and been replaced by a dense, two-metre-high box hedge. Chewing on a dry salad roll she'd picked up at the servo, she watched a junk-mailer work the street, picking her way through a mush of slippery composting leaves.

After about twenty minutes, a green early model Falcon pulled out of the Casa Rosa drive and turned towards her. She sank back into her seat, keeping an eye on the Falcon as it passed. Tickner, a hand sweeping through his thinning white hair, was driving. The glimpse she had of the figure beside him was her first sighting of Dominic.

Leaving the quiet streets of the suburb, she nearly lost sight of them in the heavy stream of traffic heading into the CBD. It was the wrong direction for the baths, and once they'd crossed the river and headed north she knew that neither the flicks nor the art gallery were on the day's agenda. Pastor Driffin's mission hall lay further into the old industrial suburb, but what business they'd have with him she couldn't think.

About halfway along the main street, the Falcon took a sharp left into a narrow lane of workshops and light industry fabricators. She pulled the Fiat over, letting the engine idle while she watched the Falcon cruise slowly down the lane. She worried that Tickner knew they were being tailed. If he was one of those nervy rear-mirror watchers, he would have noted the Fiat soon after leaving Casa Rosa. At the bottom of the lane, the Falcon's left indicator flashed, and the vehicle turned out of sight.

She moved the Fiat forward until she was within a hundred metres from where the Falcon turned. Parking her car tight against a brick wall, she walked the last stretch.

The Falcon had pulled into a small yard, shaded by neighbouring buildings. It faced a wide roller door in dire need of a coat of paint. A garage, she thought, or a storage shed; there was nothing over the door to identify the building. Built of the dull red brick typical of the suburb, there was just the whiff of oil, making her think it was maybe a private auto repair shop. A path to the side of the building led to a rear door. There were no windows other than a small grimy fanlight over the door.

Putting her ear to the door, she heard the murmur of voices. A tight, girlish giggle would have to be Dominic's. Taking her phone from her pocket, she raised it over her head and quickly snapped a photograph. Neither Dominic nor Tickner were in the grainy shot, but she'd been right about it being an auto workshop. The vehicle, what she could make of it, was one of those sleek, classy vintage jobs. Some restoration project, she guessed; Tickner must be an old car nut. Raising her phone again, she risked a second shot. Tickner was there, his head under the car's raised bonnet. In front of the car, almost out of the shot, but recognisable from Flora's photograph was the Forenzios' orphan, angelic Dominic. The Sicilian Boy.

She found Driffin where she'd met him before, in the small room at the side of the mission hall. He was alone, tinkering with the broken element of a bread toaster. Felicia would have told him the case had been dropped, but he seemed unsurprised to see her.

'The girl's death,' he said. 'You feel responsible. It's understandable.'

Valentin had convinced herself that Jane's death was down to Sal, but it wasn't something she wanted to share with Driffin. It wasn't Jane she wanted to talk about, or Dominic, particularly. It was Casa Rosa, and what Driffin knew about the deaths that occurred there eighty years ago.

The pastor sighed a little and pushed the toaster aside. 'You've been talking to Peter Tickner,' he said. 'That sordid affair is one of his pet interests.'

'I read the article he wrote,' Valentin said. 'He mentioned an unnamed suicide. And there was nothing about the cause of Little Henry's death.' She flipped the pages of her notebook.

Driffin hesitated to respond. 'Why would this interest you? It has nothing to do with Dominic and this girl.'

'I think it has,' she said. 'I think Jane's suicide is connected to it.'

Driffin rose from his chair and closed the door, though there was no one in the hall. There was a former parishioner of his, he said, a woman named Bea Holder. Valentin should talk to her. 'She's in nursing care, now. Very frail physically and almost blind, but mentally sharp as a tack. Her father was one of the investigating detectives.'

'So there was an investigation.'

'Not into his wife's death, though it was common knowledge in their circle that she was a cocaine addict. Harry Bull had a lot of influence. The boy's death was a different matter. He was found dead in the garage with his art tutor, an English woman Harry had employed during the summer holidays to teach the boy to draw. He had something of a talent, apparently. The woman's name was Alice Hopgood. Early twenties, fresh off the boat, nothing known about her. Harry never suspected. She must have been a charmer – though Harry, of course, married to a cocaine abuser, you'd have to question his judgement. I don't know how it got out, probably some servant's tittle-tattle. The consequences for Hopgood would have been dire. Impressionable boy, rapacious young woman. It was never determined who initiated the suicide, not officially, though naturally the blame fell on the tutor. Harry managed to keep it out of the newspapers.' Driffin paused to light a cigarette.

Valentin glanced up from her notebook.

The pastor looked uncomfortable, as if he'd betrayed a confidence. 'Speak to Bea Holder,' he said. 'She has her father's notes and cuttings. Tickner interviewed her, but she never took to him.'

Valentin bought a takeaway coffee to drink in the car. It was midday, but she didn't feel like eating. She skimmed her notes: Alice Hopgood

– art tutor – sex with Henry – exposed by servant – suicide… It was too much like Jane and Dominic's situation to be coincidence.

Driffin couldn't remember how the couple died; poisoned, he seemed to recall. His former parishioner would have the details. Valentin had hoped he would phone the nursing home, check on the old girl's health and lucidity. Mention her name and interest in the case.

'A cop's interest in old cases,' she said. 'I don't want her thinking I'm there on police business.'

Driffin was already regretting the information he'd given her. He was worried for Felicia's position at Casa Rosa if his blabbering got back to Flora. A pastor's pay wouldn't amount to much. He gave her the address of the nursing home and said he'd rather she kept his name out of it. He would've known from her careless words of assurance that she wouldn't.

The nursing home was across town, about half an hour's drive. Valentin tossed the coffee cup and started the car. Pulling into the traffic, her mobile rang, a number and voice she didn't recognise.

'Detective Valentin,' the voice said. 'You've been following me.'

Peter Tickner. To give her grief? Or something useful?

'I want to talk to Dominic,' she said. 'Just me and him, no police stuff. Can you arrange it?'

'Maybe. Go back to my workshop. I've left something there for you.'

'What is it?'

'You'll find it.' He paused. She could hear music in the background, some discordant jazz piece. 'It's from Dominic.'

She drove to the next junction and then doubled back through the suburb. Her driving was erratic, too fast. The coffee and lack of food was making her mind race. What would Dominic have that would interest her? What interest would Dominic have in her, other than her persistent attempts to speak to him? She worried that she was being played, that it was Tickner doing the playing. How did he get her number, unless it was from the business card she left at the house? What if she was being manipulated, as she was sure Jane was manipulated? What if she was just an extension of the game? The game both Tickner and Dominic were playing? She couldn't focus for too many questions. The Fiat sped down the lane and into the yard of Tickner's workshop.

There was a fresh oil drip where the Falcon had stood. She thought she could hear the low hum of an engine idling inside the workshop, but it was from a neighbouring building. There was nothing for her to find near the roller door. She walked down the side of the building. Behind the step of the side door was a large brown envelope, weighed down with a brick. Inside the envelope was a single sheet of paper. A portrait of a young woman, sketched expertly in pencil. She gazed at it, spellbound. Not for its exquisite execution, but its familiarity. The face was her own.

Mooney phoned as she was getting back into her car. She'd already tried ringing Tickner back, but he wasn't picking up.

Mooney was sitting in his car outside her house. 'Your mother reckons you're at work,' he said. 'You want to tell me what the fuck you're playing at?'

'I'm doing my job,' Valentin said. She was pissed with him for checking up on her, but she wanted him to know what she'd discovered.

Mooney smoked while he listened. She could hear his wheezing breath and her neighbour's kids yelling in the street.

Getting Driffin to give up what he knew about the Henry Bull/Alice Hopgood suicide as well as his informant was just police work. It was Dominic's portrait that spooked her. 'It's me,' she told Mooney. 'The spitting image. How could he even know what I look like? We've never met.'

Mooney had no answer. 'You need to steer clear of him,' he said. 'What d'you know about Tickner?'

'Nothing much. No form. Lives alone. History and old car nut. There's a fancy-looking vintage vehicle in his workshop. I'd like to get inside, take a look around.'

'You need cause for a search,' Mooney said. 'What're you looking for?'

Valentin couldn't say, specifically. She knew what she wanted: evidence of a conspiracy to get Coppin to commit an indecent act.

'Talk to the DI in the morning,' Mooney said. 'Make a case for a proper investigation into Coppin's suicide. And stay away from the nursing home. You're in enough shit already. One more formal complaint and you'll be back in uniform.'

Valentin hung up. Mooney was right, she was pushing her luck. But she wasn't done yet. If she was going to make a strong case to the DI, she needed all there was to know about Little Henry Bull and Alice Hopgood. She needed whatever it was Bea Holder had that she didn't show Tickner.

Picking up the journey she'd abandoned when Tickner phoned, she drove south. Heavy rain had settled in, the Fiat's ageing wipers barely coping. An accident on the southern outlet kept her stuck in traffic for half an hour. A text from Mooney came with a photo attachment. It was a 2011 news report pic of Flora McGregor accepting some art award. Standing beside her was a younger woman identified as the artist's daughter, Erin Forenzio. Valentin scrutinised the woman's face. A marked resemblance to Jane Coppin, Driffin had reckoned. Valentin couldn't see it. If Dominic had found something of his mother in Jane, it wasn't in her appearance.

The rain had eased by the time she reached the nursing home, a sprawling community of units and chalets on the southern fringe of the city. It was mostly residential accommodation, with a small block reserved for nursing care. Valentin dropped Driffin's name to the receptionist and said the pastor had asked her to look in on his former parishioner. The room, as neat and compact as a motel unit, smelt vaguely of a fish lunch. Valentin had a fleeting vision of Sal sitting in the wing chair under the window, thin and desiccated from years of alcoholic abuse.

Bea Holder held out a limp hand and told the receptionist to bring tea. 'The Duckworth suicides,' she murmured after Valentin had briefly detailed the reason for her visit. 'My father was the investigating detective, you know. Such a scandal.' She gestured for Valentin to bring her chair closer. Her voice was soft and precise, her gaze disconcertingly fixed on some point over Valentin's shoulder. 'They blamed the girl, of course. So much older. Henry Bull was a powerful man. Intimidating. Told my father, if there was any suggestion of perversion on his boy's part, he'd have his job.'

'He was young,' Valentin said. 'Fourteen. You think he could've initiated the affair? What was the conclusion of your father's investigation?'

'Well, they were gassed, weren't they? Fumes from the car.'

'So it was definitely suicide.'

'Gassed,' she said again. 'Sitting in the back seat. He wrote it all down.' She cocked her head, listening for the receptionist bringing the tea.

Valentin felt light-headed, a little breathless. She needed to eat; her blood sugar level was in free fall. 'Do you have it?' she said. 'What he wrote?'

There was a notebook, but she could only look at it. A reporter had come a while back, Valentin was told, writing a story on the case; he'd taken things away and not returned them. A bony finger indicated the bottom drawer of an antique tallboy. Beneath neatly folded sweaters and pants, Valentin found a yellowing, dog-eared envelope. A photograph slipped out with the notebook. Grainy, black and white. Taken at the scene. Valentin's pulse quickened.

'This was the car.'

'Henry Bull's Chevrolet. He liked flashy American cars.'

'Do you know what happened to it?'

'Afterwards? No. I expect he sold it. There was another picture. Of the girl. I gave it to that beastly reporter.'

'A photograph,' Valentin said. 'Of Alice Hopgood.'

'Not a photograph. A drawing. The boy did it. It was why she was there. To teach him to draw.'

The gardener found them. There'd been high winds overnight and he'd come in early to clear the grounds of fallen branches. Walking up the drive, he heard the car idling in the garage and smelt fumes. The rear door to the garage was unlocked. He noticed the hose trailing from the car's exhaust to the rear passenger window before managing to switch off the ignition. After opening the garage doors to clear the air, he saw the bodies slumped in the back seat. The servants were alerted, Harry Bull raised from his bed and the authorities called. Detective Ellis was the first senior police officer on the scene. Hopgood, he noted, was sitting upright, her chin on her chest. The boy had fallen across the seat away from her. Sexual activity had occurred before death; the girl's knickers had been removed, the boy's trouser buttons undone, his member exposed. Ellis interviewed Bull, servants and neighbours. A sixteen-year-old maid admitted that she'd befriended Hopgood and gained her confidence. The tutor, she said, liked talking about the English boys she'd been out with and which ones were better lovers. She confessed an attraction to her student, who was sweet-looking and had a sing-song voice. There was a falling out between the women over a borrowed skirt, returned to the maid torn and stained. She threatened to report Hopgood's dirty business with the boy if she wasn't compensated. She admitted to Ellis that she'd never actually seen the tutor acting in any way improper with the boy and that Hopgood might have been making it up to tease her. A search of Hopgood's room turned up numerous racy novels, sketches of the boy in various stages of undress and a notebook of obscene poetry. A book of paintings was left opened on her bed. *The Death of Chatterton*, Ellis wrote, depicts a young eighteenth-century poet sprawled dead on his bed after swallowing strychnine. Nothing incriminating was found in the boy's room. His sketchbooks were comprised almost entirely of copies from the Old Masters.

A block from the nursing home, Valentin pulled into a servo and ordered an egg sandwich and a can of Red Bull. She'd photographed

Ellis's notes with her phone camera, but she'd need a bigger screen to read them properly. The evidence pointed to Hopgood initiating the sex, but Valentin wasn't convinced. There was no mention of Henry's portrait of Alice, but a telling note about papers burned in the grate in the boy's bedroom. If Henry had destroyed his own incriminating drawings, how come the portrait had survived? Was it overlooked, slipped between the pages of some reference book? And how come Ellis had it? If he'd discovered it unobserved, what made him keep it for himself? And the big question for Valentin, the unnerving one of Alice's uncanny resemblance to herself. Not impossible in the world of spooky coincidences, but this was too weird to dismiss. It was as if some part of her were Alice – or, weirder still, some part of Alice was revealing itself in her. Bea Holder would have seen the likeness, if she'd not been near blind. Tickner saw it. He recognised her in the grounds of Casa Rosa before being called away. She heard it again, that birdlike cry singing his name from somewhere out of sight. Pe – ter… Pe – ter… As sweet-looking Henry might have sung out to his beloved Alice.

A cold, dry westerly replaced the squally rain. She shared a scratch meal with Sal, who'd forgotten Mooney's visit earlier, and then walked the block to her local watering hole. Drinking with Sal depressed her and she had a mind to get a little drunk, if only to dull the turmoil in her head. Bea Holder had left her with more questions than answers as well as an increasing sense of unease. The disquiet followed her along the dark street until she entered the brightly lit lobby of the hotel. Leather-clad bikers crowded the bar, lip-synching to a band pumping out eighties rock. In a back room, a group of guys she'd dated at various times kept her plied with beer and passed joints around. She left at closing time, drunker than she'd intended and a little high. Sal had already taken herself to bed, leaving dirty dishes in the sink and a near empty bottle of vodka on the table. Valentin took a nip from the bottle and smoked another joint. Her head spun as she undressed for bed and she fought back an urge to throw up. Reaching for the light switch, she noted the time on the clock: 11.43.

Sleep took her, deep and dreamless until some timeless hour of the night when she sensed movement beside her. She struggled to wake before giving herself up to a dream that was charged with a lover's presence. Whether it was Henry or Dominic, she couldn't say, but it was a soft-voiced boy with her, his sour breath in her mouth, his loins moving rhythmically between her legs. In her dream, she was neither Alice nor herself, but some spectre of lust and desire in her lover's imagination. She woke as he drew from her, his thin, pale body sliding from under the sheet into the blackness of the cold room. The dream's intensity filled her with an unaccountable horror, and she lay for a long moment until her breathing eased and the sheets felt cold and clammy against her flesh. The clock showed 3.21. Slipping free of the damp sheets, she rolled herself in the doona and fell again into a deep, dreamless sleep until the 6.30 alarm startled her awake.

Showered and dressed, she studied her drawn face in the mirror and put the dream out of her head. It was just the case getting to her, her fixation with Dominic Forenzio. Mooney was right, she'd end up as crazy as Jane Coppin if she didn't take a step back. She was too involved; she was becoming a part of the narrative. Any connection between Jane's death and an eighty-year-old double suicide had to be forensically investigated. Total detachment. And through the appropriate channel of command. Meanwhile, she had a job to go to. She lifted the blind. Early morning mist obscured a pale, wintery sun.

Sal was up, cloaked in her op shop chenille dressing gown, warming her hands on a mug of cocoa. She'd lit the stove to take the chill from the air. 'He's gone, then,' she said. A touch disapproving.

Valentin didn't ask. She dropped a slice of bread in the toaster and then noticed the brown envelope on the table, Henry's sketch of Alice half revealed. She had no recollection of leaving it there. It wasn't something she wanted Sal to see. 'Who's gone?' she said. The note of disapproval nudged memories of childhood mischief.

'Your lover,' Sal said. She lifted her long, gloomy face so Valentin could see the simmering anger. 'What're you thinking of, girl? You're sleeping with a child.'

She'd seen him. In the early hours, when she was shuffling half asleep down the hall to the toilet. He was there in front of her. And then he was gone, inside Valentin's room with the barest click of the door closing.

Valentin shook her head. 'You saw no one.' Her voice was tight. 'There's no light in the hall. You were drunk.'

There was light from the street. Filtered through coloured glass in the front door, it was light enough to see his face. A boy's face, Sal said, skin too soft for a razor.

'You dreamed it,' Valentin insisted. 'There was no one there.' She heard the toaster pop. 'I'm going to work.'

She swept the envelope with Henry's sketch from the table and took it to her room. The air felt bitterly cold after the warm kitchen. She flicked the light switch, taking a moment to get her breath. Sal was losing it. All the years of vodka and dope. There was no one there. Not in the hall, not in her room. She pulled the doona from the floor where she'd dumped it after crawling out of bed. The sheet. Where she'd lain, there was a stain. A semen stain.

Five minutes before she reached the station, her phone rang.

'Come to my workshop,' Tickner said. 'We're waiting for you.'

'I know,' Valentin said. 'I'm coming.'

She continued driving through the CBD, across the river to the north side. The morning traffic was heavy, the Fiat's worn gears crunching each time she changed down. She turned on the radio. Jazz; the notes undulating and discordant. Tickner's music. She turned the dial, but the music continued. She knew what was happening; she was no longer in charge. The case was closed. She'd made herself part of the narrative and there was no stepping back.

The traffic eased and the Fiat picked up speed. It was as if there were another's hands at the wheel, a foot heavier than hers on the pedal. Someone used to driving a vintage car. Henry Bull's Chevrolet. The time Tickner must have put in to track it down, she thought. She sees him, sitting stiffly behind the steering wheel. Like a store mannequin, expressionless. Unreal. Behind him, she can't see. But she knows he's there. Dominic. Little Henry. It doesn't matter which of them. Because they're one and the same. As she is both Valentin and Alice Hopgood…

A bus pulled out in front of her. The Fiat changed lanes, swept past. She understood now. Jane had been a mistake, or a misdirection. Or maybe a lure… They were all playthings of a force that subverted logic and rationality. Driffin had his God, Sal her channelled ghosts. Even Mooney put his faith in odds on the track. Valentin saw the futility of resisting the inevitable. Fate had her in its grip. She eased her foot off the pedal. Past the next set of lights was the lane leading to Tickner's workshop.

The Chevrolet trembles, its motor purring like a cat. The boy lies sprawled across the back seat, one leg carelessly raised. She gazes at his face, the face of a Botticelli angel. He loosens his fly, then reaches beneath her skirt. She stiffens. A whiff of something makes her gag. Fumes from the car's exhaust…

The Fiat raced down the lane, speeding Valentin to her destiny.